POETRY FROM CRESCENT MOON

Walking In Cornwall
by Ursula Le Guin

Hymns To the Night
by Novalis

Hymns To the Night: In Translation
by Novalis

Flower Pollen: Selected Thoughts
by Novalis

Novalis: His Life, Thoughts and Works
by Novalis

Edmund Spenser: *Heavenly Love: Selected Poems*
selected and introduced by Teresa Page

Edmund Spenser: *Amoretti*
edited by Teresa Page

The Visions of Petrarch and Bellay: Early Sonnets
by Edmund Spenser

Robert Herrick: *Delight In Disorder: Selected Poems*
edited and introduced by M.K. Pace

Robert Herrick: *Hesperides*
edited and introduced by M.K. Pace

Robert Herrick: *Upon Julia's Breasts: Love Poems*
edited and introduced by M.K. Pace

Sir Thomas Wyatt: *Love For Love: Selected Poems*
selected and introduced by Louise Cooper

John Donne: *Air and Angels: Selected Poems*
selected and introduced by A.H. Ninham

D.H. Lawrence: *Being Alive: Selected Poems*
edited with an introduction by Margaret Elvy

D.H. Lawrence: *Amores*
edited with an introduction by Margaret Elvy

D.H. Lawrence: *Look! We Have Come Through!*
edited with an introduction by Margaret Elvy

D.H. Lawrence: *Love Poems and Others*
edited with an introduction by Margaret Elvy

D.H. Lawrence: *New Poems*
edited with an introduction by Margaret Elvy

D.H. Lawrence: Symbolic Landscapes
by Jane Foster

D.H. Lawrence: Infinite Sensual Violence
by M.K. Pace

Percy Bysshe Shelley: *Paradise of Golden Lights: Selected Poems*
selected and introduced by Charlotte Greene

Selected Poems
by William Shakespeare

Elizabethan Sonnet Cycles
by Daniel, Drayton, Sidney,
Spenser and Shakespeare

Elizabethan Sonnet Cycles (Volume
Two)
by Lodge, Griffin, Smith,
Constable and Fletcher

Three Metaphysical Poets
edited by A.H. Ninham

Three Romantic Poets
edited by Miriam Chalk

HENRY OF OFTERDINGEN
A ROMANCE

Novalis

HENRY OF OFTERDINGEN
A ROMANCE

Novalis

Translated by Frederick S. Stallknecht
& Edward C. Sprague
Edited by Carol Appleby

CRESCENT MOON

First published 1842. This edition 2025.

Design by Radiance Graphics Set in Book Antiqua 10 on 14pt.

British Library Cataloguing in Publication data available for this title.

ISBN-13 9781861719188

ISBN-13 9781861719324

Crescent Moon Publishing

P.O. Box 1312 Maidstone, Kent ME14 5XU, Great Britain

www.crmoon.com

CONTENTS

NOTE ON THE TEXT

The text is from *Henry of Ofterdingen* by Novalis, translated by Frederick S. Stallknecht & Edward C. Sprague, and published by John Owen, 1842.

Footnotes are in square brackets: [1]

Novalis

ADVERTISEMENT

The present translation is made from the edition of Tieck and Schlegel. The life of the author is chiefly drawn from the one written by the former. The completion of the second part is also by the same writer.

Richter said, in a prophetic feeling of the fate of his own works, that translators were like wagoners who carry good wine to fairs – but most unaccountably water it before the end of the journey. Which allusion and semi-confession is meant to take the place of the usual apology; and the reader can proceed without farther preface.

Cambridge, June, 1842.

LIFE OF THE AUTHOR

Probably some of the readers of this volume will feel an interest in the author's life. Although there are but few works, in which the mind of the author is more clearly and purely reflected than in this; yet it is natural that the reader should feel some interest in the outward circumstances of one, who has become dear to him; and those friends of Novalis, who have never known him personally, will be glad to hear all that we can bring to light concerning him.

The Baron of Hardenberg, the father of the author, was director of the Saxonian salt works. He had been a soldier in his younger days, and retained even in his old age a predilection for a military life. He was a robust, ever active man, frank and energetic; – a pure German. The pious character of his mind led him to join the Moravian community; yet he remained frank, decided, and upright. His mother, a type of elevated piety and Christian meekness, belonged to the same religious community. She bore with lofty resignation the loss, within a few successive years, of a blooming circle of hopeful and well educated children.

Friedrich von Hardenberg (Novalis) was born on the second of May, in the year 1772, on a family estate in the county of Mansfield. He was the oldest of eleven children, with the exception of a sister who was born a year earlier. The family consisted of seven sons and four daughters, all distinguished for their wit and the lofty tone of their minds. Each possessed a peculiar disposition, while all were united by a beautiful and generous affection to each other and to their parents. Friedrich von Hardenberg was weak in constitution from his earliest childhood, without, however, suffering from any settled or dangerous disease. He was somewhat of a day-dreamer, silent and of an inactive disposition. He separated himself from the society of his playmates; but his character was distinguished from that of other children, only by the ardor of his love for his master. He found his companions in his own family. His spirit seemed to be wakened from its slumber, by a severe disease in his ninth year, and by the stimulants applied for his recovery; and he suddenly appeared brighter, merrier, and more active. His father, who was obliged by his business to be much of his time away from home, entrusted his education for the most part to his mother, and to family tutors. The gentleness, meekness, and the pure piety of his mother's character, as well as the religious habits of both parents, which naturally extended to the whole household, made the deepest impression upon his mind; an impression which exerted the happiest influence upon him throughout his whole life. He now applied himself diligently to his studies, so that in his twelfth year he had acquired a pretty thorough knowledge of the Latin language, and some smattering of Greek. The reading of Poetry was the favorite occupation of his leisure hours. He was particularly pleased with the higher kind of fables, and amused himself by composing them and relating them to his brothers. He was accustomed for several years to act, in concert with his brothers Erasmus and Charles, a little poetical play, in which they took the characters of spirits, one of the air, another of the water, and the other of the earth. On Sunday evenings, Novalis would explain to them the most wonderful and various appearances and phenomena of these different realms. There are still in existence some of his poems written about this period.

He now applied himself too severely to study, especially to history, in which he took a deep interest. In the year 1789, he entered a Gymnasium, and in the autumn went to Jena to pursue his studies there. Here he remained until 1792, and then with his brother Erasmus entered the University at Leipzig; he left the following year for Wittenberg, and there finished his studies.

At this time the French war broke out, which not only interrupted his studies greatly, but which also inspired him suddenly with so great a desire to enter upon a military life, that the united prayers of his parents and relations were scarcely able to restrain his wishes.

About this time he became acquainted with Frederick Schlegel, and soon became his warmest friend; he also gained the friendship of Fichte; and these two great spirits exerted a powerful and lasting influence upon his whole life. After applying himself with unwearied ardor to the sciences, he left Wittenberg for Arnstadt in Thuringia, in order to accustom himself to practical business with Just, the chief judiciary of the district. This excellent man soon became one of his nearest friends. Shortly after his arrival at Arnstadt, he became acquainted with Sophia von K., who resided at a neighboring country seat. The first sight of her beautiful and lovely form decided the fate of his whole life; or rather the passion, which penetrated and inspired his soul, became the contents of his whole life. Often even in the face of childhood, there is an expression so sweet and spiritual, that we call it supernatural and heavenly; and the fear impresses itself on our hearts, that faces, so transfigured and transparent, are too tender and too finely woven for this life; that it is death or immortality that gazes through the glancing eye; and too often are our forebodings realized by the rapid withering of such blossoms. Still more beautiful are such forms, when, childhood left behind, they have advanced to the full bloom of youth. All who knew the betrothed of our author are agreed, that no description could do justice to her beauty, grace, and heavenly simplicity. She was in her fourteenth year when Novalis became acquainted with her; and the spring and summer of 1795 were indeed the blooming season of his life. Every hour he could spare from his business was spent at Grüningen; and late in the fall of 1796, he was betrothed to Sophia with the consent of her parents. Shortly after she was taken severely sick with a fever, which, though it lasted but a few weeks, yet left her with a pain in the side, which by its intensity rendered unhappy many of her hours. Novalis was much alarmed, but was quieted by her physician, who pronounced this pain of no consequence.

Shortly after her recovery he departed for Weissenfels, where he was appointed auditor in the department of which his father was director. He passed the winter of 1795-96 in business, hearing news from Grüningen of a quieting character. He journeyed thither in the spring, and found his betrothed to all appearance recovered. At this time his brother Erasmus was taken sick, so that he left off his studies, and devoted himself in a distant place to the chase and a forest life. His brother Charles joined the army, and in the spring entered upon active service. Thus Novalis lived quietly at home, his parents and sisters forming his chief society, the other children being yet quite young. In the summer, while he was rejoicing in the prospect of being soon united to Sophia, he received information, that she was at Jena, and there on account of ulceration of the liver, had undergone a severe operation. It had been her wish, that he should not be informed of her sickness, nor of the dangerous operation, till it was over. He hastened to Jena, and found her in intense suffering. Her physician, one far famed for his ability, could allow them to hope only for a very slow recovery, if indeed she should survive. He was obliged to repeat the operation, and feared that she would want strength to support her through the healing process. With lofty courage and indescribable fortitude, Sophia bore up against all her sufferings. Novalis was there to console her; his parents offered up their sympathetic prayers; his two brothers had returned and strove to be of service to the sorrowing one, as well as to the suffering. In December Serbia desired to visit Grüningen again. Novalis requested Erasmus to accompany her on her journey. He did so, together with her mother and sisters, who had attended her at Jena. After having accompanied her to her place of residence, he returned to his residence in Franconia.

Novalis was now by turns in Weissenfels and Grüningen. With great grief, however, he was obliged to confess, that he found Sophia worse and worse at every visit. Towards the end of January, 1797, Erasmus also returned to Weissenfels very sick, and the expected deaths of two beings, so much beloved, filled the house with gloom.

The 17th of March was Sophia's fifteenth birthday, and on the 19th, about noon, she fell asleep in the arms of her sisters, and faithful instructress Mademoiselle Danscour, who loved her tenderly. No one dared bring the news to Novalis, until his brother Charles at last undertook the mournful office. For three days and nights, the mourner shut himself up from his friends, weeping away the hours, and then hastened to Arnstadt, that he might be with his truest friends, and nearer to the beloved place, which contained the remains of her who was dearest to him. On the 14th of April, he also lost his brother Erasmus. Novalis writing to his brother Charles, who had been obliged to travel to Lower Saxony, says, speaking of the death of Erasmus, "Be consoled; Erasmus has conquered; the flowers of the lovely wreath are dropping off, one by one, to be united more beautifully in Heaven."

At this time Novalis, living as he did only for suffering, naturally regarded the visible and the invisible world as one, and regarded life and death as distinguished only by our longing for the latter. At the same time life was transfigured before him, and his whole being flowed together as in a clear conscious dream of a higher existence. His sensibilities, as well as his imagination, were very much decided from the solemnity of his suffering, from his heartfelt love, and from the pious longing for death, which he cherished. It is indeed very possible, that deep sorrow at this time planted the death-seed in him; unless perhaps it was his irrevocable destiny, to be so early torn away.

He remained many weeks in Thuringia, and returned consoled and truly exalted to his business, which he pursued more eagerly than ever, though he regarded himself as a stranger upon earth. About this time, some earlier, some later, but particularly during the fall of this year, he composed most of those pieces, which have been published under the title of "Fragments," as also his "Hymns to Night."

In December of this year, he went to Freiberg, where the acquaintance and instruction of the renowned Werner awoke anew his passion for physical science, and especially for mining. Here he became acquainted with Julia von Ch.; and, strange as it may appear to all but his intimate friends, he was betrothed to her, as early as the year 1798. Sophia (as we may see from his works) remained the balancing point of his thoughts; he honored her, absent as she was, even more than when present with him; but yet he thought that loveliness and beauty could, to a certain degree, replace her loss. About this time he wrote "Faith and Love," the "Flower Dust," and some other fragments, as "The Pupils at Sais." In the spring of 1799, Serbia's instructress died; which event moved Novalis the more deeply, because he knew that sorrow for the loss of her beloved pupil had chiefly contributed to hasten her death. Soon after this event he returned to the paternal estate, and was appointed under his father Assessor and chief Judiciary of the Thuringian district.

He now visited Jena often, and there became acquainted with A. W. Schlegel, and sought out the gifted Ritter, whom he particularly loved, and whose peculiar talent for experimenting he greatly admired. Ludwig Tieck saw him this year for the first time, while on a visit to his friend Wm. Schlegel. Their acquaintance soon ripened into a warm friendship. These friends, in company with Schlegel, Schelling, and other strangers, passed many happy days in Jena. On his return, Tieck visited Novalis at his father's house, became acquainted with his family, and for the first time listened to the reading of "the Pupils at Sais," and many of his fragments. He then accompanied him to Halle, and many hours were peacefully passed in Reichardt's house. His first conception of Henry of Ofterdingen dates about this time. He had also already written some of his spiritual songs; they were to make a part of a hymn book, which he intended to accompany with a volume of sermons. Besides these labors he was very industrious in the duties of his office; all his duties were attended to with willingness, and nothing of however little importance was insignificant to him.

When Tieck, in the autumn of 1799, took up his residence at Jena, and Frederick Schlegel also dwelt there, Novalis often visited them, sometimes for a short, and sometimes for a longer time. His eldest sister was married about this time, and the wedding was celebrated at a country seat near Jena. After this marriage Novalis lived for a long time in a lonely place in the golden meadow of Thuringia, at the foot of the Kyffhauser mountain; and in this solitude he wrote a great part of Henry of Ofterdingen. His society this year was mostly confined to that of two men; a brother-in-law of his betrothed, the present General von Theilman, and the present General von Funk, to whom he had been introduced by the former. The society of the last-mentioned person was valuable to him in more than one respect. He made use of his library, among whose chronicles he, in the spring, first hit upon the traditions of Ofterdingen; and by means of the excellent biography of the emperor Frederick the Second, by General von Funk, he became entirely possessed with lofty ideas concerning that ruler, and determined to represent him in his romance as a pattern for a king.

In the year 1800, Novalis was again at Weissenfels, whence, on the 23d of February, he wrote to Tieck, – "My Romance is getting along finely. About twelve printed sheets are finished. The whole plan is pretty much laid out in my mind. It will consist of two parts; the first, I hope, will be finished in three weeks. It contains the basis and introduction to the second part. The whole may be called an Apotheosis of Poesy. Henry of Ofterdingen becomes in the first part ripe for a poet, and in the second part is declared poet. It will in many respects be similar to Sternbald, except in lightness. However, this want will not probably be unfavorable to the contents. In every point of view it is a first attempt, the print of that spirit of poesy, which your acquaintance has reawakened in me, and which gives to your friendship its chief value.

"There are some songs in it, which suit my taste. I am very much pleased with the real romance, – my head is really dizzy with the multitude of ideas I have gathered for romances and comedies. If I can visit you soon, I will bring you a tale and a fable from my romance, and will subject them to your criticism." He visited his friends at Jena the next spring, and soon repeated his visit, bringing the first part of Henry of Ofterdingen, in the same form as that of which this volume is a translation.

When Tieck, in the summer of 1800, left Jena, he visited his friend for some time at his father's house. He was well and calm in his spirits; though his family were somewhat alarmed about him, thinking that they noticed, that he was continually growing paler and thinner. He himself was more attentive than usual to his diet; he drank little or no wine, ate scarcely any meat, living principally on milk and vegetables. "We took daily walks," says Tieck, "and rides on horseback. In ascending a hill swiftly, or in any violent motion, I could observe neither weakness in his breast nor short breath, and therefore endeavored to persuade him to forsake his strict mode of life; because I thought his abstemiousness from wine and strengthening food not only irritating in itself, but also to proceed from a false anxiety on his part. He was full of plans for the future; his house was already put in order, for in August he intended to celebrate his nuptials. He spake with great pleasure of finishing Ofterdingen and other works. His life gave promise of the most useful activity and love. When I took leave of him, I never could have imagined that we were not to meet again."

When in August he was about departing for Freiberg to celebrate his marriage, he was seized with an emission of blood, which his physician declared to be mere hemorrhoidal and insignificant. Yet it shook his frame considerably, and still more when it began to return periodically. His wedding was postponed, and, in the beginning of October, he travelled with his brother and parents to Dresden. Here they left him, in order to visit their daughter in Upper Lausatia, his brother Charles remaining with him in Dresden. He became apparently weaker; and when, in the beginning of November, he learned that a younger brother, fourteen years of age, had been drowned through mere carelessness, the sudden shock caused a violent bleeding at the lungs, upon which the physician immediately declared his disease incurable. Soon after this his betrothed came to Dresden.

As he grew weaker, he longed to change his residence to some warmer climate. He thought of visiting his friend Herbert; but his physician advised against such a change, perhaps considering him already too weak to make such a journey. Thus the year passed away; and, in January 1801, he longed so eagerly to see his parents and be with them once more, that at the end of the month he returned to Weissenfels. There the ablest physicians from Leipzig and Jena were consulted, yet his case grew rapidly worse, although he was perfectly free from pain, as was the case through his whole illness. He still attended to the duties of his office, and wrote considerably in his private papers. He also composed some poems about this time, read the Bible diligently, and much from the works of Zinzendorf and Lavater. The nearer he approached his end, the stronger was his hope of recovery; for his cough abated, and, with the exception of debility, he had none of the feelings of a sick man. With this hope and longing for life, fresh powers and new talents seemed to awaken within him; he thought with renewed love of his projected labors, and undertook to write Henry of Ofterdingen anew. Once, shortly before his death, he said; "I now begin, for the first time, to see what true poetry is. Innumerable songs and poems far different from those I have written awake within me." From the 19th of March, the day on which Sophia died, he became very perceptibly weaker; many of his friends visited him, and he was particularly delighted when, on the 21st of March, his faithful and oldest friend Frederick Schlegel came to see him from Jena. He conversed much with him, particularly concerning their mutual labors. During these days his spirits were good, his nights quiet, and he enjoyed tranquil sleep. About six o'clock on the morning of the 26th, he asked his brother to hand him some books, in order to look out certain passages, that he had in mind; he then ordered his breakfast, and conversed with his usual vivacity till eight. Towards nine he asked his brother to play for him on the piano, and soon after fell asleep. Frederick Schlegel soon after entered the chamber, and found him sleeping quietly. This sleep lasted till twelve o'clock, at which hour he expired without a struggle; and unchanged in death his countenance retained the same pleasant expression, that it exhibited during life.

Thus died our author before he had finished his nine-and-twentieth year. In him we may alike love and admire his extensive knowledge and his philosophical genius, as well as his poetical talents. With a spirit much in advance of his times, his country might have promised itself great things of him, had not an untimely death cut him off. Yet his unfinished writings have already had their influence; many of his great thoughts will yet inspire futurity; and noble minds and deep thinkers will be enlightened and set on fire by the sparks of his spirit.

Novalis was slender and of fine proportions. He wore his light brown hair long, hanging over his shoulders in flowing locks, a style less singular then than now; his brown eye was clear and brilliant, and his complexion, particularly his forehead, almost transparent. His hands and feet were rather too large, and had something awkward about them. His countenance was always serene and benignant. To those, who judge men by their forwardness, or by their affectation of fashion or dignity, Novalis was lost in the crowd; but to the practised eye he appeared beautiful. The outlines and expression of his face resembled very much those of St. John, as he is represented in the magnificent picture of A. Dürer, preserved in Nuremberg and München.

His speech was clear and vivacious. "I never saw him tired," says Tieck, "even when we continued together till late at night; he only stopped voluntarily to rest, and then read before he fell asleep." He knew not what it was to be tired, even in the wearisome companionship of vulgar minds; for he always found some one, who could impart some information to him, useful, though apparently insignificant. His urbanity and sympathy for all made him universally beloved. So skilful was he in his intercourse with others, that lower minds never felt their inferiority. Although he preferred to veil the depths of his mind in conversation, speaking, however, as if inspired, of the invisible world, he was yet merry, as a child, full of art and frolic, giving himself wholly up to the jovial spirit prevailing in the company. Free from self-conceit or arrogance, a stranger to affectation or dissimulation, he was a pure, true man; the purest, loveliest spirit, ever tabernacled in the flesh.

His chief studies for many years were philosophy and physical science. In the latter he discovered and foretold truths, of which his own age was in ignorance. In philosophy he principally studied Spinoza and Fichte; but soon marked out a new path, by aiming to unite philosophy with religion; and thus what we possess of the writings of the new Platonists, as well as of the mystics, became very important to him. His knowledge of mathematics, as well as of the mechanic arts, especially of mining, was very considerable. But in the fine arts he took but little interest. Music he loved much, although he knew little about its rules. He had scarcely turned his attention to painting and sculpture; still he could advance many original ideas about those arts, and pronounce skilful judgment upon them.

Tieck mentions an argument with him, concerning landscape painting, in which Novalis expressed views, which he could not comprehend; but which in part were realized, by the rich and poetical mind of the excellent landscape painter, Friedrichs, of Dresden. In the land of Poetry he was in reality a stranger. He had read but few poets, and had not busied himself with criticism, or paid much attention to the inherited system, to which the art of poetry had been reduced. Goethe was for a long while his study, and Wilhelm Meister his favorite work; although we should scarcely suppose so, judging from his severe strictures upon it in his fragments. He demanded from poesy the most everyday knowledge and inspiration; and it was for this reason, that, as the chief masterpieces of poetry were unknown to him, he was free from imitation and foreign rule. He also loved, for this very reason, many writings, which are not generally highly prized by scholars, because in them he discovered, though perhaps painted in weak colors, that very informing and significant knowledge, which he was chiefly striving after.

Those tales, which we in later times call allegories [1] with their peculiar style, most resemble his stories; he saw their deepest meaning, and endeavored to express it most clearly in some of his poems. It became natural for him to regard what was most usual and nearest to him, as full of marvels, and the strange and supernatural as the usual and common-place. Thus everyday life surrounded him like a supernatural story; and that region, which most men can only conceive as something distant and incomprehensible, seemed to him like a beloved home. Thus uncorrupted by precedents, he discovered a new way of drawing and exhibiting his pictures; and in the manifold variety of his relation to the world, from his love and the faith in it, which at the same time was his instructress, wisdom, and religion, since through them a single great moment of life, and one deep grief and loss became the essence of his poesy and of his contemplation, he resembles among late writers the sublime Dante alone, and like him sings to us an unfathomable mystical song, very different from that of many imitators, who think, that they can assume and lay aside mysticism as they could a mere ornament. Therefore his romance is both consciously and unconsciously the representation of his own mind and fate; as he makes Henry say, in the fragment of the second part, "Fate and mind are but names of one idea." Thus may his life justly appear wonderful to us. We shudder too, as though reading a work of fiction, when we learn, that of all his brothers and sisters only two brothers are now alive; and that his noble mother, who for several years has also been mourning the death of her husband, is in solitude, devoting herself to her grief and to religion with silent resignation.

HENRY OF OFTERDINGEN
✳
PART FIRST

THE EXPECTATION

DEDICATION

Thou didst to life my noble impulse warm,
    Deep in the spirit of the world to look.
    And with thy hand a trusting faith I took,
Securely bearing me through every storm,
With sweet forebodings thou the child didst bless,
    To mystic meadows leading him away,
    Stirring his bosom to its finest play,
Ideal, thou, of woman's tenderness.
Earth's vexing trifles shall I not refuse?
    Thine is my heart and life eternally, –
Thy love my being constantly renews!
    To art I dedicate myself for thee,
For thou, beloved, wilt become the Muse
    And gentle Genius of my poesy.

In endless transmutation here below
    The hidden might of song our land is greeting;
    Now blesses us in form of Peace unfleeting,
And now encircles us with childhood's glow.
She pours an upper light upon the eye,
    Defines the sentiment for every art,
    And dwells within the glad or weary heart,
To comfort it with wondrous ecstasy.
Through her alone I woke to life the truest,
    Drinking the proffered nectar of her breast,
And dared to lift my face With joy the newest.
    Yet was my highest sense with sleep oppressed.
Till angel-like thou, loved one, near me flewest.
And, kindling in thy look, I found the rest.

CHAPTER I

The patents had already retired to rest; the old clock ticked monotonously from the wall; the windows rattled with the whistling wind, and the chamber was dimly lighted by the flickering glimmer of the moon. The young man lay restless on his bed, thinking of the stranger and his tales. "It is not the treasures," said he to himself, "that have awakened in me such unutterable longings. Far from me is all avarice; but I long to behold the blue flower. It is constantly in my mind, and I can think and compose of nothing else. I have never been in such a mood. It seems as if I had hitherto been dreaming, or slumbering into another world; for in the world, in which hitherto I have lived, who would trouble himself about a flower? – I never have heard of such a strange passion for a flower here. I wonder, too, whence the stranger comes? None of our people have ever seen his like; still I know not why I should be so fascinated by his conversation. Others have listened to it, but none are moved by it as I am. Would that I could explain my feelings in words! I am often full of rapture, and it is only when the blue flower is out of my mind, that this deep, heart-felt longing overwhelms me. But no one can comprehend this but myself. I might think myself mad, were not my perception and reasonings so clear; and this state of mind appears to have brought with it superior knowledge on all subjects. I have heard, that in ancient times beasts, and trees, and rocks conversed with men. As I gaze upon them, they appear every moment about to speak to me; and I can almost tell by their looks what they would say. There must yet be many words unknown to me. If I knew more, I could comprehend better. Formerly I loved to dance, now I think rather to the music."

The young man gradually lost himself in his sweet fancies, and feel asleep. Then he dreamed of regions far distant, and unknown to him. He crossed the sea with wonderful ease; saw many strange monsters; lived with all sorts of men, now in war, now in wild tumult, and now in peaceful cottages. Then he fell into captivity and degrading want. His feelings had never been so excited. His life was an unending tissue, of the brightest colors. Then came death, a return again to life; he loved, loved intensely, and was separated from the object of his passion. At length towards the break of day his soul became calmer, and the images his fancy formed grew clearer, and more lasting. He dreamed that he was walking alone in a dark forest, where the light broke only at intervals through the green net-work of the trees. He soon came to a passage through some rocks, which led to the top of a neighboring hill, and, to ascend which he was obliged to scramble over the mossy stones, which some stream in former times had torn down. The higher he climbed, the more was the forest lit up, until at last he came to a small meadow situated on the declivity of the mountain. Behind the meadow rose a lofty cliff, at whose foot an opening was visible, which seemed to be the beginning of a path hewn in the rock. The path guided him gently along, and ended in a wide expanse, from which at a distance a clear light shone towards him. On entering this expanse, he beheld a mighty beam of light, which, like the stream from a fountain, rose to the overhanging clouds, and spread out into innumerable sparks, which gathered themselves below into a great basin. The beam shone like burnished gold; not the least noise was audible; a holy silence reigned around the splendid spectacle. He approached the basin, which trembled and undulated with ever-varying colors. The sides of the cave were coated with the golden liquid, which was cool to the touch, and which cast from the walls a weak, blue light. He dipped his hand in the basin, and bedewed his lips. He felt as if a spiritual breath had pierced through him, and he was sensibly strengthened and refreshed. A resistless desire to bathe himself made him undress and step into the basin. Then a cloud tinged with the glow of evening appeared to surround him; feelings as from Heaven flowed into his soul; thoughts innumerable and full of rapture strove to mingle together within him; new imaginings, such as never before had struck his fancy, arose before him, which, flowing into each other, became visible beings about him. Each wave of the lovely element pressed to him like a soft bosom. The flood seemed like a solution of the elements of beauty, which constantly became embodied in the forms of charming maidens around him. Intoxicated with rapture, yet conscious of every impression, he swam gently down the glittering stream. A sweeter slumber now overcame him. He dreamed of many strange events, and a new vision appeared to him. He dreamed that he was sitting on the soft turf by the margin of a fountain, whose waters flowed into the air, and seemed to vanish in it. Dark blue rocks with various colored veins rose in the distance. The daylight around him was milder and clearer than usual; the sky was of a sombre blue, and free from clouds. But what most attracted his notice, was a tall, light-blue flower, which stood nearest the fountain, and touched it with its broad, glossy leaves. Around it grew numberless flowers of varied hue, filling the air with the richest perfume. But he saw the blue flower alone, and gazed long upon it with inexpressible tenderness. He at length was about to approach it, when it began to move, and change its form. The leaves increased their beauty, adorning the growing stem. The flower bended towards him, and revealed among its leaves a blue, outspread collar, within which hovered a tender face. His delightful astonishment was increasing with this singular change, when suddenly his mother's voice awoke him, and he found himself in his parents' room, already gilded by the morning sun. He was too happy to be angry at the sudden disturbance of his sleep. He bade his mother a kind good morning, and returned her hearty embrace.

"You sleeper," said his father, "how long have I been sitting here filing? I have not dared to do any hammering on your account. Your mother would let her dear son sleep. I have been obliged to wait for my breakfast too. You have done wisely in choosing to become one of the learned, for whom we wake and work. But a real, thorough student, as I have been told, is obliged to spend his nights in studying the works of our wise forefathers."

"Dear father," said Henry, "let not my long sleep make you angry with me, for you are not accustomed to be so. I fell asleep late, and have been much disturbed by dreams. The last, however, was pleasant, and one which I shall not soon forget, and which seems to me to have been something more than a mere dream."

"Dear Henry," said his mother, "you have certainly been lying on your back, or else your thoughts were wandering at evening prayers. Come, eat your breakfast, and cheer up."

Henry's mother went out. His father worked on industriously, and said; "Dreams are froth, let the learned think what they will of them; and you will do well to turn your attention from such useless and hurtful speculations. The times when Heavenly visions were seen in dreams have long past by, nor can we understand the state of mind, which those chosen men, of whom the Bible speaks, enjoyed. Dreams, as well as other human affairs, must have been of a different nature then. In the age in which we live, there is no direct intercourse with Heaven. Old histories and writings are now the only fountains, from which we can draw, as far as is needful, a knowledge of the spiritual world; and instead of express revelations, the Holy Ghost now speaks to us immediately through the understandings of wise and sensible men, and by the lives and fate of those most distinguished for their piety. I have never been much edified by the visions, which are now seen; nor do I place much confidence in the wonders, which our divines relate about them. Yet let every one, who can, be edified by them; I would not cause any one to err in his faith."

"But, dear father, upon what grounds are you so opposed to belief in dreams, when singular changes, and flighty, unstable nature, are at least worthy of some reflection? Is not every dream, even the most confused, a peculiar vision, which, though we do not call it sent from Heaven, yet makes an important rent in the mysterious curtain, which, with a thousand folds, hides our inward natures from our view? We can find accounts of many such dreams, coming from credible men, in the wisest books; and you need only call to mind, to support what I have said, the dream which our good pastor lately related to us, and which appeared to you so remarkable. But, without taking those writings into account, if now for the first time you should have a dream, how would it overwhelm you, and how constantly would your thoughts be fixed upon the miracle, which, from its very frequency, now appears such a simple occurrence. Dreams appear to me to break up the monotony and even tenor of life, to serve as a recreation to the chained fancy. They mingle together all the scenes and fancies of life, and change the continual earnestness of age, into the merry sports of childhood. Were it not for dreams, we should certainly grow older; and though they be not given us immediately from above; yet they should be regarded as Heavenly gifts, as friendly guides, in our pilgrimage to the holy tomb. I am sure that the dream, which I have had this night, has been no profitless occurrence in my life; for I feel that it has, like some vast wheel, caught hold of my soul, and is hurrying me along with it in its mighty revolutions."

Henry's father smiled humorously, and said, looking to his wife, who had just come in, "Henry cannot deny the hour of his birth. His conversation boils with the fiery Italian wines, which I brought with me from Rome, and with which we celebrated our wedding eve. I was another sort of man then. The southern breezes had thawed out my northern phlegm. I was overflowing with spirit and humor, and you also were an ardent, charming girl. Everything was arranged at your father's in grand style; musicians and minstrels were collected from far and wide, and Augsburg had never seen a merrier marriage."

"You were just now speaking of dreams," said Henry's mother. "Do you not remember, that you then told me of one, which you had had at Rome, and which first put it into your head to come to Augsburg as my suitor?"

"You put me opportunely in mind of it," said the old man, "for I had entirely forgotten that singular dream, which, at the time of its occurrence, occupied my thoughts not a little; but even that is only a proof of what I have been saying about dreams. It would be impossible to have one more clear and regular. Even now I remember every circumstance in it, and yet, what did it signify? That I dreamed of you, and soon after felt an irrepressible desire to possess you, was not strange; for I already knew you. The agreeable and amiable traits of your character strongly affected me, when I first saw you; and I was prevented from making love to you, only by the desire of visiting foreign lands. At the time of the dream my curiosity was much abated; and hence my love for you more easily mastered me."

"Please to tell us about that curious dream," said Henry.

"One evening," said his father, "I had been loitering about, enjoying the beauty of the clear, blue sky, and of the moon, which clothed the old pillars and walls with its pale, awe-inspiring light. My companions had gone to see the girls, and love and homesickness drove me into the open air. During my walk, I felt thirsty, and went into the first decent looking mansion I met with, to ask for a glass of wine, or milk. An old man came to the door, who perhaps at first regarded me as a suspicious visitor; but when I told him what I wished, and he learned that I was a foreigner, and a German, he kindly asked me into the house, bade me sit down, brought out a bottle of wine, and asked me some questions about my business. We began a desultory conversation, during which he gave me some information about painters, poets, sculptors, and ancient times. I had scarce ever heard about such matters; and it teemed as if I had landed in a new world. He showed me some old seals and other works of art, and then read to me, with all the fire of youth, some beautiful passages of poetry. Thus the hours fled as moments. Even now my heart warms with the recollection of the wonderful thoughts and emotions, which crowded upon me that evening. He seemed quite at home in the pagan ages, and longed, with incredible ardor, to dwell in the times of grey antiquity. At last he showed me a chamber, where I could pass the night, for it was too late for me to return to the city. I soon fell asleep and dreamed. – I thought that I was passing out of the gates of my native city. It seemed to me that I was going to get something done, but where, and what, I did not know. I took the road to Hartz, and walked quickly along, as merry as if going to a festival. I did not keep the road, but cut across through wood and valley, till I came to a lofty mountain. From its top I gazed on the golden fields around me, beheld Thuringia in the distance, and was so situated, that no other mountain could obstruct my view. Opposite lay the Hartz with its dusky hills. Castles, convents, and whole districts were embraced in the prospect. My ideas were all clear and distinct. I thought of the old man, in whose house I was sleeping; and my visit seemed like some occurrence of past years. I soon saw an ascending path leading into the mountain, and I followed it. After some time I came to a large cave; there sat a very old man in a long garment, before an iron table, gazing incessantly upon a wondrously beautiful maiden, that stood before him hewn in marble. His beard had grown through the iron table, and covered his feet. His features were serious, yet kind, and put me in mind of a head by one of the old masters, which my host had shown me in the evening. The cave was filled with glowing light. While I was looking at the old man, my host tapped me on the shoulder, took my hand, and led me through many long paths, till we saw a mild light shining in the distance, like the dawn of day. I hastened to it, and soon found myself in a green plain; but there was nothing about it to remind me of Thuringia. Giant trees, with their large, glossy leaves, spread their shade far and wide. The air was very hot, yet not oppressive. Around me flowers and fountains were springing from the earth. Among the former there was one that particularly pleased me, and to which all the others seemed to do homage."

"Dear father," eagerly exclaimed Henry, "do tell me its color."

"I cannot recollect it, though it was so fixed in my mind at the time."

"Was it not blue?"

"Perhaps it was," continued the old man, without giving heed to the peculiar vehemence of his son. "All I recollect is, that my feelings were so wrought up, that for a time I forgot all about my guide. When at length I turned towards him, I noticed that he was looking at me attentively, and that he met me with a pleasant smile. I do not remember how I came from that place. I was again on the top of the mountain; my guide stood by my side and said, 'You have seen the wonder of the world. It lies in your power to become the happiest being in the world, and, besides that, a celebrated man. Remember well what I tell you. Come on St. John's day, towards evening, to this place, and when you have devoutly prayed to God to interpret this vision, the highest earthly lot will be yours. Also take notice particularly of a little blue flower, which you will find above here; pluck it, and commit yourself humbly to heavenly guidance.' I then dreamed that I was among most splendid scenes and noble men, ravished by the swift changing objects that met my eyes. How fluent were my words! how free my tongue! How music swelled its strains! Afterwards everything became dull and insignificant as usual. I saw your mother standing before me, with a kind and modest look. A bright-looking child was in her arms. She reached it to me; it gradually grew brighter; at length it raised itself on its dazzling white wings, took us both in its arms, and soared so high with us, that the earth appeared like a plate of gold, covered with beautifully wrought carving. I only recollect, that, after this vision, the flower, the old man, and the mountain appeared before me again. I awoke soon after, much agitated by vehement love. I bade farewell to my hospitable friend, who urged me to repeat my visit often. I promised to do so, and should have kept my promise, had I not shortly after left Rome for Augsburg, my mind being much excited by the scenes I had witnessed."

CHAPTER II

St. John's day was past. Henry's mother had for a long time delayed making a journey to Augsburg, her paternal home, to present her son to his grandfather, who had never yet seen him. Some merchants, trusty friends of the elder Ofterdingen, were just about travelling to Augsburg on business. Henry's mother resolved to improve this good opportunity of fulfilling her wishes; and this more especially, because she had observed that Henry had lately been more silent, and more taken up with his own gloomy fancies than usual. She saw that he was out of spirits, or sick; and thought that a long journey, the sight of strange people and places, and, as she secretly anticipated, the charms of some young country girl would drive off the gloomy mood of her son, and make him as affable and cheerful as was his wont. Her husband agreed with her in her plans, and Henry was delighted beyond all bounds with the idea of visiting a country, which, for a long time, he had looked upon (owing to the many things he had heard concerning it, from his mother and from travellers) as an earthly Paradise, and in which he had often wished himself.

Henry was just twenty years old. He had never passed the environs of his native city; the world was known to him only by report; only a few books had come within his reach. The course of life at the Landgrave was simple and quiet, according to the customs of the times; and the splendor and comfort of princely life, in those days, could but poorly compare with the conveniences, which, in our times, a private man can obtain for himself and family, without extravagance. Yet by reason of their very scarcity, a regard, almost approaching tenderness, was felt, in those times, for household furniture, and the conveniences of life. They were considered more valuable and curious. The secrets of nature, and the origin of its bodies, hardly attracted the notice of thinking minds, more than these scarce specimens of art and workmanship. This regard, too, for these silent companions of life was much heightened, by the distance from which they were brought, and by that charm of antiquity which gathered around furniture, often the property of successive generations; an heir-loom from father to son. They were often raised to the rank of pledges of a peculiar blessing and destiny; and the weal of whole kingdoms and far-scattered families depended upon their preservation. A poverty, fair in its features, adorned that age with a simplicity, full of significance and innocence. The treasures, so sparingly scattered in that dawn, shone the more brightly, and gave rise to many significant ideas in the thoughtful mind. If it is true that a proper division of light, color, and shade reveals the hidden splendor of the visible world, and opens for itself a new eye of a higher character; such a division and splendor were to be seen then; while these newer and more prosperous times represent the monotonous and insignificant picture of a common day. In all transitions, as in an interregnum, it appears as if a higher spiritual power were revealing itself; and as, upon the surface of our earth, the countries, richest both in subterraneous and super-terraneous treasures, lie between wild, inhospitable, hoary rocks, and immense plains; so also a deep-reflecting, romantic period made its appearance between the rough ages of barbarism, and the cultivated, enlightened, and wealthy age, which under a coarse garb conceals a still more beautiful form. Who does not love to wander at twilight, when the light of day and the deep shades of night mingle together in deep coloring? On this principle, we are glad to carry ourselves, in imagination, back to the years when Henry lived, who now went to meet the new circumstances, which might encompass him, with a swelling heart. He took leave of his companions and his instructer, the old and wise preacher, who knew the fertility of Henry's genius, and who bade him farewell, with a feeling heart and a silent prayer. The countess was his grandmother. He had often visited her at Wartburg. He now separated from his protectress, who gave him good counsel, and a golden chain, and who took leave of him with expressions of friendship. It was with a sad heart that Henry left his father and his birthplace. He now experienced for the first time what separation was. His imaginings as to the journey had not been accompanied with that peculiar feeling, which now filled his breast, when, for the first time, the scenes of his youth were snatched from his view, and he was cast, as it were, upon a foreign shore. Great indeed is our youthful sorrow at this first experience of the instability of earthly things, an experience necessary and indispensable to the inexperienced mind, firmly connected with and certain as our own existence. Our first separation remains, like the first announcement of death, never to be forgotten, and becomes, after it has long terrified us like a nightly vision, when at last joy at the appearance of anew day decreases, and the longing after a fixed, safer world increases, a friendly guide and a consoling and familiar idea. It comforted the young man much, that his mother was with him. The world he was leaving did not yet appear entirely lost, and he embraced her with redoubled fondness. It was early in the day, when the travellers rode from the gates of Eisenach, and the fresh daybreak was favorable to Henry's excited mood. The clearer the day grew, the more remarkable seemed to him the new and unknown scenes which surrounded him; and when upon a hill, just as the landscape behind him was illuminated by the rays of the rising sun, there occurred to him in the gloomy change of his thoughts some of the old melodies he knew by heart. He found himself in the swell of the distance, towards which he had often gazed from the neighboring mountains, where he had often wished himself in vain, and which he had painted to himself with peculiar colors. He was on the point of dipping himself in its blue flood. The wonderful flower stood before him, and he looked towards Thuringia, which he now left behind him, with the strong idea, that he was returning to his fatherland, after long wanderings from the country, towards which they now were travelling, and as if in reality he was journeying homewards.

The company, which at first had been silent from similar causes, began by degrees to wake up, and to shorten the time by various conversation and stories. Henry's mother felt it her duty to rouse him from the dreamings, in which she saw him sunken; and began to tell him of her father's land, of her father's house, and of the pleasant life in Swabia. The merchants joined in, and confirmed what his mother said. They praised the hospitality of the old man Swaning, and could not sufficiently extol the beauteous fair ones of the country of their travelling companion.

"You do well," said they, "in taking your son thither. The customs of your native country are of the most refined and pleasing character. They know how to attend to what is useful, without despising the agreeable. Every one endeavors to satisfy his wants in a social and charming way. The merchant is well treated and respected. The arts and mechanics are increased and ennobled; work appears easier to the industrious man, because it helps him to many pleasures, and because, as a reward for steady industry, he is sure to enjoy the manifold fruits of various and profitable employments. Money, industry, and goods reciprocally produce each other, and float along in busy circles. The country, as well as the cities, flourishes. The more industriously the day is employed, the more exclusively is the evening devoted to the charming pleasures drawn from the fine arts, and to social intercourse. The mind seeks recreation and change; and where could it find it more proper or more attractive, than in those unchecked diversions, and in those productions of its noblest power, the power of embodying its conceptions into realities. Nowhere can you have such sweet singers, or find such excellent painters, or see in the dancing halls more graceful movements or lovelier forms. The neighborhood of Switzerland is distinguished for the ease of its manners and conversation. Your race adorns society; and without fear of being talked about, can excite by their charming behavior a lively emulation to chain the attention. The stern fortitude and the wild jovialty of the men make room for a mild vivacity and a tender and modest joy, and love in a thousand forms becomes the leading spirit of their happy companies. Far is it from the truth, that dissoluteness or unseemly principles are by this course of conduct developed. It seems as if the evil spirit shunned the approach of innocent or graceful amusements, and certainly there are in no part of Germany more irreproachable maidens, or more faithful wives, than in Swabia.

"Yes, my young friend, in the clear, warm air of southern Germany you will soon lay aside your bashfulness; the youthful maidens will soon render you easy and talkative. Your name alone, as a stranger and as a relative of the old Swaning, who is the delight of every pleasant company, will attract the pleasant gaze of the maidens towards you; and if you follow the will of your grandfather, you will certainly bring to our native city, as did your father, an ornament in the form of a lovely woman."

Henry's mother thanked them with a modest blush, for their distinguished praise bestowed on her fatherland, and for their good opinion of her countrywomen. Henry, full of thought, could not help listening attentively and with heart-felt pleasure to the description of the land, which he saw before him.

"Although you do not take up your father's trade," continued the merchants, "but rather, as we have been told, spend your time in the pursuit of knowledge, yet you need not become one of the clergy, or renounce the pleasantest enjoyments of this life. It is bad enough that all learning is in the hands of an order, so separated from worldly life, and that the rulers are counselled by such unsociable and really inexperienced men. In solitude, where they have no share in worldly affairs, their thoughts must take a useless turn, and cannot be applied to everyday concerns. In

Swabia you can find both wise and experienced men among the laity, and you need only choose what branch of human knowledge you prefer; for you cannot want there good teachers and advisers."

After a while Henry, whose thoughts had been led by this conversation to the old court-preacher, said; "Although ignorant as I am of the real condition of the world, I do not exactly rebel against your opinion, as to the ability of the clergy to guide and judge of worldly affairs; yet I hope I may be permitted to put you in mind of our excellent court-preacher, who certainly is a pattern of a wise man, and whose instructions and counsels I can never forget."

"We revere with our whole hearts," replied the merchants, "that excellent man; but we can agree with your opinion, only so far as you speak of that wisdom, which concerns a life well pleasing to God. If you consider him as wise in worldly affairs, as he is experienced and learned in spiritual concerns, permit us to disagree with you. Yet we do not believe that the holy man deserves any less praise, because by the depth of his knowledge of the spiritual world, he is unable to gain insight into and an understanding of earthly things."

"But," said Henry, "is it not possible that that higher knowledge would fit you to guide impartially the reins of human affairs? May it not be possible that childlike and natural simplicity more safely travels the road through the labyrinth of human affairs, than that wild, wandering, and partially restrained wisdom, which considers its own interest, and which is blinded by the unspeakable variety and perplexity of present occurrences? I do not know, but it seems to me, that there are two ways, by which to arrive at a knowledge of the history of man; the one laborious and boundless, the way of experience; the other apparently but one leap, the way of internal reflection. The wanderer of the first must find out one thing from another by wearisome reckoning; the wanderer of the second perceives the nature of everything and occurrence directly by their very essence, views all things in their continually varying connexions, and can easily compare one with another, like figures on a slate. You will pardon me, that I address you, as it were, from my childish dreams; nothing could have emboldened me to speak but my confidence in your kindness, and the remembrance of my teacher, who for a long time has pointed the second way out to me as his own."

"We willingly grant you," said the kind merchants, "that we are not able to follow your train of thought; yet it pleases us that you so warmly remember your excellent teacher, and treasure up so well his lessons. It seems to us that you have a talent for poetry, you speak your fancies out so fluently, and you are so full of choice expressions and apt comparisons. You are also inclined to the wonderful, – the poet's element."

"I do not know whence it comes," said Henry; "I have heard poets spoken of before now; but have never yet seen one. I cannot even form an idea of their curious art; but yet have a great desire to hear about it. I feel that I wish to know many things, of which dark hints only are in my mind. I have often heard people speak of poems, but I have never yet seen one, and my teacher never had occasion to learn the art. Nor have I been able to comprehend everything that he has told me concerning it. Yet he always considered it a noble art, to which I would devote myself entirely, if I should become acquainted with it. In old times it was much more common than now, and every one had some knowledge of it, though in different degrees; moreover it was the sister of other arts now lost. He thought that divine favor had highly honored the minstrels, so that inspired by spiritual intercourse, they had been able to proclaim heavenly wisdom upon earth in entrancing tones."

The merchants then said; "We have in truth not troubled ourselves much with the secrets of the poets, though we have often listened with pleasure to their songs. Perhaps it is true that no man is a poet, unless he is born under a particular star, for there is something curious in this respect about this art. The other arts are very different from it, and much easier to comprehend. The secrets of painters and musicians can much more easily be imagined; and both can be learned with industry and patience. The sound lies already in the strings, and ability is all that is wanting, in order to move them, and stir up each into a delightful harmony. In painting, nature is the best instructress. She brings forth numberless beautiful and wonderful forms, gives to them color, light, and shade; and a practised hand, an exact eye, and a knowledge of the preparation and mixing of colors can imitate nature to the life. How natural for us then to comprehend the effect of these arts, and the pleasure derived from their productions. The song of the nightingale, the whistling of the wind, and the splendors of light, color, and form please us, because they strike our senses agreeably; and as our senses are fitted for this by nature, which also has the same effect, so must the artful imitation of nature please us also. Nature herself will also draw enjoyment from the power of art, and thence has she changed into man, and thus she now rejoices herself over her noble splendors, separates what is agreeable and lovely, and brings it forth by itself in such a way, that she can possess and enjoy it in all ways and at all times and places. In the art of poetry, on the contrary, there is nothing tangible to be met with. It creates nothing with tools and hands. The eye and the ear perceive it not; for the mere hearing of the words has no real influence in this secret art. It is all internal; and as other artists fill the external senses with agreeable emotions, so in like manner the poet fills the internal sanctuary of the mind with new, wonderful, and pleasing thoughts. He knows how to awaken at pleasure the secret powers within us, and by words gives us force to see into an unknown and glorious world. Ancient and future times, innumerable men, strange countries, and the most singular events rise up within us, as from deep hiding places, and tear us away from the known present. We hear strange words and know not their import. The language of the poet stirs, up a magic power; even ordinary words flow forth in charming melody, and intoxicate the fast-bound listener."

"You change every curiosity into ardent impatience," said Henry. "I cannot hear enough of these strange men. It seems to me all at once, as if I had heard them spoken of somewhere in my earliest youth; but I can remember nothing more about it. But what you have said to me is very clear and easy to comprehend, and you give me great pleasure by your beautiful descriptions."

"It is with pleasure," continued the merchants, "that we have looked back upon the many pleasant hours we have spent in Italy, France, and Swabia in the society of minstrels, and we are glad that you take so lively an interest in our discourse about them. In travelling through so many mountains, there is a double delight in conversation, and the time passes pleasantly away. Perhaps you would be pleased to hear some of the pretty tales concerning poets, that we have learned in our travels. Of the poems themselves, which we have heard, we can say but little, both because the pleasure and charm of the moment prevent the memory from retaining much; and because our constant occupations in business destroy many such recollections.

"In olden times, all nature must have been more animate and spiritual than now. Operations, which now animals scarcely seem to notice, and which men alone in reality feel and enjoy, then put animate bodies into motion; and it was thus possible for men of art to perform wonders and produce appearances, which now seem wholly incredible and fabulous. Thus it is said that there were poets in very ancient times, in the regions of the present Greek empire, (as travellers, who have discovered these things by traditions among the common people there, have informed us,) who by the wonderful music of their instruments stirred up a secret life in the woods, those spirits hidden in their trunks; who gave life to the dead seeds of plants in waste and desert regions, and called blooming gardens into existence; who tamed savage beasts, and accustomed wild men to order and civilization; who brought forth the tender affections, and the arts of peace, changed raging floods into mild waters, and even tore away the rocks in dancing movements. They are said to have been at the same time soothsayers and priests, legislators and physicians, whilst even the spirits above were drawn down by their bewitching song, and revealed to them the mysteries of futurity, the balance and natural arrangement of all things, the inner virtues and healing powers of numbers, of plants, and of all creatures. Then first appeared the varied melody, the peculiar harmony and order, which breathe through all nature; while before all was in confusion, wild and hostile. And here one thing is to be noticed; that although these beautiful traces for the recollection of these men remain, yet has their art, or their delicate sensibility to the beauties of nature been lost. Among other occurrences, it once happened that one of this peculiar class of poets or musicians, – although music and poetry may be considered as pretty much the same thing, like mouth and ear, of which the first is only a movable and answering ear, – that once this poet wished to cross the sea to a foreign land. He had with him many jewels and costly articles, which he had received as tributes of gratitude. He found a ship ready to sail, and easily agreed upon a price for his passage. But the splendor and beauty of his treasures so excited the avarice of the sailors, that they resolved among themselves to take him, throw him overboard, and afterwards to divide his goods with each other. Accordingly, when they were far from land, they fell upon him, and told him that he must die, because they had resolved to cast him into the sea. He begged them to spare his life in the most touching terms, offered them his treasures as a ransom, and prophesied that great misfortunes would overtake them, should they take his life. But they were not to be moved, being fearful lest he should sometime reveal their wickedness. When he saw at last that their resolution was taken, he prayed them that at least they would suffer him to play his swan song, after which he would willingly plunge into the sea, with his poor, wooden instrument, before their eyes. They knew very well that, should they once hear his magic song, their hearts would be softened and overwhelmed with repentance; therefore they granted his last request indeed, but stopped their ears, that not hearing his song, they might abide by their resolution. Thus it happened. The minstrel began a beautiful song, pathetic beyond conception. The whole ship accorded, the waters resounded, the sun and the stars appeared at once in the sky, and the inhabitants of the deep issued from the green flood about them, in dancing hosts. The people of the ship stood alone by themselves, with hostile intent waiting impatiently for the end of his song. It was soon finished. Then the minstrel plunged with serene brow down the dark abyss, carrying with him his wonder-working instrument. Scarcely had he touched the glittering wave, when a monster of the deep rose up beneath him, and quickly bore the astonished minstrel away. It swam directly to the shore whither he had been journeying, and landed him gently among the rushes. The poet sang a song of gratitude to his saviour, and joyfully went his way. Sometime after the occurrence of these events, he again visited the seashore, and lamented in sweetest tones his lost treasures, which had been dear to him as remembrances of happier hours, and as tokens of love and gratitude. While he was thus singing, his old friend came swimming joyfully through the waves, and rolled from his back upon the sand the long-lost treasures. The boatmen, after the minstrel had leaped into the sea, began immediately to divide the spoil. During the division a murderous quarrel arose between them, which cost many of them their lives. The few that remained were not able to navigate the vessel; it struck the shore and foundered. They with difficulty saved their lives, and reached the beach with torn garments and empty hands. Thus by the aid of the grateful sea-monster, who had gathered them up from the bottom of the sea, the treasures came into the hands of their original possessor." [See Note I. at the end.]

CHAPTER III

There is another story, continued the merchants after a pause, certainly less wonderful and taken from later times, which yet may please you and give you a clearer insight into the operations of that wonderful art. There was once an old king, whose court was the most splendid of his age. People streamed thither from far and near, in order to share in the splendor of his mode of life. There was not wanting the greatest abundance of costly delicacies at his daily entertainments. There was music, splendid decorations, a thousand different dramatic representations, with other amusements to pass away the time. Nor did intellect fail to be represented there in the persons of sage, pleasant, and learned men, who added to the entertainment and inspiration of the conversation. Finally, there were added many chaste and beautiful youth of both sexes, who constituted the real soul of the charming festivals. The old king, otherwise a strict and stern man, entertained two inclinations, which were the true causes of the splendor of his court, and to which it owed its thanks for its beautiful arrangement. The first of these inclinations was his love for his daughter, who was infinitely dear to him, as a pledge of the love of his wife, who had died in her youth, and to whom, for her marvellous loveliness, he would have sacrificed all the treasures of nature, and all the powers of human minds, in order to create for her a heaven upon earth. The other was a real passion for poesy and her masters. He had from his youth read the works of the poets with heart-felt delight, and had spent much labor and great sums of money in the collection of the poetical works of every tongue, and the society of minstrels was especially dear to him. He invited them from all quarters to his court, and loaded them with honors. He never grew wearied with their songs, and for the sake of some new and splendid production often forgot the most important business affairs, and even the necessaries of life. Amidst such strains had his daughter grown up, and her soul became, as it were, a tender song, the artless expression of longing and of sadness. The beneficent influence, which the protected and honored poets exerted, showed itself through the whole land, but particularly at the court. Life, like some precious potion, was enjoyed in lingering and gentle draughts, and in its purer pleasures; because all low and hateful passions were shunned, as jarring discords to the harmony which ruled all minds. Peace of soul, and beautiful contemplations of a self-created happy world, had become the possession of this wonderful time, and dissension appeared only in the old legends of the poets, as a former enemy of man. It seemed as if the spirits of song could have given no lovelier token of their gratitude to their protector, than his daughter, who possessed all that the sweetest imagination could unite in the tender form of a fair maiden. When you beheld her at the beautiful festivals, amid a band of charming companions in glittering white dress, intensely listening to the rival songs of the inspired minstrels, and with blushes placing the fragrant garland around the locks of the happy one, who had won the prize, you would have taken her for the beautiful and embodied spirit of this art, conspiring with its magic language; and you would cease to wonder at the ecstasies and melodies of the poets.

Yet a mysterious fate seemed to be at work in the midst of this earthly paradise; The sole concern of the people of that country was about the marriage of the blooming princess, upon which the continuation of their blissful times, and the fate of the whole land, depended. The king was growing old. This care lay heavy at his heart; and yet no opening for marriage showed itself, that was agreeable to the wishes of all. A holy reverence for the royal family forbade any subject to harbor the idea of proposing for the hand of the princess. She was hardly regarded as a creature of this earth, and all the princes, who had appeared at court with proposals, seemed so inferior to her, that no one thought that the princess or the king could fix their eye on any one of them. A sense of inferiority had by degrees deterred any suitors from visiting the court, and the wide-spread report of the excessive pride of the royal family seemed to take away from all others the desire to see themselves equally humbled. Nor was this report entirely without foundation. The king, with all his mildness of disposition, had almost unconsciously imbibed a feeling of lofty superiority, which rendered every thought of a connexion of his daughter with a man of lower rank and obscurer origin unendurable and impossible to be entertained. Her high and unparalleled worth had heightened this feeling within him. He was descended from a very old royal family of the East. His consort had been the last of the descendants of the renowned hero Rustan. His minstrels continually sang to him of his relationship to those superhuman beings, who formerly ruled the world. In the magic mirror of their art the difference between the origin of his family and that of other men, and the splendor of his descent, appeared yet clearer, so that it seemed to him that he was connected with the rest of the human family through the nobler class of the poets alone. He looked around in vain for a second Rustan, whilst he felt that the heart of his blooming daughter, the situation of his kingdom, and his increasing age rendered her marriage, in all points of view, most desirable. Not far from the capital, there lived, upon a retired country-seat, an old man, who occupied himself exclusively with the education of his only son, except that he occasionally assisted the country people by his advice in cases of dangerous sickness. The young man was of a serious disposition, and devoted himself exclusively to the study of nature, in which his father had instructed him from childhood. The old man many years before had arrived from a distance at this peaceful and blooming region, and was content while enjoying the beneficent peace, which the king had spread abroad through this retreat. He took advantage of this peace to search into the powers of nature, and impart the piecing knowledge to his son, who gave evidence of much talent for the pursuit, and to whose penetrating mind nature willingly confided her secrets. Without a lofty power of understanding, the secret expression of his noble face, and the peculiar brilliancy of his eyes, you would have called the appearance of this youth ordinary and insignificant. But the longer you gazed upon him, the more attractive he became; and you could scarcely tear yourself from him, when you had once beard his soft impressive voice, and the utterances which his glorious talents prompted. One day, the princess, whose pleasure-garden adjoined the forest, which concealed the country house of the old man in a little valley, had betaken herself thither alone on horseback, that she might follow out her fancies undisturbed, and sing to herself her favorite songs. The fresh air of the lofty trees enticed her gradually deeper into their shade, until at last she came to the house where the old man lived with his son. Happening to feel thirsty, she alighted, fastened the horse to a tree, and stepped into the house, to ask for a glass of milk. The son was present, and was well nigh confounded by the enchanting appearance of a majestic female form, which seemed almost immortal, adorned as it was by all the charms of youth and beauty, and by that indescribable fascinating transparency, revealing the tender, innocent, and noble soul. While he hastened to gratify her desire, the old man addressed her with modest respect, and invited her to be seated at their simple hearth, which was placed in the middle of the house, and on which there glimmered noiselessly a light blue flame. Immediately on entering, the princess was struck with the varied ornaments of the room, the order and cleanliness of the whole, and the peculiar sanctity of the place; and her impression was heightened yet more by the venerable appearance of the old man, poorly clad as he was, and by the modest behavior of the son. The former recognised her immediately as a lady of the court, judging this from her costly dress and noble carriage. While the son was absent, the princess asked him about some curiosities which had caught her eye, and especially concerning some old and singular pictures, which stood at her side over the hearth, and which he kindly undertook to explain to her. The son soon returned with a pitcher of fresh milk, which he artlessly and respectfully handed her. After some interesting conversation with the hosts, she gracefully thanked them for their hospitality, and with blushes asked the old man's permission to visit his house again, that she might enjoy his instructive conversation concerning his wonderful curiosities. She then rode back without having divulged her rank, as she noticed that neither the father nor the son knew her. Although the capital was situated thus near, they were both so buried in their studies, that they strove to shun the busy world; and the young man had never been seized with the desire of being present at the festivities of the court. He had never been accustomed to leave his father alone for more than an hour at the utmost, while roaming through the woods searching for insects and plants, and sharing the inspiration of the mute spirit of nature through the influence of its various outward charms. The simple occurrences of this day were equally important to the old man, the princess, and the youth. The first easily perceived the novel and deep impression, which the unknown lady had made upon his son. He knew his character perfectly, and was fully aware that such a deep impression would last as long as his life. His youth, and the nature of his heart, would of necessity render the first feeling of this nature an unconquerable passion. The old man had for a long time looked forward to such an occurrence. The exceeding loveliness of the stranger excited an involuntary sympathy in the soul of his son, and his unsuspicious mind harbored no troublesome anxiety about the issue of this singular adventure. The princess had never been conscious of experiencing such emotions as arose in her mind, while riding slowly homeward. She could form no exact idea of the curiously mixed, wondrously stirring feelings of a new existence. A magical veil was spread in wide folds over her clear consciousness. It seemed to her that, when it should be withdrawn, she would find herself in a more spiritual world than this. The recollection of the art of poetry, which hitherto had occupied her whole soul, seemed now like a far distant song, connecting her peculiarly delightful dream with the past. When she reached the palace, she was almost frightened at its varied splendor, and yet more at the welcome of her father, for whom for the first time in her life she experienced a distant respect. She thought it impossible for her to mention her adventure to him. Her other companions were too much accustomed to her reveries, and her deep abstractions of thought and fancy, to notice anything extraordinary in her conduct. She seemed now to lose some of her affable sweetness of disposition. She felt as if she were among strangers, and a peculiar anxiety harassed her until evening, when the joyful song of some minstrel, who chanted the praises of hope, and sang with magic inspiration of the wonders which follow faith in the fulfilment of our wishes, filled her with consolation, and lulled her with the sweetest dreams.

As soon as the princess had taken leave, the youth plunged into the forest. He had followed her among the bushes as far as the garden gate, and then sought to return by the road. As he was walking along, he saw some bright object shining before his feet. He stooped and picked up a dark red stone, one side of which was wonderfully brilliant, and the other was graved with ciphers. He knew it to be a costly carbuncle, and thought that he had observed it in the middle of the necklace which the unknown lady wore. He hastened with winged footsteps home, as if she were yet there, and brought the stone to his father. They decided that the son should return next morning to the road, and see whether any one was sent to look for it; if not, they would keep it till they received a second visit from the lady, and then return it to her. The young man passed much of the night gazing at the carbuncle, and felt towards morning irresistibly inclined to write a few words upon the paper in which he wrapt it. He hardly knew himself the meaning of the words which he wrote:

A mystic token deeply graved is beaming
Within the glowing crimson of the stone,
Like to a heart, that, lost in pleasant dreaming,
Keepeth the image of the fair unknown.
A thousand sparks around the gem are streaming,
A softened radiance in the heart is thrown;
From that, the light's indwelling essence darts.
But ah, will this too have the heart of hearts?

As soon as the morning dawned, he took his way in haste to the garden gate.

In the mean while the princess in undressing on the previous evening, had missed the jewel from her necklace. It was a memento from her mother, and moreover a talisman, the possession of which insured to her the liberty of her person, since with it she could never fall into another's power against her will.

This loss surprised more than it frightened her. She remembered that she had it the day before when riding, and was quite certain that it was lost, either in the house of the old man, or on the way back through the woods. She still remembered the exact road she had taken, and concluded to go in search of it as soon as the day should break. This idea caused her so much joy, that it seemed as if she was not at all sorry for her loss, in the good pretence it gave to take the same road once more. At daybreak she passed through the garden to the forest; as she walked with unwonted speed, it was natural that her bosom should feel oppressed, and her heart beat faster than usual. The sun was beginning to gild the tops of the old trees, which moved with a gentle whispering, as if they would waken each other from their drowsy night-faces, in order to greet the sun together; when the princess, startled by a rustling at some distance, looked down the road, and saw the young man hastening towards her. He at the same time observed her.

He remained a while standing as if enchained, and gazed fixedly upon her, as if to assure himself that her appearance was real and no illusion. They greeted each other with subdued expressions of joy at their meeting, as if they had long known and loved each other. Before the princess could explain to him the reason of her early walk, he handed her with blushes and a beating heart the stone in the inscribed billet. It seemed as if the princess anticipated the meaning of the lines. She took the billet silently and with a trembling hand, and almost unconsciously hung a golden chain, which she wore about her neck, upon him, as a reward for his fortunate discovery. He knelt abashed before her, and could hardly find words to answer her inquiries about his father. She told him in a half whisper, and with downcast eyes, that she would with pleasure soon visit them again, and take advantage of his father's promise to make her acquainted with his curiosities.

She thanked the young man again with unusual feeling, and returned slowly on her way without once looking back. The youth was speechless. He bowed respectfully and gazed after her for a long time, until she vanished behind the trees. In a few days she visited them again, and after this her visits became frequent. The youth by degrees became the companion of her walks. He accompanied her from the garden at an appointed hour, and escorted her back again. She observed a strict silence with respect to her rank, confiding as she otherwise was to her attendant, from whom no thought of her heavenly soul was ever hidden. The loftiness of her descent seemed to pour a secret fear into her. The young man gave up to her likewise his whole soul. Both father and son considered her a maiden of quality from the court. She clung to the old man with the tenderness of a daughter. Her caresses lavished upon him were the rapturous prophets of her tenderness towards his son. She was soon perfectly at home in the wonderful house; and while she sang to her lute her charming song with an unearthly voice, the old man and the son sitting at her feet, the latter of whom she instructed in the divine art; she learned on the other hand from his inspired lips the solution of those riddles, which everywhere abound in the secrets of nature. He taught her how by a mysterious sympathy the world had arisen, and the stars been united in their harmonious order. The history of the past became clear to her mind from his holy fables; and how delightful it became, when in the height of his inspiration her scholar seized the lute, and broke out with incredible skill into the most admirable songs. One day, when seized by a peculiar romance of feeling, she was in his company, and her powerful, long-cherished love overcame at returning her customary, maiden timidity; they both almost unconsciously sank into each other's arms, and the first glowing kiss melted them into one forever. As the sun was setting, the roaring of the trees gave notice of a mighty tempest. Threatening thunder-clouds with their deep, night-like darkness gathered over them. The young man hastened to carry his charge in safety from the fearful hurricane and the crashing branches. But through the darkness and his fear for his beloved, he missed the road, and plunged deeper and deeper into the forest. His fear increased when he perceived his mistake. The princess thought of the terror of the king and of the court. An unutterable anxiety pierced at times like a consuming ray into her soul; and the voice of her lover, who continually spoke consolation to her heart, alone restored courage and confidence, and eased her oppressed bosom.

The storm raged on; all endeavors to find the road were in vain, and they both thought themselves fortunate, when, by a flash of lightning, they discovered a cave near at hand on the declivity of a woody hill, where they hoped to find a safe refuge from the dangers of the tempest, and a resting place from their fatigue. Fortune realized their wishes. The cave was dry and overgrown with clean moss. The young man quickly lighted a fire of brushwood and moss, by which they could dry their garments; and the two lovers saw themselves thus strangely separated from the world, saved from a dangerous situation, and alone at each other's side in a warm and comfortable shelter.

A wild almond branch, loaded with fruit, hung down into the cave; and a neighboring stream of trickling water quenched their thirst. The youth had preserved his lute; and now they were entertained by its consoling and cheering music, as they sat by the crackling fire. A higher power seemed to have taken upon itself to loosen the knot more quickly, and to have brought them under peculiar circumstances into this romantic situation. The innocence of their hearts, the magic harmony of their minds, the united, irresistible power of their sweet passion, and their youth, soon made them forget the world and their relations to it, and lulled them, under the bridal song of the tempest and the nuptial torches of the lightning, into the sweetest intoxication, by which a mortal couple ever has been blessed. The break of the light blue morning was to them the awakening of a new, blissful world. Nevertheless a stream of hot tears, which soon gushed forth from the eyes of the princess, revealed to her lover the thousand-fold anxieties, which were awakening in her heart. In one night he had grown old in years, and had passed from youth to manhood. With an inspiring enthusiasm, he consoled his mistress, reminded her of the holiness of true love, and of the high faith which it inspired, and prayed her to look forward with confidence from the good spirit of her heart to the brightest future. The princess felt that his consolation was founded on truth, revealed to him that she was the daughter of the king, and that she feared only on account of the pride and anxiety of her father. After mature consideration, they concluded what course to pursue, and the young man immediately started to seek his father, and to make him acquainted with their plan. He promised to be with her again soon, and left her lost in sweet imaginings of what would be the issue of these occurrences. The youth soon reached the dwelling of his father, who was right glad to see his son return to him in safety. He listened to the story and the plans of the lovers, and seemed willing to assist them. His house was retired, and contained some subterraneous chambers, which could not easily be discovered. Here the princess was to dwell. She was brought thither at twilight, and received by the old man with deep emotion. She afterwards often wept in her solitude, when her thoughts reverted to her mourning father; yet she concealed her grief from her lover, and told it only to the old man, who consoled her kindly, and painted to her imagination her early return to her father.

In the mean time the court had fallen into the greatest alarm, when, at evening, the princess was missing. The king was entirely beside himself, and sent people in every direction to seek her. No man could explain her absence. No one mistrusted that she was entangled in a love affair, and therefore an elopement was not thought of. Moreover no other person of the court was missing, nor was there any cause for the remotest suspicion. The messengers returned without having accomplished anything, and the king sank into the deepest dejection. It was only at evening, when his minstrels came before him, bringing with them their beautiful songs, that his former pleasure appeared renewed to him; his daughter seemed near him, and he conceived the hope that he should soon behold her again. But when he was again alone, his heart seemed like to break, and he wept aloud. Then he thought within himself; "of what advantage to me now is all this splendor and my high birth? Without her, even these songs are mere words and delusions. She was the charm that gave them life and joy, power and form. Would rather that I were the lowest of my subjects. Then my daughter would still be with me; perhaps also I should have a son-in-law, and my grandson would sit upon my knees; then indeed I should be another king than I am now. It is not the crown or the kingdom that makes the king; it is the full, overflowing feeling of happiness, the satiety of earthly possessions, the consciousness of perfect satisfaction and content. In this way am I now punished for my pride. The loss of my wife did not sufficiently humble me; but now my misery is boundless." Thus complained the king in his hours of ardent longing. Yet at times his old austerity and pride broke forth. He was angry with his own complaints; he would endure and be silent as becomes a king. He thought even then that he suffered more than all others, and that royalty was burdened with heavy care; but when it became darker, and stepping into the chamber of his daughter he beheld her clothes hanging there, and her little effects scattered around, as if she had but a moment before left the chamber; then he forgot his resolutions, exhibited all the gestures of sorrow, and called upon his lowest servant for sympathy. All the city and country wept and condoled with him, with their whole hearts. It is worthy of remark, that it was noised abroad that the princess yet lived, and would soon return with a husband. No one knew whence this report arose; but every one clung to it with joyous belief, and awaited her return with impatient expectation. Thus several months passed on, until spring again drew nigh. "What will you wager," said some of sanguine disposition, "that the princess will not return also?" Even the king grew more serene and hopeful. The report seemed to him like a promise from some kind power. The accustomed festivals were again renewed, and nought seemed wanting but the princess to fill up the bloom of their former splendor. One evening, exactly a year from the time when she disappeared, the whole court was assembled in the garden. The air was warm and serene; and no sound was heard but that of the gentle wind in the tops of the old trees, announcing, as it were, the approach of some far off joy. A mighty fountain, arising amid the torches, which with their innumerable lights relieved the duskiness of the sighing tree-tops, accompanied the varied songs with melodious murmurs sounding through the forest. The king sat upon a costly carpet, and the court in festal dress was gathered around him. The multitude filled the garden, and encircled the splendid scene. The king at this moment was sitting plunged in profound thought. The image of his lost daughter appeared before him with unwonted clearness. He thought of the happy days, which ended with the last year about that time. A burning desire overpowered him, and the tears flowed fast down his venerable cheeks; yet he experienced a hope, as clear as it was unusual. It seemed as if the past year of sorrow were but a heavy dream, and he raised his eyes as if seeking her lofty, holy, captivating form amidst the people and the trees. The minstrel had just ended, and deep silence gave evidence of deep emotion; for the poets had sung of the joys of meeting, of spring, and of the future, as hope is accustomed to adorn them.

The silence was suddenly interrupted by the low sound of an unknown but beautiful voice, which seemed to proceed from an aged oak. All looks were directed towards it, and a young man in simple, but peculiar dress, was seen standing with a lute upon his arm. He continued his song, yet saluted the king, as he turned his eyes towards him, with a profound, bow. His voice was remarkably fine, and the song of a nature strange and wonderful. He sang the origin of the world, the stars, plants, animals, and men, the all-powerful sympathy of nature; the remote age of gold, and its rulers Love and Poesy; the appearance of hatred and barbarism, and their battles with these beneficient goddesses; and finally, the future triumph of the latter, the end of affliction, the renovation of nature, and the return of an eternal golden age. Even, the old minstrels, wrapped in ecstasy, drew nearer to the singular stranger. A charm, they had never before felt, seized all listeners, and the king was carried away in feeling, as upon a tide from Heaven. Such music had never before been heard. All thought that a heavenly being had appeared among them; and especially so, because the young man appeared, during his song, continually to grow more beautiful and resplendent, and his voice more powerful. The gentle wind played with his golden locks. The lute in his hands seemed inspired, and it was as if his intoxicated gaze pierced into a secret world. The child-like innocence and simplicity of his face appeared to all transcendant. Now the glorious strain was finished. The elder poets pressed the young man to their bosoms with tears of joy. A silent inward exultation shot through the whole assembly. The king, filled with emotion, approached him. The young man threw himself reverently at his feet. The king raised him up, embraced him, and bade him ask for any gift. Then, with glowing cheeks he prayed the king to listen to another song, and to decide as to his request. The king stepped a few paces back, and the young stranger began: –

Through many a rugged, thorny pass,
With tattered robe, the minstrel wends;
He toils through flood and deep morass,
Yet none a helping hand extends.
Now lone and pathless, overflows
With bitter plaint his wearied heart;
Trembling beneath his lute he goes,
And vanquished by a deeper smart.

There is to me a mournful lot,
Deserted quite I wander here; –
Delight and peace to all I brought,
But yet to share them none are near.
To human life, and everything
That mortals have, I lent a bliss;
Yet all, with slender offering
My heart's becoming claim dismiss.

They calmly let me take my leave,
As spring is seen to wander on;
And none she gladdens, ever grieve
When quite dejected she hath gone.
For fruits they covetously long,
Nor wist she sows them in her seed;
I make a heaven for them in song,
Yet not a prayer enshrines the deed.

With joy I feel that from above
Weird spirits to these lips are bann'd,
O, that the magic tie of love
Were also knitted to my hand!
But none regard the pilgrim lone,
Who needy came from distant isles;
What heart will pity yet his own,
And quench his grief in winning smiles?

The lofty grass is waving, where

He sinks with tearful cheeks to rest;
But thither winnowing the air,
Song-spirits seek his aching breast;
Forgetting now thy former pain,
Its burden early cast behind, –
What thou in huts hast sought in vain,
Within the palace wilt thou find.

Awaiteth thee a high renown,
The troubled course is ending now;
The myrtle-wreath becomes a crown,
Hands truest place it on thy brow.
A tuneful heart by nature shares
The glory that surrounds a throne;
Up rugged steps the poet fares,
And straight becomes the monarch's son.

So far he had proceeded in his song, and wonder held the assembly spell-bound; when, during these stanzas, an old man with a veiled female of noble stature, carrying in her arms a child of wondrous beauty, who playfully eyed the assembly, and smilingly outstretched its little hands after the diadem of the king, made their appearance and placed themselves behind the minstrel. But the astonishment was increased, when the king's favorite eagle, which was always about his person, flew down from the tops of the trees with a golden headband, which he must have stolen from the king's chamber, and hovered over the head of the young man, so that the band fastened itself around his tresses. The stranger was frightened for a moment; the eagle flew to the side of the king, and left the band behind. The young man now handed it to the child, who reached after it; and sinking upon one knee towards the king, continued his song with agitated voice: –

From fairy dreams the minstrel flies
Abroad, impatient and elate;
Beneath the lofty trees he hies
Toward the stately palace-gate.
Like polished steel the walls oppose,
But over swiftly climb his strains;

And seized by love's delicious throes,
The monarch's child the singer gains.

They melt in passionate embrace,
But clang of armor bids them flee;
Within a nightly refuge place
They nurse the new-found ecstasy.
In covert timidly they stay,
Affrighted by the monarch's ire;
And wake with every dawning day
At once to grief and glad desire.

Hope is the minstrel's soft refrain,
To quell the youthful mother's tears;
When lo, attracted by the strain,
The king within the cave appears.
The daughter holds in mute appeal
The grandson with his golden hair;
Sorrowed and terrified they kneel,
And melts his stern resolve to air.

And yieldeth too upon the throne
To love and song a Father's breast;
With sweet constraint he changes soon
To ceaseless joy the deep unrest.
With rich requital love returns
The peace it lately would destroy,
And mid atoning kisses burns
And blossoms an Elysian joy.

Spirit of Song! oh, hither come,
And league with love again to bring
The exiled daughter to her home,
To find a father in the king!
To willing bosom may he press
The mother and her pleading one,
And yielding all to tenderness,
Embrace the minstrel as his son.

The young man, on uttering these words, which softly
swelled through the dark paths, raised with trembling hand the
veil. The princess, her eyes streaming with tears, fell at the feet of
the king, and reached to him the beauteous child. The minstrel

knelt with bowed head at her side. An anxious silence seemed to hold the breath of every one suspended. For a few moments the king remained grave and speechless; then he took the princess to his bosom, pressed her to himself with a warm embrace, and wept aloud. He also raised the young man, and embraced him with heart-felt tenderness. Exulting joy flew through the assembly, which began to crowd eagerly around them. Taking the child, the king raised it towards Heaven with touching devotion; and then kindly greeted the old man. Countless tears of joy were shed. The poets burst forth in song, and the night became a sacred festive eve of promise to the whole land, where life henceforth was but one delightful jubilee. No one can tell whither that land has fled. Tradition only whispers us that mighty floods have snatched Atlantis from our eyes.

CHAPTER IV

Several days' journey was accomplished without the least interruption. The road was hard and dry, the weather refreshing and serene, and the countries, through which they passed, fertile, inhabited, and continually varied. The fertile Thuringian forest lay behind them. The merchants, who had often travelled by the same road, were acquainted with the people, and experienced everywhere the most hospitable reception. They avoided the retired regions, and such as were infested with robbers, or took a sufficient escort for their protection, when obliged to travel through them. Many proprietors of the neighboring castles were on good terms with the merchants. The latter visited them, seeking orders for Augsburg. Much friendly hospitality was shown them, and the old ladies with their daughters pressed around them with hearty curiosity. Henry's mother immediately won their affection by her good-natured complaisance and sympathy. They were rejoiced to see a lady from the capital, who was willing to tell them new fashions, and who taught them the recipes for many pleasant dishes. The young Ofterdingen was praised by knights and ladies, on account of his modesty and artless, mild behavior. The ladies lingered, too, with pleasure upon his captivating form, which resembled the simple word of some Unknown, which perhaps one scarcely regards, until, long after he has gone, it gradually opens its bud, and at length presents a beautiful flower in all the colored splendor of deeply interwoven leaves, so that one never forgets it, nor is ever wearied of its remembrance, but finds in it an exhaustless and ever-present treasure. We now begin to divine the Unknown more exactly; and our presages take form, till at once it becomes clear, that he was an inhabitant of a higher world. The merchants received many orders, and parted from their hosts with mutual hearty wishes, that they might see each other soon again. In one of these castles, where they arrived towards evening, the people were enjoying themselves right jovially. The lord of the castle was an old soldier, who celebrated and interrupted the leisure of peace, and the solitude of his situation, with frequent banquets; and who, besides the tumult of war and the chase, knew no other means of pastime, except the brimming beaker.

He received the new guests with brotherly heartiness, in the midst of his noisy companions. The mother was conducted to the lady of the castle. The merchants and Henry were obliged to seat themselves at the merry table, where the beaker passed bravely around. Henry, after much intreaty, was, in consideration of his youth, excused from pledging every time; the merchants, on the contrary, did not find it much against their tastes, and smacked the old Frank-wine with tolerable gusto. The conversation turned upon the adventures of past years. Henry listened attentively to what was said. The knights spoke of the holy land, of the wonders of the sacred tomb, of the adventures of their enterprise and voyage, of the Saracens in whose power some of them had been, and of the joyous and wonderful life of field and camp. They expressed with great animation their indignation, when they learned that the heavenly birth-place of Christendom was in the power of the unbelieving heathen. They exalted those great heroes, who had earned for themselves an immortal crown, by their persevering endeavors against this lawless people. The lord of the castle showed the rich sword, which he had taken from their leader with his own hand, after he had conquered his castle, slain him, and made his wife and children prisoners, which deeds, by the permission of the emperor, were represented on his coat of arms. All examined the splendid sword. Henry took it and felt suddenly inspired with warlike ardor. He kissed it with fervent devotion. The knight rejoiced at his sympathy with their feelings. The old man embraced him, and encouraged him to devote his hand also forever to the deliverance of the holy sepulchre, and to have affixed to his shoulder the marvel-working cross. He was enraptured, and seemed hardly able to release the sword. "Think, my son," cried the old knight, "a new crusade is on the point of departure. The emperor himself will lead our forces into the land of the morning. Throughout all Europe the cry of the cross is sounding anew, and everywhere heroic devotion is excited. Who knows that we may not, a year hence, be sitting at each other's side in the great and far renowned city of Jerusalem, as joyful conquerors, and think of home over the wine of our fatherland? You will see here, at my house, a maiden from the holy land. Its maidens appear very charming to us of the West; and if you guide your sword skilfully, beauteous captives shall not be wanting." The knights sang with a loud voice the Crusade-song, which at that time was a favorite throughout Europe.

> The grave in heathen hands remaineth;
> The grave, wherein the Savior lay,
> Their cruel mockery sustaineth,
> And is unhallowed every day.
> Its sorrow comes in stifled plea, –
> Who saves me from this injury?
>
> Where bides each valorous adorer?
> The zeal of Christendom has gone!
> Where is the ancient Faith's restorer?
> Who lifts the cross and beckons on?
> Who'll free the grave and rend in twain
> The haughty foe's insulting chain?
>
> A holy storm o'er earth and billow
> Is rushing through the midnight hour;
> To stir the sleeper from his pillow,
> It roars round city, camp, and tower,

In wailful cry from battlements, –
Up, tardy Christian, get thee hence.

Lo, angels everywhere commanding
With solemn faces, voicelessly, –
And pilgrims at the gates are standing
With tearful cheeks, appealingly!
They sadly mourn, those holy men,
The fierceness of the Saracen.

There breaks a red and sullen morrow
O'er Christendom's extended field;
The grief, that springs from love and sorrow,
In every bosom is revealed;
The hearth is left in sudden zeal,
And each one grasps the cross and steel.

The armèd bands are chafing madly,
To rescue the Redeemer's grave;
Toward the sea they hasten gladly,
The holy ground to reach and save.
And children too obey the spell,
The consecrated mass to swell.

High waves the cross, its triumph flinging
On scarrèd hosts that rally there,
And Heaven, wide its portal swinging,
Is all revealed in upper air;
For Christ each warrior burns to pour
His blood upon the sacred shore.

To battle, Christians! God's own legion
Attends you to the promised land,
Nor long before the Paynim region
Will smoke beneath His terror-hand.
We soon shall drench in joyous mood
The sacred grave with heathen blood.

The Holy Virgin hovers, lying
On angel wings, above the plain.
Where all, by hostile weapon dying,
Upon her bosom wake again.
She bends with cheeks serenely bright
Amid the thunder of the fight.

Then over to the holy places!
That stifled plea is never dumb!
By prayer and conquest blot the traces,
That mark the guilt of Christendom!
If first the Savior's grave we gain,
No longer lasts the heathen reign.

Henry's whole soul was in commotion. The tomb rose before him like a youthful form, pale and stately, upon a massive stone in the midst of a savage multitude, cruelly maltreated, and gazing with sad countenance upon a cross, which shone in the background with vivid outlines, and multiplied itself in the tossing waves of the ocean.

Just at this time, his mother sent for him to present him to the knight's lady. The knights were deep in the enjoyments of the banquet, and in their imaginations as to the impending crusade, and took no notice of Henry's departure. He found his mother in close conversation with the old, kindhearted lady of the castle, who welcomed him pleasantly. The evening was serene, the sun began to decline, and Henry, who was longing after solitude and was enticed by the golden distance, which stole through the narrow, deep-arched windows into the gloomy apartment, easily obtained permission to stroll beyond the castle. He hastened, his whole soul in a state of excitement, into the free air. He looked from the height of the old rock down into the woody valley, through which a little rivulet brawled along, turning several mills, the noise of which was scarcely audible from the greatness of the elevation. Then he gazed toward the immeasurable stretch of woods and mountain-passes, and his restlessness was calmed, the warlike tumult died away, and there remained behind only a clear, imaginative longing; He felt the absence of a lute, little as he knew its nature and effects. The serene spectacle of the glorious evening soothed him to soft fancies; the blossom of his heart revealed itself momently like lightning-flashes. He rambled through the wild shrubbery, and clambered over fragments of rock; when suddenly there arose from a neighboring valley a tender and impressive song, in a female voice accompanied by wonderful music. He was sure that it was a lute, and standing full of admiration he heard the following song in broken German.

If the weary heart is living
Yet, beneath a foreign sky;
If a pallid Hope is giving
Fitful glimpses to the eye;
Can I still of home be dreaming?
Sorrow's tears adown are streaming,
Till my heart is like to die.

Could I myrtle-garlands braid thee,
And the cedar's sombre hair!
To the merry dances lead thee,
That the youths and maidens share!
Hadst thou seen in robes the fairest,
Glittering with gems the rarest,
Thy belov'd, so happy there!

Ardent looks my walk attended,
Suitors lowly bent the knee,
Songs of tenderness ascended
With the evening star to me.
In the cherished there confiding, –
Faith to woman, love abiding,
Was their burden ceaselessly.

There, around the crystal fountains
Heaven fondly sinks to rest,
Sighing through the wooded mountains
By its balmy waves caressed;
Where among the pleasure-bowers,
Hidden by the fruits and flowers,
Thousand motley songsters nest.

Wide those youthful dreams are scattered!
Fatherland lies far away!
Long ago those trees were shattered,
And consumed the castle gray.
Came a savage band in motion
Fearful like the waves of ocean,

And Elysium wasted lay.

Terribly the flames were gushing
Through the air with sullen roar,
And a brutal throng came rushing
Fiercely mounted to the door.
Sabres rang, and father, brother,
Ne'er again beheld each other, –
Us away they rudely tore.

Though my eyes with tears are thronging,
Still, thou distant motherland,
They are turned, how full of longing,
Full of love, toward thy strand!
Thou, O child, alone dost save me
From the thought that anguish gave me,
Life to quench with hardy hand.

Henry heard the sobbing of a child and a soothing voice. He descended deeper through the shrubbery, and discovered a pale, languishing girl sitting beneath an old oak tree. A beautiful child hung crying on her neck, and she herself was weeping; a lute lay at her side upon the turf. She seemed a little alarmed when she saw the young stranger, who was drawing near with a saddened countenance.

"You have probably heard my song," said she kindly. "Your face seems familiar to me; let me think. My memory fails me, but the sight of you awakens in me a strange recollection of joyous days. O! it appears as if you resembled my brother, who before our disasters was separated from us and travelled to Persia, to visit a renowned poet there. Perhaps he yet lives and sadly sings the misfortunes of his sisters. Would that I yet remembered some of the beautiful songs he left us! He was noble and kind-hearted, and found his chief happiness in his lute."

The child, who was ten or twelve years old, looked at the strange youth attentively, and clung fast to the bosom of the unhappy Zulima. Henry's heart was penetrated with sympathy. He consoled the songstress with friendly words, and prayed her to relate to him her history circumstantially. She seemed not unwilling to do so. Henry seated himself before her, and listened to her tale, interrupted as it was by frequent tears. She dwelt principally upon the praises of her countrymen and fatherland. She portrayed their loftiness of soul, and their pure, strong susceptibility of life's poetry, and the wonderfully mysterious charms of nature, She described the romantic beauties of the fertile regions of Arabia, which lay like happy islands in the midst of impassable, sandy wastes, refuge places for the oppressed and weary, like colonies of Paradise, – full of fresh wells, whose streams trilled over dense meadows and glittering stones, through venerable groves, filled with every variety of singing birds; regions attractive also in numerous monuments of memorable past time.

"You would look with wonder," she said, "upon the many-colored, distinct, and curious traces and images upon the old stone slabs. They seem to have been always well known; nor have they been preserved without a reason. You muse and muse, you conjecture single meanings, and become more and more curious to arrive at the deep coherence of these old writings. Their unknown meaning excites unwonted meditation; and even though you depart without having solved the enigmas, you have yet made a thousand remarkable discoveries in yourself, which give to life a new refulgence, and to the mind an ever profitable occupation. Life, on a soil inhabited in olden time, and once glorious in its industry, activity, and attachment to noble pursuits, has a peculiar charm. Nature seems to have become there more human, more rational; a dim remembrance throws back through the transparent present the images of the world in marked outline; and thus you enjoy a twofold world, purged by this very process from the rude and disagreeable, and made the magic poetry and fable of the mind. Who knows whether also an indefinable influence of the former inhabitants, now departed, does not conspire to this end? And perhaps it is this hidden bias, that drives men from new countries, at a certain period of their awakening, with such a restless longing for the old home of their race, and that emboldens them to risk their property and life, for the sake of possessing these lands."

After a pause she continued.

"Believe not what you are told of the cruelties of my countrymen. Nowhere are captives treated more magnanimously; and even your pilgrims to Jerusalem were received with hospitality; only they seldom deserved it. Most of them were worthless men, who distinguished their pilgrimages by their evil deeds, and who, for that reason, often fell into the hands of just revenge. How peacefully might the Christian have visited the holy sepulchre, without being under the necessity of commencing a terrible and useless war, which embitters everything, spreads abroad continued misery, and which has separated forever the land of the morning from Europe! What is there in the name of possessor? Our rulers reverentially honored the grave of your Holy One, whom we also consider a divine person; and how beautifully might his sacred tomb become the cradle of a happy union, the source of an alliance blessing all forever!"

Night overtook them during this conversation, darkness approached, and the moon rose in quiet light from the dark forest. They descended slowly towards the castle. Henry was full of thought, and his warlike inspiration had entirely vanished. He observed a strange confusion in the world; the moon assumed the appearance of a sympathizing spectator, and raised him above the ruggedness of the earth's surface, which there seemed so inconsiderable, however wild and insurmountable it might appear to the wanderer below. Zulima walked silently by his side, hand in hand with the child. Henry carried the lute. He endeavored to revive the sinking hope of his companion, to revisit once again her home, whilst he felt within him an earnest prompting to be her deliverer, though in what manner he knew not. A strange power seemed to lie in his simple words, for Zulima felt an unwonted tranquillity, and thanked him in the most touching manner for his consolation.

The knights were yet in their cups, and the mother was engaged in household gossip. Henry had no desire to return to the noisy hall. He felt weary, and with his mother soon betook himself to the chamber, that was set apart for them. He told her before he fell asleep, what had happened, and soon sank into pleasant dreams. The merchants had also retired betimes, and were early astir. The knights were in deep sleep, when they started on their journey; but the lady of the house tenderly took leave of them. Zulima had slept but little; an inward joy had kept her awake; she made her appearance as they were departing, and humbly but eagerly assisted the travellers. Before they started, she brought with many tears her lute to Henry, and touchingly besought him to take it with him as a remembrance of Zulima.

"It was my brother's lute," she said, "who gave it to me at our last parting; it is the only property I have saved. It seemed to please you yesterday, and you leave me an inestimable gift, – *sweet hope*. Take this small token of my gratitude, and let it be a pledge, that you will remember the poor Zulima. We shall certainly see each other again, and then perhaps I shall be much happier."

Henry wept. He was unwilling to take the lute, so indispensable to her happiness.

"Give me," said he, "the golden hand in your hair ornamented with the strange characters, unless it be memorial of your parents, sisters, or brothers, and take in return a veil which my mother will gladly resign to you."

She finally yielded to his persuasions; and gave him the band, saying;

"It is my name in my mother tongue, which I myself in better times embroidered on this band. Let it be a pleasure for you to gaze upon it, and to think that it has bound up my hair during a long and sorrowful period, and has grown pale with its possessor." Henry's mother loosed the veil and gave it to her, while she embraced her with tears.

CHAPTER V

After a few days' journey they arrived at a small village, situated at the foot of some sharp hill-tops, interspersed with deep defiles. The country in other respects was fruitful and pleasant, though the hilly ridge presented a dead, repulsive appearance. The inn was neat, the people attentive; and a number of men, partly travellers, partly mere drinking guests, sat in the room entertaining themselves with various cheer.

Our travellers mingled with them, and joined in their conversation. The attention of the company was particularly directed to an old man strangely dressed, who sat by a table and answered pleasantly whatever questions of curiosity were put to him. He had come from foreign lands, and early that day had been examining the surrounding country. He was now explaining his business, and the discoveries he had made during the day. The people here called him a treasure-digger. But he spoke very modestly of his power and knowledge; yet what he said bore the impress of quaintness and novelty. He said that he was born in Bohemia. From his youth he had been very curious to know what might be hidden in the mountains, whence water poured its visible springs, and where gold, silver, and precious stones were found, so irresistibly attractive to man. He had often in the neighboring cloister-chapel beheld their solid light appended to the pictures and relics, and only wished that they would speak to him in explanation of their wonderful origin. He had indeed sometimes heard that they came from far distant regions; but had always wondered why such treasures and jewels might not also be found in his own land. The mountains would not be so extensive and lofty, and so closely guarded, without some purpose; he also imagined that he had found shining and glimmering stones upon them. He had climbed about industriously among the clefts and caves, and had peered into their antiquated halls and arches with unspeakable pleasure.

At length he met a traveller who told him that he must become a miner in order to satisfy his curiosity. There were miners in Bohemia, and he needed only descend the river for ten or twelve days, to Eula, where to gratify his desire he had only to mention it. He waited for no further confirmation of this, but set off on the next day. After a fatiguing journey of several days he reached Eula.

"I cannot describe how gloriously I felt, when I saw from the hill the piles of rock overgrown with thickets, upon which stood the board huts, and watched the smoke-wreaths rising over the forest from the valley below. A distant murmur increased my eager anticipations. With incredible curiosity and full of silent reverence, I soon stood over a steep descent, which led precipitously down into the mountain, from among the huts. I hastened towards the valley, and soon met some men dressed in black, with lamps in their hands, whom I not improperly took to be miners, and to whom I told my desire with anxious timidity. They listened to me kindly, and told me that I must go to the smelting-houses and inquire for the overseer, who supplied the place of director and master, and who would tell me whether I could be admitted. They thought my request would be granted, and told me that 'good luck' was the customary form of greeting the overseer. Full of joyous expectations I pursued my way, constantly repeating to myself the new and significant greeting. I found a venerable old man who received me with kindness, and after telling him my history and my warm desire to be instructed in his rare and mysterious art, he readily promised to fulfil my wishes. He seemed pleased with me, and entertained me in his own house. I could scarcely wait for the moment when I should descend the pit, and behold myself in the long-coveted apparel. That very evening he brought me a mining-dress, and explained to me the use of some tools which were kept in a chamber. At evening the miners came to him, and not a word of their conversation did I lose, however foreign and unintelligible the chief part of their language appeared to me. The little, however, that I seemed to understand heightened the ardor of my curiosity, and busied me at night with strange dreams. I awoke early, and found myself at the house of my new host, where the miners were gradually collecting to receive orders. A little side-room was fitted up as a chapel. A monk appeared and read mass, and afterwards pronounced a solemn prayer, in which he invoked Heaven to give the miners its holy protection, to assist them in their dangerous labors, to defend them from the temptations and snares of evil spirits, and to grant them abundant ore. I never prayed more fervently, and never realized so vividly the deep significance of the mass. My companions appeared to me like heroes of the lower earth, who were obliged to encounter a thousand perils, but possessing an enviable fortune in their precious knowledge, and prepared, by grave and silent intercourse with the primeval children of nature, in their sombre, mystic chambers, for the reception of heavenly gifts, and for a blessed elevation above the world and its troubles. When the service was concluded, the overseer, giving me a lamp and a small wooden crucifix, accompanied me to the shaft, as we are accustomed to call the steep entrance into the subterraneous abodes. He taught me the method of descent, acquainted me with the necessary precautions, as well as with the names of the various objects and divisions. He led the way, and slid down a round beam, grasping with one hand a rope, which was knotted to a transverse bar, and with the other his lamp. I followed his example, and in this manner we soon reached a considerable depth. I have seldom felt so solemnly; and the distant light glimmered like a happy star, pointing out the path to the secret treasures of nature. We came below to a labyrinth of paths. My kind master was ever ready to answer my inquisitive questions, and to teach me concerning his art. The roaring of the water, the distance from the inhabited surface, the darkness and intricacy of the paths, and the distant hum of the working miners, delighted me extremely, and I joyfully felt myself in full possession of all that for which I had most ardently sighed. This complete satisfaction of our innate taste, this wonderful delight in things which perhaps have an intimate relation to our secret being, and in occupations for which one is destined from the cradle, cannot be explained or described. Perhaps they might appear to every one else common, insignificant, and unpleasant; but they seemed to me necessary as air to the lungs, or food to the stomach. My good master was pleased at my inward delight, and promised me that, with such zeal and attention, I should advance rapidly and become an able miner. With what reverence did I behold for the first time in my life, on the sixteenth of March, more than five-and-forty years ago, the king of metals in small, delicate leaves between the fissures of the rocks! It seemed as if, having been doomed here to close captivity, it glittered kindly towards, the miner, who with so many dangers and labors breaks a way to it through its strong prison-walls, that he may remove it to the light of day, and exalt it to the honor of royal crowns, vessels, and holy relics, and to dominion over the world in the shape of genuine coin, adorned with emblems, cherished by all. From that time I remained at Eula, and advanced gradually from the business of removing the hewn pieces of ore in baskets, to the degree of hewer, who is the real miner, and who performs the observations upon the stone."

The old man paused a moment in his narration, and drank, while the attentive listeners pledged his good luck, as they drained their cups. Henry was delighted with the old man's discourse, and was desirous to hear still more from him.

His listeners related descriptions of the dangers and strangeness of the miner's life, and had many marvels to tell, at which the old man often smiled, and endeavored to correct their odd representations.

After a while Henry said, "you must have experienced much that is wonderful since then, I hope you have never repented your selection of a mode of life. Be kind enough to tell us how you have employed yourself since, and why you are now travelling. You must have looked farther into the world, and I am certain that you are now something more than a common miner."

"I take great pleasure," said the old man, "in the recollection of past times, in which I find cause to bless the divine mercy and goodness. Fate has led me through a joyful and serene life, and not a day has passed, at the close of which I could not retire to rest with a thankful heart. I have always been fortunate in my undertakings, and our common Father in Heaven has guarded me from evil, and brought me to a gray old age with honor. Next to him I must thank my old master for all these blessings, who long since was gathered to his fathers, and of whom I never can think without tears. He was a man of the old school, after God's own heart. He was gifted with deep penetration, yet childlike and humble in every action. Through his means mining has become in high repute, and has helped the duke of Bohemia to immense treasures. The whole region has become by its influence settled and prosperous, and is now a blooming land. All the miners honored him as a father, and as long as Eula stands, his name will be mentioned with emotion and gratitude. His name was Werner, and he was a Lausatian by birth. His only daughter was a mere child when I came to his house. My industry, faithfulness, and devoted attachment daily won his affection. He gave me his name and adopted me as his son. The little girl grew to be an open-hearted, merry creature, whose countenance was as beautifully clear and pure as her own mind. The old man, when he saw that she was attached to me, that I loved to play with her, and that I could never cease gazing at her eyes, which were as blue and open as heaven and glittering as crystal, often told me that when I became a worthy miner, he would not refuse her to me. He kept his word. The day I became hewer he laid his hands upon us, blessed us as bride and bridegroom, and a few weeks afterward I called her my wife. Early on that day, although a mere apprentice, I struck upon a rich vein. The Duke sent me a golden chain, with his likeness engraven on a large medallion, and promised me the office of my father-in-law. How happy was I when on my marriage day I hung the chain around the neck of my bride, and the eyes of all were turned upon her. Our old father lived to see some merry grand-children, and his declining years were more joyous than he had ever anticipated. With joy could he finish his task, and fare forth from the dark mine of this world, to rest in peace, and await the final day.

"Sir," said the old man, as he turned his gaze upon Henry, and wiped some tears from his eyes, "it must be that mining is blessed by God; for there is no art, which renders those who are occupied in it happier and nobler, which awakens a deeper faith in divine wisdom and guidance, or which preserves the innocence and childlike simplicity of the heart more freshly. Poor is the miner born, and poor he departs again. He is satisfied with knowing where metallic riches are found, and with bringing them to light; but their dazzling glare has no power over his simple heart. Untouched by the perilous delirium, he is more pleased in examining their wonderful formation, and the peculiarities of their origin and primitive situation, than in calling himself their possessor. When changed into property, they have no longer any charm for him, and he prefers to seek them amid a thousand dangers and travails, in the fastnesses of the earth, rather than to follow their vocation in the world, or aspire after them on the earth's surface, with cunning and deceitful arts. These severe labors keep his heart fresh and his mind strong; he enjoys his scanty pay with inward thankfulness, and comes forth every day from the dark tombs of his calling, with new-born enjoyment of life. He now appreciates the pleasure of light and of rest, the charms of the free air and prospect; his food and drink are right refreshing to one, who enjoys them as devoutly as if at the Lord's Supper; and with what a warm and tender heart he joins his friends, or embraces his wife and children, and thankfully shares the delights of heart-felt intercourse."

"His lonely occupation cuts off a great part of his life from day and the society of man. Still he does not harden himself in dull indifference as to these deep-meaning matters of the upper world; and he retains a childlike simplicity, which recognises the interior essence, and the manifold, primitive energies of all things. Nature will never be the possession of any single individual. In the form of property it becomes a terrible poison, which destroys rest, excites the ruinous desire of drawing everything within the reach of its possessor, and carries with it a train of wild passions and endless sorrows. Thus it undermines secretly the ground of the owner, buries him in the abyss which breaks beneath him, and so passes into the hands of another, thus gradually satisfying its tendency to belong to all.

"How quietly, on the contrary, the poor miner labors in his deep solitudes, far from the restless turmoil of day, animated solely by a thirst for knowledge and a love of harmony. In his solitude he tenderly thinks of his friends and family, and his sense of their value and relationship is continually renewed. His calling teaches indefatigable patience, and forbids his attention to be diverted by useless thoughts. He deals with a strange, hard, and unwieldly power, which will yield only to persevering industry and continual care. But what a glorious flower blooms for him in these awful depths, – a firm confidence in his heavenly Father, whose hand and care are every day visible to him in signs not easily mistaken! How often have I sat down, and by the light of my lamp gazed upon the plain crucifix with the most heart-felt devotion! Then for the first time I clearly understood the holy meaning of this mysterious image, and struck upon a heart-vein of the richest golden ore, and which has yielded me an everlasting reward."

After a pause the old man continued: –

"Truly must he have been divine, who first taught men the noble art of mining, and who has hidden in the bosom of the rock this sober emblem of human life. In one place the veins are large, easily broken, but poor; in another a wretched and insignificant cleft of rock confines it; and here the best ores are to be found. It often splits before the miner's face into a thousand atoms, but the patient one is not terrified; he quietly pursues his course, and soon sees his zeal rewarded, whilst working it open in a new and more promising direction.

"A specious lump often entices him from the true direction; but he soon discovers that the way is false, and breaks his way by main strength across the grain of the rock, until he has found the true path that leads to the ore. How thoroughly acquainted does the miner here become with all the humors of chance, and how assured that energy and constancy are the only sure means of overcoming them and of raising the hidden treasure."

"Certainly you are not without cheering songs," said Henry. "I should think that your calling would involuntarily inspire you with music, and that songs would be your welcome companions."

"There you have spoken the truth," said the old man. "The song and the guitar belong to the miner's life, and no occupation can retain their charm with more zest than ours. Music and dancing are the pleasures of the miner; like a joyful prayer are they, and the remembrance and hope of them help to lighten weary labor and shorten long solitude.

"If you would like it now, I will give you a song for your entertainment, which was a favorite in my youth.

"Who fathoms her recesses,
Is monarch of the sphere, –
Forgetting all distresses,
Within her bosom here.

"Of all her granite piling
The secret make he knows,
And down amid her toiling

Unweariedly he goes.

"He is unto her plighted,
And tenderly allied, –
Becomes by her delighted,
As if she were his bride.

"New love each day is burning
For her within his breast,
No toil or trouble shunning,
She leaveth him no rest.

"To him her voice is swelling
In solemn, friendly rhyme,
The mighty stories telling
Of long-evanished time.

"The Fore-world's holy breezes
Around his temples play,
And caverned night releases
To him a quenchless ray.

"On every side he greeteth
A long familiar land,
And willingly she meeteth
The labors of his hand.

"For helpful waves are flowing
Along his mountain course,
And rocky holds are showing
Their treasures' secret source.

"Toward his monarch's palace
He guides the golden stream,
And diadem and chalice
With noble jewels gleam.

"Though faithfully his treasure
He renders to the king,
He liveth poor with pleasure,
And makes no questioning.

"And though beneath him daily
They fight for gold and gain,

Above here let him gaily \
The lord of earth remain."

The song pleased Henry exceedingly, and he begged the old man to sing another. He was willing to gratify him, saying, "I know one song that is very strange, and of whose origin we ourselves are ignorant. A travelling miner, who came to us from a distance, and who was a curious diviner with a wand, brought it with him. The song became a favorite because it was so peculiar, – nearly as dark and obscure as the music itself; but on that very account singularly attractive, and like a dream between sleeping and waking.

"I know where is a castle strong,
With stately king in silence reigning,
Attended by a wondrous throng,
Yet deep within its walls remaining.
His pleasure-hall is far aloof,
With viewless warders round it gliding,
And only streams familiar sliding
Toward him from the sparry roof.

"Of what they see with lustrous eyes,
Where all the stars in light are dwelling,
They faithfully the king apprize,
And never are they tired of telling.
He bathes himself within their flood,
So daintily his members washing,
And all his light again is flashing
Throughout his mother's [2] paly blood.

"His castle old and marvellous,
From seas unfathomed o'er him closing,
Stood firm, and ever standeth thus,
Escape to upper air opposing;
An inner spell in secret thrall
The vassals of the realm is holding,
And clouds, like triumph-flags unfolding,
Are gathered round the rocky wall.

"Lo, an innumerable race

Before the barred portals lying;
And each the trusty servant plays,
The ears of men so blandly plying.
So men are lured the king to gain,
Divining not that they are captured;
But thus by specious longing raptured,
Forget the hidden cause of pain.

"But few are cunning and awake,
Nor ever for his treasures pining;
And these assiduous efforts make,
The ancient castle undermining.
The mighty spell's primeval tie
True insight's hand alone can sever;
If so the Inmost opens ever,
The dawn of freedom's day is nigh.

"To toil the firmest wall is sand,
To courage no abyss unsounded;
Who trusteth in his heart and hand,
Seeks for the king with zeal unbounded.
He brings him from his secret hill,
The spirit foes by spirits quelling,
Masters the torrents madly swelling,
And makes them follow at his will.

"The more the king appears in sight,
And freely round the earth is flowing,
The more diminishes his might,
The more the free in number growing.
At length dissolves that olden spell, –
And through the castle void careering,
Us homeward is the ocean bearing
Upon its gentle, azure swell."

Just as the old man ended, it struck Henry that he had somewhere heard that song. He asked him to repeat it and wrote it down. The old man then departed, and the merchants conversed with the other guests on the pleasures and hardships of mining. One said "I don't believe the old man is here without some object. He has been climbing to-day among the hills, and has doubtless discovered good signs. We will ask him when he comes in again."

"See here," said another, "we might ask him to hunt up a well for our village. Good water is far off, and a well would be right welcome to us."

"It occurs to me," said a third, "that I might ask him to take with him one of my sons, who has already filled the house with stones. The youngster would certainly make an able miner, and the old man seems honest, and one who would bring him up in the way he should go."

The merchants were thinking whether they might not establish, by aid of the miner, a profitable trade with Bohemia, and procure metals thence at low prices. The old man entered the room again, and all wished to make use of his acquaintance, when he began to say: –

"How dull and depressing is this narrow room! The moon is without there in all her glory, and I have a great desire to take a walk. I saw to-day some remarkable caves in this neighborhood. Perhaps some of you would like to go with me; and if we take lights, we shall be able to view them without any difficulty."

The inhabitants of the village were already acquainted with the existence of these caves, but no one had as yet dared to enter them. On the contrary they were deceived by frightful traditions of dragons and other monsters, which were said to dwell therein. Some went so far as to say that they had seen them, and insisted that the bones of men who had been robbed, and of animals which had been devoured, were to be found at the entrances of these caves. Others thought that a ghost haunted them, for they had often seen from a distance a strange human form there, and songs had been heard thence at night.

The old man was rather incredulous upon the point, and laughingly assured them that they could visit the caves with safety under the protection of a miner, since such monsters must shun him; and as for a singing spirit, that must certainly be a beneficent one. Curiosity rendered many courageous enough to accept his proposition. Henry wished also to accompany him, and his mother at length yielded to his entreaties, and the persuasion and promises of the old man, who agreed to have a special eye to his safety. The merchants promised to do the same. Long sticks of pitch-pine were collected for torches; part of the company provided themselves plentifully with ladders, poles, ropes, and all sorts of defensive weapons, and thus finally they started for the neighboring hills. The old man led the way with Henry and the merchants. The boor had brought that inquisitive son of his, who full of joy held a torch and pointed out the way to the caves. The evening was clear and warm. The moon shone mildly over the hills, prompting strange dreams in all creatures. Itself lay like a dream of the sun, above the introverted world of visions, and restored nature, now living in its infinite phases, back to that fabulous olden time, when every bud yet slumbered by itself, lonely and unquickened, longing in vain to expand the dark fulness of its immeasurable existence. The evening's tale mirrored itself in Henry's mind. It seemed as if the world lay disclosed within him, showing him as a friendly visitor all her hidden treasures and beauties. So clearly was the great yet simple apparition revealed to him. Nature seemed incomprehensible, only because the near and the true loomed around man with such a manifold lavishment of expression. The words of the old man had opened a secret door. He saw a little dwelling built close to a lofty minster, from whose stone pavement arose the solemn foreworld, while the clear, joyous future, in the form of golden cherubs, floated from the spire towards it with songs. Loud swelled the notes in their silvery chanting, as all creatures were entering at the wide gate, each audibly expressing in a simple prayer and proper tongue their interior nature. How strange it seemed that this clear view, so necessary to his existence, had been so long unknown to him. He now reviewed at a glance all his relations to the wide world around him. He felt what he had become, and was to become, through its influence, and comprehended all the peculiar conceptions and presages, which he had already often stumbled upon in contemplation. The story which the merchants had related of the young man, who studied nature so assiduously, and who became the son-in-law of the king, recurred to his mind, with a thousand other recollections of his past life, weaving themselves involuntarily on his part into a magic thread. While Henry was thus occupied in his inward musings, the company had approached the cave. The entrance was low, and the old man took a torch and first clambered over some fragments of rock. A perceptible current of air blew towards them, and the old man assured them that they could follow with confidence. The most timorous brought up the rear, holding their weapons in readiness. Henry and the merchants were behind the old man, and the boy walked merrily at his side. The path, at first narrow, emerged into a spacious and lofty cave, which the gleam of the torches could not fully illumine. Some openings, however, were seen in the rocky wall opposite. The ground was soft and quite even; the walls and ceiling were also neither rough nor irregular. But the innumerable bones and teeth which covered the ground, chiefly attracted the attention of all. Many were in a full state of preservation, some bore marks of decay, while some projecting here and there from the walls seemed petrified. Most of them were of extraordinary size and strength. The old man was much gratified at seeing these relics of gray antiquity; they added little courage, however, to the farmers, who considered them downright evidence, that beasts of prey were near at hand, although the old man pointed out the signs upon them of a remote antiquity, and asked them whether they had ever heard of destruction among their flocks, or the seizure of men in the neighborhood, and whether they thought these relics the bones of known beasts or men. The old man wished to penetrate farther into the cave, but the farmers deemed it advisable to retreat to its mouth, and there await his return. Henry, the merchants, and the boy remained with him, having provided themselves with ropes and torches. They soon reached a second cave, where the old man did not forget to mark the path by which they entered, by a figure of bones which he erected before the mouth. This cave resembled the other, and was equally full of the remains of animals. Henry's mind was affected by wonder and awe; he felt as if passing through the outer-court of the central earth-palace. Heaven and earth lay at once far distant from him; these dark and vast halls seemed parts of some strange subterraneous kingdom. "May it not be possible," thought he to himself, "that beneath our feet there moves by itself a world in mighty life, that strange productions derive their being from the bowels of the earth, which sends forth the internal heat of its dark bosom into gigantic and preternatural shapes? Might not these awful strangers have been driven forth once by the piercing cold, and appeared amongst us, while perhaps at the same time heavenly guests, living, speaking energies of the stars, were visible above our heads? Are these bones the remains of their wandering upon the surface, or of their flight into the deep?"

Suddenly the old man called them to him, and showed them the fresh track of a human foot upon the ground. They could discover no more, so that the old man concluded they might follow the track without fear of meeting robbers. They were about to do this, when suddenly, as from a great depth beneath their feet, a distinct strain arose. They listened attentively, with not a little astonishment.

"In the vale I gladly linger,
Smiling in the dusky night,
For to me with rosy finger
Proffers Love his cup of light.

"With its dew my spirit sunken
Wafted is toward the skies,
And I stand in this life drunken
At the gate of paradise.

"Lulled in blessed contemplation,
Vexes me no petty smart;
O, the queen of all creation
Gives to me her faithful heart.

"Many years of tearful sorrows
Glorified this common clay, –
Thence a graven form it borrows,
Life securing it for aye.

"Here the lapse of days evanished
But a moment seems to me;
Backward would I turn, if banished,
Gazing hither gratefully."

All were most agreeably surprised and eagerly wished to discover the singer.

After some search, they found in an angle of the right wall a deep sunken path, to which the footsteps seemed to lead them. Soon they thought they perceived a light, which became clearer as they approached. A new vault of greater extent than those they had yet passed opened before them, in the further extremity of which they saw a human form sitting by a lamp, with a great book before him upon a slab, in which he appeared to be reading.

The figure turned towards them, arose, and came forward. He was a man whose age it were impossible to guess. He seemed neither old nor young, and no traces of time were discoverable, except in his smooth silvery hair, which was parted on his forehead. An indescribable air of serenity dwelt in his eyes, as if he were looking down from a clear mountain into an infinite spring.

He had sandals upon his feet, and wore no other dress except a large mantle cast around him, which added dignity to his noble form. He expressed no surprise at their unexpected arrival, and greeted them as old acquaintances and expected guests.

"It is pleasant indeed," said he, "that you have sought me. You are the first friends I have ever seen, though I have dwelt here a long season. It seems that men are beginning to examine our spacious and wonderful mansion a little more closely."

The old man answered, "We did not expect to find here so friendly a host. We had been told of wild beasts and spectres, but we now find ourselves most agreeably deceived. If we have disturbed your devotions or deep meditations, pardon it to our curiosity."

"Can any sight be more delightful," said the unknown, "than the joyous and speaking countenance of man? Think not that I am a misanthrope, because you find me in this solitude. I have not shunned the world, but have only sought a retirement, where I could apply myself to my meditations undisturbed."

"Have you never grieved for your own desolation, and do not hours sometimes come, when you are fearful, and long to hear a human voice?"

"Now, no more. There was a time in my youth, when a highly wrought imagination induced me to become a hermit. Dark forebodings busied my youthful fancy. I thought to find in solitude full nourishment for my heart. The fountain of my inner life seemed inexhaustible. But I soon learned that fulness of experience must be added to it, that a young heart cannot dwell alone; nay, that man, by manifold intercourse with his race, reaches a certain self-subsisting independence."

"I myself believe," said the old man, "that there is a certain natural impulse to every mode of life; and that perhaps the experiences of increasing age lead of themselves to a withdrawal from human society. It then seems as if society were devoted to activity as much for gain as for maintenance. It is powerfully impelled by a great hope, by a common object, and children and the aged seem not at home. Helplessness and ignorance exclude the first from it, while the latter, with every hope fulfilled, every object attained, and new hopes and objects no longer woven into their circle, turn back into themselves, and find enough employment in preparing for a higher existence. But more peculiar causes seem to have separated you entirely from men, and influenced you to resign all the comforts of society. Methinks that the tension of your mind must often relax, and give place to the most disagreeable emotions."

"I have indeed felt that; but have learned to avoid it by a

strict regularity in my mode of living. For this purpose I endeavor by exercise to preserve my health, and then there is no danger. Every day I walk for several hours and enjoy the light and air as much as possible; or I remain in these halls, and busy myself at certain times with basket-braiding and carving. I exchange my ware at distant places for provisions; I have brought many books with me, and thus time passes like a moment. In these places I have acquaintances who know where I live, and from whom I learn what is going on in the world. These will bury me when I die, and take away my books."

He led them nearer his seat, which was against the wall of the cave. They noticed several books and a guitar lying upon the ground, and upon the wall hung a complete suit of armor apparently quite costly. The table consisted of five great stone slabs, put together in the form of a box. Upon the upper one were two sculptured male and female figures large as life, holding a garland of lilies and roses. Upon the side was inscribed,

"Frederick and Mary of Hohenzollern here returned to their native dust."

The hermit inquired of his guests concerning their fatherland, and how they had journeyed into these regions. He was kind and communicative, and displayed great knowledge of the world.

The old man said, "I see you have been a warrior; the armor betrays you."

"The dangers and vicissitudes of war, the deep, poetic spirit connected with an armed host, tore me from my youthful solitude and determined the destiny of my life. Perhaps the long tumult, the innumerable events among which I have dwelt, awakened in me a yet stronger inclination for solitude, where numberless recollections make pleasant companions; and this the more, in proportion as our view of them is varied; a view which now first discovers their true connexion, their significance, and their occult tendency. The peculiar sense for the study of man's history develops itself but tardily, and rather through the silent influence of memory than by the more forcible impressions of the present.

The nearest events seem but loosely connected, yet they sympathize so much the more curiously with the remote. And it is only when one is able to comprehend in one view a lengthened series, neither interpreting too literally, nor confounding the proper method with capricious fancies, that he detects the secret chain which binds the past to the future, and learns to rear the fabric of history from hope and memory. Yet only he can succeed in discovering the simple laws of history, to whom the whole past is present. We arrive only at incomplete and cumbrous formulas, and are well content to find for ourselves an available pre-scription, that may sufficiently expound the riddle of our own short lives. But I can truly say that each rigorous view of the events of life causes us deep and inexhaustible pleasure, and raises us, of all speculations, the highest above earthly evils. Youth reads history only from curiosity, as it cons a story; to maturity it becomes a divinely consoling and edifying comp-anion, preparing it gently by its wise discourses for a higher and more embracing sphere of action, and acquainting it through intelligible images with the unknown world. The church is the dwelling-house of history, the church-yard its symbolic flower-garden. History should only be written by old and pious men, whose own is drawing to its close, and who have nothing more to hope for, but transplantation to the garden. Their descriptions will be neither obscure nor dull; on the contrary a ray from the spire will exhibit everything in the most exact and beautiful light, and the Holy Spirit will hover above these rarely stirred waters."

"How true and obvious are your remarks," said the old man. "We ought certainly to spend more labor in faithfully recording the occurrences of our own times, and should leave our record as a devout bequest for posterity. There are a thousand remoter matters to which care and labor are devoted, while we trouble ourselves little with the nearer and weightier, the occurrences of our lives, and those of our relatives and generation, whose fleeting destiny we have comprehended in the idea of a Providence. We heedlessly suffer all traces of these to escape from our memories. Like consecrated relics, all facts of the past will be sought for by a wiser future, not indifferent to the biography of the most insignificant man, since in his life the lives of all his greater contemporaries will be more or less reflected."

"It is also much to be regretted," said the count of Hohenzollern, "that even the few, who have undertaken to report the deeds and events of their times, have not carried out their designs, nor striven to give order and completeness to their observations; but have proceeded almost wholly at random in the choice and collection of their facts. Any one may easily see that he only can describe plainly and perfectly, that which he knows exactly, whose origin and consequences, object and use, are present to his mind; for otherwise there will be no description, but a bewildering mixture of imperfect statements. Let a child describe an engine, or a farmer a ship, and no one can gain anything useful or instructive from their words; and so is it with most historians, who are perhaps able enough even to be wearisome in relating and collecting facts; but who forget what is most note-worthy, what first makes history historical, and connects so many varied events in an agreeable and instructive whole. If I understand all this rightly, it appears to me necessary that a historian should be also a poet; for poets alone know the art of skilfully combining events. In their tales and fables I have often noticed, with silent pleasure, a tender sympathy with the mysterious spirit of life. There is more truth in their romances than in learned chronicles. Though the heroes and their fates are inventions, yet the spirit in which they are composed is true and natural. In some degree it matters not whether those persons, in whose fates we trace our own, ever did or did not exist. We seek to contemplate the great and simple spirit of an age's phenomena; and if this wish be gratified, we are not cumbered about the certainty of the existence of their external forms."[See Note II.]

"I have also been much attached to the poets on that account," said the old man. "Life and the world have become through them more clear and perceptible to me. It has appeared to me that they must be in alliance with the acute spirits of light, which penetrate and divide all natures, and spread over each a peculiar, softly tinted veil. By their songs I felt my own nature gently developed, and it could move, as it were, more freely, enjoy its social disposition and desires, poise with silent pleasure its limbs against each other, and in various forms excite delight a thousand-fold."

"Were you so happy in your country as to have some poets?" asked the hermit.

"There have been a few with us at times; but travelling seemed their chief pleasure, and therefore they scarcely ever remained long with us. But during my wanderings in Illyria, Saxony, and Sweden, I have met some, the remembrance of whom is ever pleasant."

"You have, travelled far, and doubtless must have seen much during your life, that is wonderful."

"Our art almost compels us to look industriously around the world, and it is as if the miner were driven by a subterraneous fire. One mountain sends him to another. He never ceases his scrutiny, and during his whole life is gaining knowledge from that wonderful architecture, which has so curiously floored and wainscotted the earth under our feet. Our art is very ancient and extended. It may indeed, like our race, have migrated with the sun from the East toward the West, from the middle to the extremities. It has been obliged everywhere to combat with other difficulties; and as necessity continually urges the human spirit to wise inventions, so the miner can increase his knowledge and ability, and enrich his home with youthful experience."

"You are well nigh inverted astrologers," said the hermit; "as they ceaselessly regard the sky, wandering through its immeasurable spaces, so do you turn your gaze to the earth, exploring its construction. Astrologers study the forces and influences of the stars, while you are discovering the forces of rocks and mountains, and the manifold properties of earth and stone strata. To them the higher world is a book of futurity; to you the earth is a memorial of the primeval world."

"This connexion is not without its meaning," said the old man; "these shining prophets play perhaps a chief part in that old history of the wonderful creation. Men perhaps in the course of time will learn to understand them better, and to explain them by their operations, and inversely. Perhaps also the great mountain-chains exhibit the traces of their former ways, and perhaps they desired to support themselves without foreign aid, to take their own way to Heaven. Many raised themselves boldly enough that they might become stars, and therefore must now be deprived of the fair green vesture of the lower regions. They have therefore gained nothing, except the power of influencing the weather for their fathers, and of becoming prophets for the lower world, which now they protect, and now deluge with tempests."

"Since I have dwelt in this cave," the hermit answered, "I have been accustomed to reflect more on ancient times. I cannot describe how attractive such meditations are, and I can imagine the love which a miner must cherish for his trade. When I look upon these strange old bones, which are collected in such great numbers here; when I picture to myself the savage period when those strange and monstrous beasts crowded in dense bands into these caves, driven thither perhaps by fear and terror, and finding here their death; when again I go back to the times when these caves were formed, and wide-spread floods covered the land; then I seem to myself like a dream of futurity; like a child of eternal peace. How quiet and peaceful, how mild and dear is out present nature, when compared with violent and gigantic times! The mightiest tempests, the most terrible earthquakes of our day, are but weak echoes of the throes of that first birth. Perhaps also the animal and vegetable kingdoms, and even the men who then existed, if any were found on the different islands of the ocean, were of firmer and ruder organization; at least we should not then be obliged to accuse the traditions of a giant race of being mere poetic fancies."

"It is pleasant," said the old man, "to notice the gradual pacification of nature. A concord ever becoming deeper, a more friendly intercourse, reciprocal aid and encouragement, seem gradually to have been formed; and we can look forward continually to better times. It may perhaps be possible, that here and there a little of the old leaven is fermenting, and that still more violent convulsions are to follow; yet these mighty struggles for a free and harmonious existence are visible; and in this spirit will every convulsion pass over and draw nearer to the great goal. It may be that nature is no longer so fertile, that at present no metals or precious stones, rocks or mountains are springing into existence, that plants and animals do not increase to such an astonishing size and strength; but the more that physical powers are exhausted, the more have plastic, ennobling, and social powers increased. The mind has become more susceptible and tender, the fancy more varied and symbolical, the hand more free and artistic. Nature approaches man; and if she were once an uncouthly teeming rock, then is she now a quietly thriving plant, a silent human artist And of what service would be the multiplication of these treasures, of which there are now enough for the most distant age? How small is the space I have surveyed; and yet what mighty stores have I at a single glance discovered, the use of which is left for future generations! What riches are enclosed in the northern mountains, what favorable signs I discovered throughout my native land, in Hungary, at the foot of the Carpathian hills, and in the rocky vales of Tyrol, Austria, and Bavaria. I might have been a rich man, if I had taken with me what I might only have picked up and broken off. In many places I saw myself as in a magic garden. On every side costly and skilfully framed metals met my sight. From the beautiful tresses and branches of silver hung glittering, ruby-red, transparent fruits; and the heavy-laden shrubs, stood upon crystal ground of inimitable workmanship. One can scarcely trust his senses in these wonderful regions, and can never grow weary of rambling through these charming solitudes, or of gloating over their jewels. I have seen much that is wonderful during my present journey, and certainly in other lands the earth is equally plentiful and fruitful."

"When," said the unknown, "one remembers the treasures which are hidden in the East, he cannot doubt what you remark; and have not distant India, Africa, and Spain been distinguished even from antiquity, by the richness of their soil? Though a soldier is not apt to take very exact notice of the veins and the clefts of mountains, yet at times I have reflected upon these shining tracts of land, which, like rare birds, indicate an unexpected bloom and fruit. How little did I imagine, when I passed these dark dwellings joyously by the light of day, that I should ever finish my life in the bosom of a mountain! My love carried me proudly above the surface of the earth, and I hoped in later years to fall asleep in her embrace. The war having ended, I returned home, full of glad expectations of a refreshing harvest. But the spirit of the war seemed to have become the spirit of my fortune. My Maria had borne me two children in the East. They were the joy of our existence. The voyage and the rough air of the West destroyed their bloom; they were buried a few days after my arrival in Europe. Sorrowfully I carried my disconsolate wife to our home. A silent grief weakened the thread which bound her to life. During a journey which I was obliged to take, and on which, as was her wont, she accompanied me, she gently but suddenly expired in my arms. It was near this place, where her earthly pilgrimage was finished. My resolution was taken in a moment; I found, what I had never expected; a heavenly illumination came over me; and from the day when I buried her here with my own hands, a divine hand freed my heart from all sorrow. Since then I have caused this monument to be erected. An event often seems to be endings when in fact it is beginning; and thus has it been with my life. May God grant you an old age as happy, and a spirit as quiet as mine."

Henry and the merchants had listened attentively to the conversation; and the first particularly was conscious of new developments in his prophetic soul. Many words, many thoughts, fell like quickening seeds into his breast, and soon drew him from the narrow circle of his youth to the heights of the world. The hours just passed lay behind him like long-revolving years; and it seemed as if he had always thought and felt as now.

The hermit showed him his books. They consisted of old histories and poems. Henry turned over the leaves of these huge and beautifully illuminated works, and his curiosity was strongly excited by the short lines of the verses, the titles, some of the passages, and the beautiful pictures which appeared here and there, like embodied words, to assist the imagination of the reader. The Hermit observed his inward gratification and explained these singular pictures. All the varied scenes of life were represented among them. Battles, funereal trains, marriage ceremonies, shipwrecks, caves, and palaces, kings, heroes, priests, men in singular costume, strange beasts, were delineated in different alternations and connexions. Henry could not sate himself with gazing at them, and wished nothing more than to remain with the hermit, who irresistibly attracted him, and to be instructed by him in these books. In the mean time the old man asked whether there were any more caves; and the hermit told him, that there were some extensive ones near, to which he would accompany him. The old man was ready; and the hermit, who observed Henry's interest in the books, induced him to remain, and to examine them more closely during their absence. Henry was glad to stay where the books were, and thanked the hermit heartily for his permission to do so. He turned over their leaves with indescribable pleasure. At last a book fell into his hands, written in a foreign tongue, which appeared to him somewhat like Latin or Italian. He longed greatly to know the language, for the book pleased him greatly, though he did not understand a syllable of it. It had no title; but after a little search he found some engravings. They seemed strangely familiar to him; and on examination, he discovered his own form quite discernible among the figures. He was terrified, and thought that he must be dreaming; but after having examined them again and again, he could no longer doubt their perfect resemblance. He could hardly trust his senses, when in one of the pictures he discovered the cave, the hermit, and the old man by his side. By degrees he found among the pictures the girl from the holy land, his parents, the count and countess of Thuringia, his friend the court chaplain; and many others of his acquaintance; yet their dress was changed, and seemed to belong to another period. There were many forms he could not call by name, but which nevertheless seemed known to him. He saw the exact portraits of himself, in different situations. Towards the end he appeared larger and nobler. The guitar rested in his arms, and the countess handed him a wreath. He saw himself at the imperial court, on shipboard, now in warm embrace with a beautifully formed and lovely girl, now in battle with fierce-looking men, and again in friendly conversation with Saracens and Moors. He was frequently accompanied by a man of grave aspect. He felt a deep reverence for this august form, and was glad to see himself arm in arm with him. The last pictures were obscure and incomprehensible; yet some of the shapes of his dream surprised him with the most intense rapture. The conclusion of the book was wanting. Henry was very sorrowful, and wished for nothing more earnestly than to be able to read and thoroughly understand the book. He looked over the pictures repeatedly, and was almost abashed when the company returned. A strange sort of shame overcame him. He did not suffer himself to make known his discovery, and merely asked the Hermit generally about its title and language. He learned that it was written in the Provence tongue.

"It is long since I have read it," said the Hermit; "I do not now remember its contents very distinctly. As far as I recollect, it is a romance, relating the wonderful fortune of a poet's life, wherein the art of poesy is represented and extolled in all its various relations. The conclusion is wanting to the manuscript, which I brought with me from Jerusalem, where I found it left with a friend, and took it, away, an a memorial of him."

They now took leave of each other. Henry was moved to tears; the cave had become so remarkable and the hermit so dear to him.

All embraced the hermit heartily, and he himself seemed to have become attached to them. Henry thought that he noticed his kind and penetrating gaze fixed upon him. His farewell words to him were full of meaning. He seemed to know of his discovery and to have reference to it. He followed them to the entrance of the cave, after having requested them, and particularly the boy, not to tell the farmers concerning him, as it would only expose him to their troublesome acquaintance.

They all promised this. As they separated from him, and commended themselves to his prayers, he said,

"But a short time and we shall see each other again, to smile at the conversation of this day. A heavenly dawn will surround us, and we shall rejoice that we greeted each other kindly in this vale of probation, and were inspired with like sentiments and anticipations. There are angels who guide us here in safety. If your eye is fixed upon Heaven, you will never lose the way to your home."

They separated with a silent feeling of devotion, soon found their timorous companions, and amid general conversation shortly reached the village, where Henry's mother, who had been somewhat anxious about him, received them with a thousand expressions of joy.

CHAPTER VI

Men, who are born for business, for action, cannot too soon contemplate for themselves and animate all things. They must themselves grapple with and pass through many relations, must harden their whole being against the influence of new situations, and the dissipation which a multitude and variety of objects engenders; and they must accustom themselves, even in the urgency of great occasions to hold fast to the thread of their object. They should not yield to the invitations of inactive contemplation. Their soul must not be gazing at self; it must be ceaselessly directed to outward things, a handmaid to the understanding, active and prompt in discrimination. They are heroes; and events press about them which must be fulfilled, and their problems solved. By their influence all occurrences of chance become history, and their life is an unbroken chain of remarkable and splendid, intricate and singular events.

Far otherwise is it with those quiet, unknown men, whose world is their own mind, whose activity the action of the contemplative intellect, and whose life a gentle development of their inner powers. No desquietude drives them to outward things. A tranquil possession satisfies them; and the immense drama without does not entice them to engage in it themselves; but they regard it as significant and wonderful, a source of contemplation for their leisure moments. Longings for the spirit hold them in the distance; and it is this spirit that destines them to act the mysterious part of the mind in this human worlds while others represent the outer limbs and senses, the mind's projected powers. They would be disturbed by great and various events. A simple life is their lot, and they become acquainted with the rich subject-matter and countless phenomena of the world from relations and writings alone. But seldom in the course of their lives does any occurrence draw them along with it in its sudden vortex, in order to acquaint them by a few experiences more accurately with the situation and character of active men. On the contrary, their susceptible minds are already sufficiently busied with near and insignificant phenomena, which represent the great world as it were renewed; and they will advance no step, without making the most surprising discoveries in themselves, concerning the nature and significance of these phenomena. They are poets, those men of rare inspiration, who at times wander through our dwelling-place, and everywhere renew the ancient, venerable, service of humanity, and of its first gods, – the stars, spring, love, happiness, fertility, health, and the joyous heart; they, who are already here in possession of heavenly rest, and, driven about by no foolish desires, breathe only the fragrance of earthly fruits, without devouring them, then to be irrevocably chained to the lower world. They are free guests whose golden feet tread softly, and whose presence involuntarily outspreads its wings around. A poet may be known, like a good king, by cheerful and bright faces, and he alone justly bears the name of sage. If you compare him with heroes, you will find that the songs of the poets frequently awake heroic courage in youthful hearts; but heroic deeds have probably never awakened the spirit of poesy in any mind whatever. Henry was a poet by nature. Many events seemed to conspire to aid his development, and as yet nothing had disturbed the elasticity of his soul. All that he saw and heard seemed only to remove new bars within him, and to open new windows for his spirit. The world, with its great and changing relations, lay before him. But as yet it was silent; and its soul, its language was not yet awakened. Soon did a poet approach, holding a lovely girl by the hand, that by the sound of the mother tongue, and by the movement of a sweet and tender mouth; the soft lips might unlock and the simple harmony unfold in unending melodies.

The journey was now ended. It was towards evening when our travellers, in safety and good spirits, arrived at the far-famed city of Augsburg, and, full of expectation, rode through the high streets to the spacious mansion of the old Swaning.

The surrounding country had already appeared delightful to the eyes of Henry. The animated bustle of the city, and the great houses of stone affected him strangely, yet agreeably. He experienced a real pleasure in thinking of his future abode. His mother was very much pleased to see herself in her native city after her wearisome journey, soon to embrace again her father and old acquaintances, to introduce Henry to them, and for once be able quietly to forget all household cares in the cordial remembrances of her youth. The merchants hoped by the pleasures there to indemnify themselves for the discomforts of their journey, and to do a profitable business.

Lights gleamed from the house of the old Swaning, and joyous music swelled towards them. "What will you bet," said the merchants, "that your grandfather is not giving a merry party? We came as if invited. How much his uninvited guests will astonish him. He is not dreaming that now the true festivity is about to commence." Henry felt embarrassed, and his mother was only anxious about their dress. They alighted; the merchants remained with the horses, and Henry and his mother entered the splendid mansion. Not a soul belonging to the house was to be seen below. They were obliged to ascend the lofty stairs. Some servants ran past them; they asked them to inform the old Swaning of the arrival of some strangers who wished to speak with him. The servants made some objection at first, for the travellers did not appear in very good condition as to dress, yet finally they announced them to the master of the house. The old

Swaning came out. He did not know them at first, and asked them their names and business. Henry's mother wept and fell upon his neck.

"Do you not know your own daughter?" she exclaimed weeping. "I bring you my son."

The aged father was extremely moved. He pressed her long to his bosom. Henry sank upon his knee and tenderly kissed his hand. He raised him to himself and held both mother and son in his embrace.

"Come right in," said Swaning, "I have only my friends and acquaintances here, who will rejoice with me." Henry's mother hesitated, but had no time to consider. The father led them both into the lighted hall.

"Here I bring my daughter and grandson from Eisenach," cried Swaning, in the merry crowd of gaily dressed guests.

All eyes were turned towards the door; all ran to it; the music ceased, and the two travellers stood bewildered and dazzled in their dusty dresses, in the midst of the motley throng. A thousand joyful exclamations passed from mouth to mouth. All her acquaintances pressed around the mother. Innumerable were the questions which were asked. Each one wished to be recognised and welcomed first. Whilst the elder part of the company were attending to the mother, the attention of the younger portion was directed to the strange youth, who was standing with downcast eyes, not daring to look again upon the unknown faces. His grandfather introduced him to the company, and inquired after his father and about the occurrences of his journey.

The mother thought of the merchants, who out of politeness had remained below by the horses. She told her father, who sent down for them immediately, and invited them to ascend. The horses were led into the stable, and the merchants appeared.

Swaning thanked them heartily for the friendly escort they had afforded his daughter. They were acquainted with many who were present, and exchanged friendly greetings. The mother asked permission to change her dress. Swaning led her to her chamber, and Henry followed for the same purpose.

The appearance of one man was very striking to Henry, who thought that he had seen him in that book. His noble bearing distinguished him from all the rest. His face wore an expression of serene gravity, an open, finely arched forehead, large, black, penetrating, and tranquil eyes, a humorous expression about his pleasant mouth, and his full manly proportions, gave to him a meaning and fascinating appearance. He was strongly built, his movements quiet and expressive, and where he stood he seemed about to stay forever. Henry asked his grandfather about him.

"I am glad," said the old man, "that you noticed him. It is my excellent friend Klingsohr, the poet. You should be prouder of his acquaintance than of the emperor's. But how is your heart? He has a beautiful daughter, who perhaps will surpass the father in your eyes. It would be strange if you had not noticed her."

Henry blushed; "my mind has been distracted, dear grandfather. The company is numerous, and I was looking only at your friend."

"We see that you came from the North," replied Swaning; "we shall soon thaw you out here. You shall learn soon to look after pretty faces."

They were now ready, and returned to the hall, where in the mean time preparations for supper had been made. The old Swaning led Henry to Klingsohr, and told him that Henry had noticed him particularly, and ardently desired to become acquainted with him.

Henry was confused. Klingsohr spoke kindly to him of his fatherland and of his journey. There was so much to inspire confidence in his voice, that Henry soon gained courage and conversed with him freely. After a little while Swaning came to them again, bringing with him the beautiful Matilda.

"You must receive my grandson kindly, and pardon him that he has noticed your father before you. Your bright eyes will awaken his youth within him. In his native land Spring comes too late."

Henry and Matilda blushed. They gazed admiringly upon each other. She asked him, with scarcely audible words, whether he was fond of dancing. While he was answering in the affirmative, the merry music struck up. He silently offered her his hand; she accepted it, and they mingled among the rows of waltzers. Swaning and Klingsohr looked on. The mother and the merchants were delighted with Henry's grace and with his lovely partner. The mother had enough to converse about with the friends of her youth, who wished her much happiness from so well educated and hopeful a son.

Klingsohr said to Swaning, – "Your grandson has an attractive countenance; it indicates a clear and comprehensive mind, and his voice comes deep from his heart."

"I hope," replied Swaning, "that he will become your docile pupil. It seems to me that he is born for a poet. May your spirit fall upon him. He looks like his father, only he seems more ardent and excitable. The former was a youth of superior talents. He was wanting, however, in a certain liberality of mind. He might hare become something more than an industrious and able mechanic."

Henry wished that the dance would never end. With heartfelt pleasure his eyes rested on the roses of his partner. Her innocent eye did not avoid his. She appeared like the spirit of her father in the most lovely disguise. Eternal youth spoke from her full and quiet eyes. Upon a light blue ground lay the mild splendor of the brown stars. Her forehead and nose were beautifully formed. Her face was like a lily inclined towards the rising sun, and from her slender white neck, the blue veins clung round her tender cheeks in gentle curves. Her voice was like a distant echo, and her small head with its brown tresses seemed but to hover over her airy form.

Refreshments were brought in, and the dances closed. The elder people seated themselves on one side, the younger on the other.

Henry remained with Matilda. A young relative seated

herself at his left, and Klingsohr sat opposite him. If Matilda said but little, his other neighbor, Veronika, was so much the more talkative. She immediately played the familiar with him, and soon made him acquainted with all present. Henry lost much of her conversation. He was still with his partner, and wished to turn much oftener to the right. Klingsohr made an end to their talking. He asked about the band with the strange devices, which Henry had fastened to his coat. He told him with much emotion of the girl from the holy land. Matilda wept; and now Henry could scarcely hide his tears. For this reason he entered into conversation with her. All were enjoying themselves, and Veronika joked and laughed with her acquaintances. Matilda described Hungary, where her father often dwelt, and the mode of life in Augsburg. The enjoyment was at its height. The music put all restraint to flight, and all the affections into a joyful play. Baskets of flowers in all their splendor exhaled their odors upon the table, and the wine danced about between the dishes and the flowers, shook its golden wings, and formed many varied pictures between the guests and the world. Henry now understood for the first time what was meant by a festival. A thousand happy spirits seemed to gambol around the table, and to live in silent sympathy with the joys of the happy people, and to intoxicate themselves with their pleasures. The enjoyment of life stood before him, like a tinkling tree full of golden fruits. Pain had vanished, and it seemed impossible that ever human inclination should have turned from this tree to the dangerous fruit of knowledge, the tree of strife. He now learned what were wine and food. They tasted very richly to him. A heavenly oil seasoned them for him, and from the beaker sparkled the splendor of earthly life. Some of the maidens brought a fresh garland to the old Swaning. He put it on, and kissing them, said, "You must bring one also to our friend Klingsohr, and for thanks he will teach you a couple of new songs. You shall have mine immediately. He beckoned for the music to commence, and sang with a clear voice: –

"Surely life is most distressing,
And a mournful fate we meet!
Stress and need our only blessing,
Practised only in deceit;
And our bosoms never daring
To unfold their soft despairing.

"What the elders all are telling,
To the youthful heart is waste;
Throes of longing are we feeling
The forbidden fruit to taste;
Would the gentle youths but deign us,
And believe that they could gain us!

"Thinking so then are we sinning?
All our thoughts are duty-free.
What indeed to us remaining,
Wretched wights, but fantasy?
Do we strive our dreams to banish,
Never, never will they vanish.

"When in prayer at even bending
Frightens us the loneliness,
Favor and desire are wending
Thitherward to our caress;
How disdain the fair offender,
Or resist the soft surrender?

"Mothers stern our charms concealing,
Every day prescribe anew.
What availeth all our willing?
Spring they not again to view?
Warm desire is ever riving
Closest fetters with its striving.

"Every impulse harshly spurning
Hard and cold to be as stone,
Never glances bright returning,
Close to be and all alone,
Heed to no entreaty giving, –
Call you that the flower of living?

"Ah, how great a maid's annoyance,

Sick and chafed her bosom is, –
And to make her only joyance,
Withered lips bestow a kiss!
Will the leaf be turning never,
Elders' reign to end forever?"

Both old and young laughed. The girls blushed and smiled aside. Amidst a thousand railleries a second garland was brought and put upon Klingsohr. They begged him, however, very earnestly not to give them such a gay song. "No," said Klingsohr, "I will take good care not to speak so lightly of your secrets; say yourselves what kind of a song you would prefer."

"Anything but a love song," cried the girls; "let it be a drinking song if you like." Klingsohr sang: –

"On verdant mountain-side is growing
The god, who heaven to us brings;
The sun's own foster-child, and glowing
With all the fire its favor flings.

"In Spring is he conceived with pleasure,
The bud unfolds in silent joy,
And mid the Autumn's harvest-treasure
Forth springs to life the golden boy.

"Within his narrow cradle lying,
In vaulted rooms beneath the ground,
He dreams of feasts and banners flying
And airy castles all around.

"Near to his dwelling none remaineth,
When chafeth he in restless strife,
And every hoop and fetter straineth
In all the pride of youthful life.

"For viewless watchmen round are closing,
Until his lordly dreams are o'er,
With air-enveloped spears opposing
The loiterer near the sacred door.

"So when unfold his sleeping pinions,
With sparkling eyes he greets the day,

Obeys in peace his priestly minions,
And forth he cometh when they pray.

"From cradle's murky bosom faring,
He winketh through a crystal dress,
The rose of close alliance bearing,
Expressive in its ruddiness.

"And everywhere around are pressing
His merry men in jubilee,
Their love find gratitude confessing
To him with jocund tongue and free.

"He scatters o'er the fields and valleys
His innerlife in countless rays,
And Love is sipping from his chalice,
And pledged forever with him stays.

"As spirit of the golden ages,
The Poet alway he beguiles,
Who everywhere in reeling pages
Doth celebrate his pleasant wiles.

"He gave him, his allegiance sealing,
To every pretty mouth a right,
And this the god through him revealing,
That none the edict dare to slight."

"A fine prophet!" exclaimed the girls. Swaning was heartily
pleased. They made some objections, but all to no purpose. They
were obliged to reach out their sweet lips to him. Henry blushed
only on account of his earnest neighbor; otherwise he would have
loudly rejoiced in the privilege of the poet. Veronika was among
the garland bearers. She came suddenly back and said to Henry,
"truly, is it not a fine thing to be a poet?"

Henry did not trust himself to take advantage of this question.
Excess of joy and the earnestness of first love were contending in
his breast. The charming Veronika was joking with the others,
and in the meanwhile he found time somewhat to quench his joy.
Matilda told him that she played the guitar. "Ah!" said he, "how I
should love to learn it from you. I have for a long time desired it."

"My father instructed me; he plays it matchlessly," said she blushing.

"I believe, however," said Henry, "that I can learn it more easily from you. How delighted I should be to hear you sing."

"Do not expect too much."

"O!" said Henry, "what may I not expect, since your speech merely is song, and your form is expressive of heavenly music."

Matilda was silent. Her father commenced a conversation, in which Henry spoke with the most lively spirit Those who were near wondered at the fluency of the young man's speech, and the richness of his imagery. Matilda gazed upon him with silent attention. She seemed to delight in his words, which were still more clearly explained by his speaking features. His eyes appeared unusually brilliant. He turned at times towards Matilda, who was astonished by the expression of his face. In the warmth of conversation, he involuntarily seized her hand, and she could not but sanction much of what he said, with a gentle pressure. Klingsohr knew how to keep up his enthusiasm, and gradually drew his whole soul from his lips. At last all rose. There was a general confusion. Henry remained by the side of Matilda. They stood apart unobserved. He clasped her hand and kissed it tenderly. She suffered him to hold it without opposition, and looked upon him with unspeakable kindness. He could not restrain himself, bent towards her, and kissed her lips. She was taken unawares and involuntarily returned his ardent kiss. "Sweet Matilda," – "Dear Henry," – this was all they could say to each other. She pressed his hand, and then mingled with her companions. Henry stood as if in Heaven. His mother came to him. He told her all concerning his love.

"Is it not a good thing that we have visited Augsburg?" said she. "Does it not in truth please you?"

"Dear mother," said Henry, "I had not represented it to myself thus. It is most glorious."

The remainder of the evening passed away in infinite pleasure. The old people played, talked, and observed the dancing. The music undulated through the hall like a pleasure-sea, and bore along the enraptured youth upon its surface.

Henry felt the rapturous presages of the first buoyancy of love. Matilda also willingly suffered herself to be carried away by the flattering waves, and only concealed from him her tender trust, her budding inclination, behind a light flower veil. The old Swaning noticed the growing intimacy between them, and teazed them both about it. Klingsohr had taken a liking to Henry, and was pleased with his tenderness towards his daughter. – The other young men and girls soon noticed it. They brought the sober Matilda forward with the young Thuringian, and did not conceal that they were glad no longer to be obliged to shun Matilda's observation of the secrets of their hearts.

It was late in the evening when the company separated. "The first and only feast of my life," said Henry, when he was alone, and his mother had retired wearied to rest. "Do I not feel as I felt in that dream about the blue flower? What peculiar connexion is there between Matilda and that flower? That face, which bowed towards me from the petals, was Matilda's heavenly countenance, and I also now remember that I saw it in that book. But why did it not there thus move my heart? O! she is the visible spirit of song, the worthy daughter of her father. She will dissolve me into music. She will become my inmost soul, the guardian spirit of my holy fire. What an eternity of faithful love do I feel within me? I was born only to revere her, to serve her forever, to think of and to feel her. Does there not belong a peculiar, undivided existence to her contemplation and worship? Am I the happy one, whose being may be the echo, the mirror of her's? It is not owing to chance that I have seen her at the end of my journey, that a happy feast has encircled the highest moment of my life. It could not have been otherwise; for does not her presence render every thing a feast?"

He stepped to the window. The choir of the stars stood in the dusky sky, and in the east a white glimmer announced the coming day.

Full of rapture, Henry exclaimed, "Ye eternal stars, ye silent wanderers, I call upon you as witnesses of my sacred oath. For Matilda will I live, and eternal constancy shall bind her to my heart. The morning of eternal day is also opening for me. The night is past. I kindle myself to the rising sun, for an inextinguishable offering."

Henry was heated, and only fell asleep late in the morning. The thoughts of his soul flowed together into a wonderful dream. A deep blue stream glimmered from the green plains. A boat was floating upon the smooth surface. Matilda was sitting in it, and steering. She was adorned with garlands, singing a simple song, and looked over to him with sweet sadness. His bosom was oppressed, he knew not why. The sky was clear; the flood quiet. Her heavenly face was reflected in the waves. Suddenly the boat began to whirl. He cried out to her earnestly. She smiled and laid down the helm in the boat which continued its whirling. He was seized with overwhelming fear. He plunged into the stream, but could not move, and was hurried along. She beckoned to him, as if she had something to tell him, and though the boat was fast filling with water, yet she smiled with unspeakable tenderness, and looked down serenely into the abyss. Suddenly it drew her in. A gentle breath of air passed over the stream, which, flowed on as quiet and glittering as ever. His intense anxiety robbed Henry of all consciousness. His heart no longer throbbed. On recovering, his senses, he was on the dry land. He must have floated a long distance. It was a strange country. He knew not what had happened to him. His mind had vanished. Thoughtlessly he plunged deeper and deeper into the country. He was excessively weary. A little spring gushed from the side of a hill, sounding like the music of bells. In his hand he caught a few drops, and with them wetted his parched lips. The terrible occurrence lay behind him like a fearful dream. He walked on farther and farther; – flowers and trees spoke to him.

Now he felt in high spirits and at home. He heard that song again. He ran to the place whence the sounds proceeded.

Suddenly some one held him by the clothes. "Dear Henry," cried a well known voice. He looked round, and Matilda clasped him in her arms.

"Why did you run from me, dear heart," cried she panting. "I could scarcely overtake you."

Henry wept. He clasped her to himself, "Where is the stream?" cried he with tears.

"Do you not see its blue waves above us?"

He looked up, and the blue stream was flowing gently over his head.

"Where are we, dear Matilda?"

"With our fathers."

"Shall we remain together?"

"Forever," she replied, while she pressed her lips to his, and so embraced him that she could not tear herself from him. She put a wondrous, secret word into his mouth, and it rang through his whole being. He was about to repeat it, when his grandfather called, and he awoke. He would have given his life to remember that word.

CHAPTER VII

Klingsohr stood before his bed and kindly bade him good morning. He was in high spirits, and fell upon Klingsohr's neck. "That is not meant for you," cried Swaning. Henry smiled, and hid his blushes on his mother's cheeks.

"Would you like to go with me," said Klingsohr, "and breakfast on a beautiful eminence just before the city? The fine morning would refresh you. Dress yourself. Matilda is already waiting for us."

Henry with a thousand joyful feelings thanked him for his welcome invitation. In a moment he was ready, and kissed Klingsohr's hand with much fervor. They went to Matilda, who looked wonderfully lovely in her simple morning dress, and who greeted him kindly. She had already packed her breakfast into a little basket which she hung upon one arm, and without ceremony gave the other to Henry. Klingsohr followed them, and thus they passed through the city, already full of animation, to a little hill by the river, where a wide and full prospect opened between some lofty trees.

"Though I have often," said Henry, "delighted in the unfolding of varied nature in the peaceful neighborhood of her manifold possessions; yet never has such a creative and pure serenity filled me, as today. Those distant points seem so near to me, and the rich landscape is like an inward fantasy. How changeable is nature, however unchangeable appears its surface! How different is it when an angel, a spirit of power is at our side, than when a person in distress utters his complaints before us, or a farmer tells us how unfortunate the weather is for him, or how much he needs some rainy days for his crops. To you, dearest master, do I owe this bliss; yes, this bliss, – for there is no other word that can more truly express my heart's condition. Joy, desire, transport, are merely the members of that bliss which inspires them with a higher life. He pressed Matilda's hand to his heart, and his ardent gaze sank deep into her mild and susceptible eyes.

"Nature," replied Klingsohr, "is for our mind, what a body is for light. It reflects it, separates it into its proper colors, kindles a light on its surface or within it, when it equals its opacity: when it is superior, it rays forth in order to enlighten other bodies. But eyen the darkest bodies can, by water, fire, and air, be made clear and brilliant."

"I understand you," dear master. "Men are crystals for our minds. They are the transparent nature. Dear Matilda, I might call you a pure and costly sapphire. You are clear and transparent as the heavens; you beam with the mildest light. But tell me, dear master, whether I am right; it seems to me that at the very point when one is most intimate with nature, he can and would say the least concerning her."

"That depends upon your view of her," said Klingsohr. "Nature is one thing for our enjoyment and our disposition, but another for our intellect, the guiding faculty of our earthward powers. We must take good care not to lose sight of one more than the other. There are many who only know the one side, and think but little of the other. But we can unite them both, and that too with profit. A great pity it is, that so few think of being able to move freely and fitly in their inner natures, and to insure for themselves, by a necessary separation, the most effectual and natural use of their faculties. Usually the one hinders the other; and thus a helpless sluggishness gradually arises, so that, if such men should ever arise with united powers, a great confusion and contention would ensue, and all things would be tossed here and there in an ungainly manner. I cannot sufficiently impress upon you, to endeavor with industry and care to be acquainted with your own intellect and natural bias. Nothing is more indispensable to the poet, than insight into the nature of every occupation, acquaintance with the means by which every object may be attained, and the power of fitly regulating the presence of the spirit according to time and circumstances. Inspiration without intellect is useless and dangerous; and the poet will be able to perform few wonders, when he is astonished by wonders."

"But is not an implicit faith in man's dominion over destiny indispensable to the poet?"

"Certainly indispensable, because he cannot represent fate to himself in any other light, when he maturely reflects upon it. But how distant is this calm certainty from that anxious doubt, which proceeds from the blind fear of superstition! And thus also the steady, animating warmth of a poetic mind is exactly the reverse of the wild heat of a sickly heart; The one is poor, overwhelming, and transient; the other perfectly distinguishes all forms, favors the culture of the most manifold relations, and is in itself eternal. The youthful poet cannot be too cool and considerate. A far-reaching, attentive, and quiet disposition belongs to the true, melodious ease of address. It becomes a confused prattling, when a violent storm is raging in the breast; and the attention is lost in a trembling emptiness of thought. Once more I repeat it; the true mind is like the light; even as calm and sensitive, as elastic and penetrating, as powerful and as imperceptibly active, as that costly element, which with its native regularity scatters itself upon all objects, and exhibits them in charming variety. The poet is pure steel, as sensitive as a brittle thread of glass, as hard as the unyielding flint."

"I have indeed at times felt," said Henry, "that in the moments when my inner nature was most awake, I was less excited than at other times, when I could run about freely and attend to all occupations with pleasure. A spiritual, penetrative essence permeated me, and I could employ every sense at pleasure, could revolve every thought like an actual body, and view it from all sides. I stood with silent sympathy in my father's work-shop, and rejoiced when I could help him to accomplish anything properly. Propriety has a peculiarly strengthening charm, and it is true that the consciousness of it gives rise to a more lasting and distinct enjoyment, than that overflowing feeling of an incomprehensible, superfluous splendor."

"Believe not," said Klingsohr, "that I disregard the latter; but it must come of itself and not be bought. The rarity of its appearance is beneficent; if more frequent, it would weary and weaken. One cannot quickly enough tear himself from the sweet rapture which it leaves behind, and return to a regular and laborious occupation. It is as with pleasant morning dreams, from whose sleepy vortex one must extricate himself by force, if he would not fall into a lassitude, continually more oppressive, and so struggle through the whole day in sickly exhaustion."

"Poetry," continued Klingsohr, "will be cultivated strictly as an art. As mere enjoyment it ceases to be poetry. The poet must not run about unoccupied the whole day in chase of figures and feelings. That is the very reverse of the proper method. A pure, open mind, dexterity in reflection and contemplation, and ability to put forth all the faculties in a mutually animating effort, and to keep them so, – these are the requisites of our art. If you will commit yourself to my care, no day shall pass in which you shall not add stores to your knowledge, and obtain some useful views. The city is rich in artists of all descriptions. There are some experienced statesmen and educated merchants here. One can get acquainted with all ranks without much difficulty, with people of all pursuits, and with all social circumstances and requirements. I will with pleasure instruct you in the mechanical part of our art, and read its most remarkable productions with you. You may share Matilda's hours of instruction, and she will willingly teach you to play the guitar. Each occupation will usher in the rest; and when you have thus well spent the day, the conversation and pleasures of a social evening, and the views of the beautiful landscapes around, will continually renew to you the calmest enjoyment."

"What a glorious life you here lay open to me, dear master. Under your guidance I shall for the first time understand what a noble mark is before me, and how by your counsel alone I can hope to attain it."

Klingsohr embraced him tenderly. Matilda brought them the breakfast, and Henry asked her with a tender voice, whether she would be kind enough to receive him as fellow pupil, and her own scholar. "I shall probably be your scholar forever," said he, as Klingsohr turned away. She nodded slightly towards him. He threw his arms around the blushing maiden, and kissed her soft lips. Gently she retreated from him, yet handed him with childish grace a rose which she wore in her bosom. She then busied herself about her basket. Henry watched her with silent rapture, kissed the rose, fixed it on his breast, and walked to Klingsohr's side, who was gazing down at the city.

"By what road, did you come here," asked Klingsohr.

"Down over that hill," replied Henry, "where the road loses itself in the distance."

"You must have seen some fair landscapes."

"We travelled through an almost uninterrupted series of beautiful ones."

"Perhaps your native town is pleasantly situated?"

"The country is varied enough; it is rude, however, and a noble river is wanting. Streams are the eyes of a landscape."

"Your account of your journey," said Klingsohr, "agreeably entertained me last evening. I have indeed observed that the spirit of poesy is your kind companion. Your friends have unobservedly become its voices. Where a poet is, poetry everywhere breaks out. The land of poetry, romantic Palestine, has greeted you with its sweet sadness; war has addressed you in its wild glory, and nature and history have met you in the forms of a miner and a hermit."

"You forget the best, dear master, the heavenly appearance of love. It depends upon you, whether this appearance shall forever remain with me."

"What do you think," cried Klingsohr as he turned to Matilda who was just approaching; "would you like to become Henry's inseparable companion? Where you are, I remain also."

Matilda was terrified. She flew into her father's arms. Henry trembled with infinite joy. "Shall he then be with me forever, dear father?"

"Ask him for yourself," said Klingsohr With emotion.

She looked upon Henry with the most heart-felt tenderness.

"My eternity is indeed thy work," cried Henry, whilst the tears rolled down his blooming cheeks.

They embraced each other. Klingsohr caught them in his arms. "My children," he cried, "be faithful to each other unto death! Love and constancy will make your life eternal poesy."

CHAPTER VIII

In the afternoon Klingsohr led to his room his new son, in whose happiness his mother and grandfather took the tenderest interest, honoring Matilda as his protecting spirit, and made him acquainted with his books. Afterward they spoke of poetry.

"I know not," said Klingsohr, "why the representation of nature as a poet is commonly considered poetry. She is not so at all times. Dull desire, stupid apathy and sluggishness, are in her, as in men, exposing qualities which wage a restless strife With poesy. This mighty battle would be a fine subject for a poem. Many lands and ages seem, like the majority of men, to stand entirely under the dominion of this enemy to poesy; in others, on the contrary, poesy is at home and everywhere visible. The periods of this battle are very worthy of the historian's notice, and its representation is a pleasant and profitable employment. It is usually the season of the poet's birth. Nothing is more disagreeable to its adversary than that she, herself being opposed to poesy, becomes a poetic personage, and often in the heat of the engagement changes weapons with poesy, and is violently struck by her own venomous darts; while, on the other hand, the wounds of poesy, which she receives from her own weapons, heal readily, and only serve to render her yet more charming and powerful."

"On the whole," said Henry, "war seems to me poetical.

People fancy that they must fight for a possession no matter how miserable, and do not observe that the spirit of romance excites them to annihilate all useless baseness. They carry arms for the cause of poesy, and both hosts follow an invisible standard."

"In war," replied Klingsohr, "the primeval fluid is stirred up. New continents are to arise, new races to spring forth from the great dissolution. The true war is the war of religion; its direct end is destruction; and men's madness appears in its full dimensions. Many wars, particularly those which originate in national hate, belong to this class, and are real poems. Here true heroes are at home, who, being the noblest antitypes of poesy, are but earthly powers involuntarily penetrated by poesy. A poet, who at the same time were a hero, would be indeed a heavenly messenger; but our poetry is not equal to the work of representing him."

"How am I to understand that, dear father," said Henry. "Can any object be too lofty for poesy?"

"Certainly. We cannot on the whole speak for poesy itself, but only for her earthly means and instruments. If indeed there is for every single poet a proper district within which he must remain, in order not to lose all breath and vantage, then there is also for the whole sum of human powers a determinate boundary line to the capacity for representation; beyond which representation cannot retain the necessary strength or form, but loses itself in an empty, delusive nonentity. Particularly as a pupil, one cannot guard enough against these extravagances; since a lively fancy loves too well to fly to the extreme bounds, and arrogantly endeavors to seize upon and express the supersensual and exuberant. Riper experience first teaches us to shun this disproportion of objects, and to leave the investigation of what is simplest and loftiest to worldly wisdom. The older poet rises no higher than is needful to arrange, his vast stock in a comprehensible order, and he is careful to omit the manifoldness, which afforded him the requisite material, and also the necessary points of agreement. I might almost say that in every line chaos should shine through the well-clipped foliage of order. A graceful style merely renders the richness of the thought more comprehensible and agreeable; regular symmetry, on the contrary, has all the dryness of numbers. The best poesy lies very near us, and an ordinary matter is not seldom the object of its most tender love. With the poet, poetry is confined to limited instruments, and just so far becomes an art. Language especially has its fixed sphere. The compass of one's native tongue is yet narrower. By practice and reflection the poet learns to understand his own language. He knows exactly what he can accomplish by its aid, and will make no fruitless attempt to strain it beyond its powers. Seldom will he collect all its powers upon a single point; for otherwise he becomes wearisome, and even destroys the rich effect of a well applied exhibition of its strength. No poet, but a quack, aims at wonderful efforts."[See Note III.]

"Poets on the whole cannot learn too much from musicians and painters. In these arts it is very striking, how necessary it is to take sparing advantage of the auxiliary means of the art, and how much depends upon proper relations. Those artists, on the contrary, can certainty accept from us the poetic independence, and the inner spirit of each composition and invention; particularly of every genuine work. The execution, not the material, is the object of the art. They should be more poetical, we more musical and graphic; yet both according to the manner and method of our art. You yourself will soon see in what songs you can best succeed; they will certainly be those, the subjects of which are easiest and nearest at hand. Therefore it can be said that poetry rests entirely upon experience. I know that in my younger days an object could hardly seem too distant and too unknown, for such I delighted most to sing. What was the result? An empty, meagre flash of words, without a spark of true poetry. Thence the tale [3] is the most difficult of tasks, and a young poet will seldom perform it correctly."

"I should like to hear one of yours," said Henry. "The few I have heard, though insignificant, have delighted me exceedingly."

"I will satisfy your wish this evening. I remember one which I composed when quite young, which is sufficiently evident still; yet it will entertain you the more instructively, for it will recall much that I have told you."

"Language," said Henry, "is indeed a little world in signs and sounds. As man rules over it, so would he rule the great world, and in it express himself freely. And in this very joy of expressing in the world what is without it, and of doing that which in reality was the primal object of our existence, lies the origin of poetry."

"It is very unfortunate," said Klingsohr, "that poetry has a particular name, and that poets constitute a particular class. It is not, however, strange. It arises from the natural action of the human sprit. Does not every man strive and compose at every moment?"

Just then Matilda entered the room. Klingsohr continued. "Consider love, for instance. In nothing is the necessity of poetry for the continuance of humanity so clear as in that. Love is silent; poesy alone can speak for it. Or rather love itself is nothing but the highest poetry of nature. Yet I will not tell you of things, with which you are better acquainted than I."

"Thou art indeed the father of love;" cried Henry, as he threw his arms around Matilda, and they both kissed his hand.

Klingsohr embraced them and went out.

"Dear Matilda," said Henry after a long kiss, "it seems to me like a dream, that thou art mine; yet it seems still more wonderful, that thou hast not been so always."

"It seems to me," said Matilda, "that I knew thee long, long ago."

"Canst thou then love me?"

"I know not what love is; but this can I tell thee, that it is as if I now first began to live, and that I am so devoted to thee that I would this instant die for thee."

"My Matilda, now for the first time do I feel what it is to be immortal."

"Dear Henry, how infinitely good thou art. What a glorious spirit speaks from thee. I am a poor, insignificant girl."

"How thou dost make me blush! Indeed I am what I am only through thee. Without thee I were nothing. What were a spirit without a heaven; and thou art the heaven that upbears and supports me."

"How divinely happy should I be, wert thou as faithful as my father. My mother died shortly after my birth; yet my father weeps for her every day."

"I deserve it not, yet may I be happier than he!"

"I would joyfully live long by thy side, dear Henry. Certainly through thee I should become much better."

"O! Matilda, even death shall not separate us."

"No, Henry, where I am, wilt thou be."

"Yes, where thou art, Matilda, will I forever be."

"I comprehend not the meaning of eternity; yet I fancy that what I feel, when I think of thee, must constitute eternity."

"Yes, Matilda, we are eternal, because we love each other."

"Thou canst not believe, dearest, how fervently, when we came home early this morning, I knelt before the image of the holy mother, what unspeakable things I prayed to her. I thought that I should melt away in tears. It seemed as if she smiled upon me. I now for the first time know what gratitude is."

"O beloved, Heaven has given me thee to adore. I worship thee. Thou art the holy one that carriest my wishes to God, through whom He reveals himself to me, through whom He makes known to me the fulness of His love. What is religion but an infinite harmony, an eternal unison of loving hearts? Where two are gathered together, He is indeed among them. Thou wilt be my breath eternally. My bosom will never cease to draw thee to itself. Thou art divine majesty, eternal life in the loveliest of forms."

"Alas, Henry, thou knowest the fate of the roses. Wilt thou also press the pale cheek, the withered lips, with tenderness to thy own? Will not the traces of age be also the traces of bygone love?"

"O that thou couldst see through my eyes into my spirit! But thou lovest me, and canst also believe me. I cannot comprehend what is said of the withering of charms. They are unfading! That which draws me so inseparably to thee, that has awakened in me such everlasting desire, is not of this world. Couldst thou but see how thou appearest to me, what a wonderful form penetrates thy shape, and everywhere is raying towards me, thou wouldst not fear age. Thy earthly shape is but a shadow of this form. The earthly faculties strive and swell that they may incarnate it; but nature is yet unripe; the form is only an eternal archetype, a fragment of the unknown holy world."

"I understand thee, dear Henry, for I see something similar when I look upon thee."

"Yes, Matilda, the higher world is nearer to us than we usually believe. Here already we live in it, and we see it closely interwoven with our earthly nature."

"Thou wilt yet reveal much that is glorious to me, beloved?"

"O! Matilda, from thee alone cometh the gift of divination. Everything that I have is indeed thine. Thy love will lead me into the sanctuaries of life, and the most sacred recesses of the mind; thou wilt fill me with enthusiasm, wilt excite me to the highest contemplation. Who knows that our love will not change to wings of flame bearing us upward, and carrying us to our heavenly home, ere old age and death reach us? Is it not a miracle already that thou art mine, that I hold thee in my arms, that thou lovest me, and that thou wilt be mine forever?"

"To me also everything seems possible, and I plainly feel a gentle flame kindling within me. Who knows that it does not transfigure us, and gradually dissolve all earthly ties? Only tell me, Henry, whether thou hast that boundless confidence in me, that I have in thee. Yet I never have felt towards any one as I do towards thee; not even to my father, whom I love so dearly."

"Dear Matilda, it really torments me, that I cannot tell thee everything at once, that I cannot at once give my whole heart to thee. For the first time in my life am I perfectly frank. No thought, no feeling can I longer conceal from thee, – thou must know everything. My whole being shall mingle itself with thine. A most boundless resignation to thee can alone satisfy my love. In that indeed it consists. It is truly a most mysterious flowing together of our most secret and personal existence."

"Henry, two beings can never thus have loved each other."

"I cannot believe it possible, for till now no Matilda has lived."

"And no Henry!"

"Swear to me once more that thou art mine. Love is an endless repetition."

"Yes, Henry, by the invisible presence of my good mother, I swear to be thine forever."

"I swear to be thine forever, Matilda, as surely as love, God's presence, is with us."

A long embrace and countless kisses sealed the eternal alliance of the blessed pair.

CHAPTER IX

At evening some guests were present; the grandfather drank the health of the young bridal pair, and promised to give them soon a splendid marriage feast. "Of what use is long waiting?" said the old man. "Early marriages make long love. I have always observed that marriages early contracted were the happiest. In latter years there is no longer such a devotion in the marriage relation as in youth. Youth, enjoyed in common, forms an inseparable tie. Memory is the safest ground of love."

After the meal more people came in. Henry asked his new father to fulfil his promise. Klingsohr said to the company, "I have promised Henry to-day to relate a tale. If it would please you I am ready to do so."

"That was a wise idea of Henry's," said Swaning. "We have heard nothing from you for a long time."

All seated themselves by the fire, which was sparkling on the hearth. Henry sat by Matilda, and stole his arm around her. Klingsohr began.

"The long night had just set in. The old hero struck his shield, so that it resounded far through the solitary streets of the city. Thrice he repeated the signal. Then the lofty, many-colored windows of the palace began to shed abroad their light, and their figures were put in motion. They moved the more quickly, as the ruddy stream which began to illumine the streets became stronger. Also by degrees the immense pillars and walls began to shine. At length they stood in the purest milk-blue glimmer, and flickered with the softest colors. The whole region was now visible, and the reflection of the figures, the clashing of the spears, swords, shields, and helmets, which bowed from all sides towards crowns appearing here and there, and finally closed round a simple green garland in a wide circle, as the crowns vanished before it; all this was reflected from the frozen sea that surrounded the hill on which the city stood, – and even the far distant mountain range, which girdled the sea, was half enwrapped with a mildly reflected splendor. Nothing could be plainly distinguished; yet a strange sound was heard, as if from an immense workshop in the distance. The city, on the contrary, was light and clear. Its smooth transparent walls reflected the beautiful beams; and the perfect symmetry, the noble style, and fine arrangement of all the buildings were well defined. Before every window stood earthern pots with ornaments, full of every variety of ice and snow flowers, which sparkled most brilliantly.

"But fairest of all appeared the garden upon the great square in front of the palace, consisting of metal plants and crystal trees, hung with varied jewel-blossoms and fruits. The manifold and delicate shapes, the lively lights and colors, formed a lordly spectacle, made still more magnificent by a lofty fountain, frozen in the midst of the garden. The old hero walked slowly past the palace doors. A voice from within called his name. He turned towards the door, which opened with a gentle sound, and stewed into the hall. His shield was held before his eyes.

"'Hast thou yet discovered nothing,' plaintively cried the beautiful daughter of Arcturus. She lay on silken cushions, upon a throne artfully fashioned from a huge pyrite-crystal, and some maidens were assiduously chafing her tender limbs, which seemed a rare union of milk and purple. On all sides streamed from beneath the hands of the maidens that charming light, which so wondrously illuminated the palace. A perfumed breeze was waving through the hall. The hero was silent.

"'Let me touch thy shield,' said she softly.

"He approached the throne and stepped upon the costly carpet. She seized his hand, pressed it with tenderness to her heavenly bosom, and touched his shield. His armor resounded, and a penetrating force inspired his frame. His eyes flashed, and the heart beat loudly against his breastplate. The beautiful Freya appeared more serene, and the light that streamed from her became more brilliant.

"'The king is coming,' cried a splendid bird that was perched behind the throne. The attendants threw an azure veil over the princess, which concealed her heaving bosom. The hero lowered his shield, and looked upward to the dome, whither two broad staircases wound from each side of the hall. Soft music preceded the king, who soon appeared in the dome, and descended with a numerous train.

"The beautiful bird unfolded its shining wings, and gently fluttering, sang to the king as with a thousand voices:

"The stranger fair delay no longer maketh.
Warmth draweth near, Eternity begins.
From long and tedious dreams the Queen awaketh,
When land in eddying love with ocean spins.
Her farewell hence the chilly midnight taketh,
When Fable first the ancient title wins.
The world will kindle upon Freya's breast,
And every longing in its longing rest."

The King embraced his daughter with tenderness. The spirits of the stars surrounded the throne, and the hero took his place in the order. A numerous crowd of stars filled the hall in splendid groups. The attendants brought a table and a little casket, containing a heap of leaves, upon which were inscribed mystic figures of deep significance, constructed of constellations. The king reverently kissed these leaves, mixed them carefully together, and handed some to his daughter; the rest he kept. The princess placed them in a row upon the table; then the king closely examined his own, and chose with much reflection before he added one to them. At times he seemed forced to choose this or that leaf. But often his joy was evident, when he could complete by a lucky leaf a beautiful harmony of signs and figures. As the play commenced, tokens of the liveliest sympathy were visible among all the by-standers, accompanied by peculiar looks and gestures, as if each one had an invisible instrument in his hands which he plied diligently. At the same time a gentle but deeply moving music was heard in the air, seeming to arise from the stars gliding past each other in a wondrous motion, and from the other movements so peculiar. The stars floated round, now slowly, now quickly, in continually changing lines, and curiously imitated, to the swell of the music, the figures on the leaves. The music changed incessantly with the images upon the table; and though the transitions were often strange and intricate, yet a simple theme seemed to unite the whole. With incredible adroitness the stars flew together according to the images. Now in great confusion, but now again beautifully arranged in single clusters, and now the long train was suddenly scattered, like a ray, into innumerable sparks, but soon came together, through smaller circles and patterns ever increasing, into one great figure of surprising beauty. The varied shapes in the windows remained all this time at rest. The bird unceasingly ruffled its costly plumage in every variety of form. Hitherto the old hero had also pursued an unseen occupation, when suddenly the king full of joy exclaimed, "all is well. Iron, throw thy sword into the world, that it may know where peace rests."

The hero snatched the sword from his thigh, raised it with the point to heaven, and hurled it from the window over the city and the icy sea. It flew through the air like a comet, and seemed to penetrate the mountain chain with a clear report, as it fell downward in brilliant flakes of fire.

At this time the beautiful child Eros lay in his cradle and slumbered gently, whilst Ginnistan his nurse rocked him, and held out her breast to his foster-sister Fable. She had spread her variegated wimple over the cradle, so that the bright lamp which stood before the scribe might not trouble the child. Busily he wrote, at times looking morosely at the children, and gloomily towards the nurse, who smiled upon him kindly and kept silence.

The father of the children walked in and out continually, at each turn gazing upon them, and greeting Ginnistan kindly. He always had something to dictate to the scribe. The latter observed his words exactly, and when he had written, handed them to an aged and venerable woman, who was leaning on an altar, where stood a dark bowl of clear water, into which she looked with serene smiles. When she dipped the leaves in the water, and found on withdrawing them, that some of the writing remained still glittering, she gave them to the scribe, who fastened them in a great book, and seemed much out of humor when his labor had been in vain, and all the writing had been obliterated. The woman turned at times towards Ginnistan and the children, and dipping her finger in the bowl, sprinkled some drops upon them, which, as soon as they touched the nurse, the child, or the cradle, dissolved into a blue vapor, exhibiting a thousand strange images, and floating and changing constantly around them. If one of these by chance touched the scribe, many figures and geometrical diagrams fell down, which he strung with much diligence upon a thread, and hung them for an ornament around his meagre neck. The child's mother, who was sweetness and loveliness itself, often came in. She seemed to be constantly occupied, always carrying with her some domestic utensil. If the prying scribe observed it, he began a long reproof, of which no one took any notice. All seemed accustomed to his fruitless fault-finding. The mother sometimes gave the breast to little Fable, but was soon called away, and Ginnistan took the child back again, for it seemed to love her best. Suddenly the father brought in a small slender rod of iron, which he had found in the court. The scribe looked at it, twirled it round quickly, and soon discovered, that being suspended from the middle by a thread, it turned of itself to the north. Ginnistan also took it in her hand, bent it, pressed it, breathed upon it, and soon gave it the form of a serpent biting, its own tail. The scribe was soon weary of looking at it. He wrote down everything that had occurred, and was very diffuse about the utility of such a discovery. But how vexed was he when all he had written did not stand the proof, and when the paper came blank from the bowl. The nurse continued to play with it. She chanced to touch with it the cradle; the child awoke, threw off his covering, and holding one hand towards the light, reached after the serpent with the other. As soon as he received it, he leaped so quickly from the cradle that Ginnistan was frightened, and the scribe fell nearly out of his chair from wonder; the child stood in the chamber, covered only by his long golden hair, and gazed with speechless joy upon the prize, which pointed in his hands, towards the North, and seemed to awake within him deep emotion. He grew visibly.

"Sophia," said he with a touching voice to the woman, "let me drink from the bowl."

She gave it him without delay, and he could not cease drinking; yet the bowl continued full. At last he returned it, while embracing the good woman heartily. He pressed Ginnistan to his heart, and asked her for the variegated cloth, which he bound becomingly around his thigh. He took little Fable in his arms. She appeared greatly to delight in him, and began to prattle. Ginnistan devoted all her attention to him. She looked exceedingly charming and gay, and pressed him to herself with the tenderness of a bride. She led him with whispered words to the chamber door, but Sophia nodded earnestly and pointed to the serpent. Just then the mother entered, to whom he immediately flew, and with warm tears welcomed her. The scribe had departed in anger. The father entered: and as he saw mother and son in silent embrace, he approached the charming Ginnistan behind them and caressed her. Sophia ascended the stairs. Little Fable took the scribe's pen and began to write. Mother and son were deeply engaged in conversation. The father availed himself of the opportunity, and lavished many a tender word and look upon Ginnistan, who returned them willingly; and in their sweet interchange of love, both the presence or absence of any was forgotten. After some time Sophia returned, and the scribe entered. He drove little Fable with many rebukes from his seat, and took a long time to put his things in order. He handed to Sophia the leaves that Fable had written over, that they might be returned clean; but his displeasure was extreme, when Sophia drew the writing brilliant and uneffaced from the bowl, and laid it before him. Fable clang to her mother, who took her to her breast, and put the chamber in order, opened the windows for the fresh air, and made preparations for a costly meal. A beautiful landscape was visible from the windows, and a serene sky overarched the earth. The father was busily employed in the court. When he was weary, he looked up towards the window, where Ginnistan stood and threw to him all sorts of sweetmeats. Mother and son went out in order to assist in any manner, and to prepare for the resolution they had taken. The scribe twitched his pen, and always made a wry face, when he was forced to ask any information of Ginnistan, who had a good memory and recollected everything that transpired. Eros soon returned, clad in beautiful armor, round which the varigated cloth was wound like a scarf. He asked Sophia's advice as to when and how he should commence his journey. The scribe was very troublesome, and wanted to furnish him with a complete traveller's guide, but his instructions were not regarded.

"You can commence your journey immediately," said Sophia, "Ginnistan can guide you. She knows the road and is acquainted everywhere. She will take the form of your mother, that she may not lead you into temptation. If you find the king, think of me; for then I shall soon come to assist you."

Ginnistan exchanged forms with the mother, whereat the father seemed much pleased. The scribe was rejoiced that they were both going away; particularly when Ginnistan on taking leave presented him with a pocket-book, in which the chronicles of the house were circumstantially recorded. Yet the little Fable remained a thorn in his eye, and he desired nothing more for his peace and content, than that she might also be among the number of the travellers. Sophia pronounced a blessing upon the two who knelt down before her, and gave them a vessel full of water from the bowl. The mother was very sad. Little Fable, would willingly have gone with them; the father was too much occupied out of doors, to concern himself much about it. It was night when they left, and the moon stood high in the sky.

"Dear Eros," said Ginnistan, "we must hasten, that we may come to my father, who has not seen me for a long time, and has fought for me anxiously everywhere upon earth. Do you not see his emaciated face? Your testimony will cause him to recognise me in this strange form."

Love hies along in dusky ways,
The moon his only light;
The shadow-realm itself displays,
And all uncouthly dight.

An azure mist with golden rim
Around him floats in play,
And quickly Fancy hurries him
O'er stream and land away.

His teeming bosom beating is
In wondrous spirit-flow;
A presagement of future bliss
Bespeaks the ardent glow.

And Longing sat and wept aloud,
Nor knew that Love was near;
And deeper in her visage ploughed
The hopeless sorrow's tear.

The little snake remaineth true,
It pointeth to the North,
And both in trust and courage new
Their leader follow forth.

Love hieth through the hot Simoon,
And through the vapor-land,
Enters the halo of the moon,

The daughter in his hand.

He sat upon his silver throne,
Alone with his unrest;
When heareth he his daughter's tone,
And sinketh on her breast.

Eros stood deeply moved by their tender embrace. At length the tottering old man collected himself and bade his guest welcome. He seized his great horn and blew a mighty blast. The ringing echo vibrated through the ancient castle. The pointed towers with their shining balls, and the deep black roofs, trembled.

The castle stood firm, for it had settled upon the mountain from beyond the deep sea.

Servants were gathering from every quarter; their peculiar forms and dresses delighted Ginnistan infinitely, and did not frighten the brave Eros. They first greeted her old acquaintances, and all appeared before them in new strength, and in all the glory of their natures. The impetuous spirit of the flood followed the gentle ebb. The old hurricanes rested upon the beating breast of the hot, passionate earthquake. The gentle showers looked around for the many-colored bow which stood so pallid, far from the sun that most attracts it. The rude thunder resounded through the play of the lightning, behind the innumerable clouds which stood in a thousand charms, and allured the fiery youth. The two sisters Morning and Evening were especially delighted by their arrival. Tears of tenderness were mingled in their embraces. Indescribable was the appearance of this wonderful court. The old king could not gaze long enough upon his daughter. She was tenfold happy in her father's castle, and could not grow weary of looking at the well known wonders and rarities. Her joy was unspeakable, when the king gave her the key to the treasure-chamber, and permission to arrange there a spectacle for Eros, which could entertain him until the signal for breaking up. The treasure-place was a large garden, the variety and richness of which surpassed all description. Between the immense cloud-trees lay innumerable air-castles of surprising architecture, each succeeding one more costly than the others. Large herds of little sheep with silver-white, golden, and rose-colored wool, were wandering about, and the most singular animals enlivened the grove. Remarkable pictures stood here and there, and the festive processions, the strange carriages which met the eye on every side, continually occupied the attention. The beds were filled with many-colored flowers. The buildings were crowded with every species of weapon, and furnished with the most beautiful carpets, tapestry, curtains, drinking-cups, and all kinds of furniture and utensils arranged in an endless order. From the hill they saw a romantic region overspread with cities and castles, temples and sepulchres; every delight of inhabited plains united to the fertile charms of the wilderness and the mountain steep. The fairest colors were most happily blended. The mountain peaks shone like pyramids of fire in their hoods of ice and snow. The plain lay smiling in the freshest green. The distance was arrayed in every shade of blue, and from the sombre bosom of the sea waved countless pennons of varied hue from numerous fleets. In the distance a shipwreck was to be seen; here in the foreground a rustic cheerful meal of country people; there the terribly grand eruption of a volcano, the desolating earthquake; and in front beneath shady trees a loving couple in sweet caresses. Further on was a fearful battle, and beyond it a theatre full of the most ludicrous masks. In another spot of the foreground was a youthful corpse upon its bier, to which an inconsolable lover clung, and the weeping parents at its side; beyond was seen a lovely mother with her child at her breast, and angels sitting at her feet, and gazing from the branches over head. The series were continually shifting, and at last all flowed together into one mysterious picture. Heaven and earth were in complete uproar. All terrors had broken loose. A mighty voice cried, "to arms!" A terrible host of skeletons, with black standards, rushed like a tempest from the dark mountain, and attacked the life which was feasting merrily in youthful bands among the open plains, anticipating no danger. Terrible tumults arose, the earth trembled, the tempest howled, fearful meteors lighted the gloom. With unheard of cruelty, the host of phantoms tore the tender limbs of the living. A funeral pyre towered on high, and amid shrieks which made the blood run cold, the children of life were consumed by the flames. Suddenly a milk-blue stream broke on all sides from the dark heap of ashes. The phantoms hastened to fly, but the flood visibly swelled and swallowed up the detestable brood. Soon all fear was allayed. Heaven and earth flowed together in sweet music. A flower, wonderful in beauty, floated glittering upon the gentle billows. A shining bow half circled the flood, and on both sides of it sat celestial shapes on splendid thrones. Sophia sat highest with the bowl in her hands, near a majestic man, whose locks were bound by a garland of oak leaves, and who bore in his right hand a palm of peace instead of a sceptre. A lily leaf bent over the chalice of the floating flower. The little Fable sat upon it, and sang to the harp the sweetest song. In the chalice sat Eros himself, bending over a beautiful, slumbering maiden who held him fast embraced. A smaller blossom closed around them both, so that from the thighs they seemed changed to a flower.

Eros thanked Ginnistan with thousand fold rapture. He embraced her tenderly, and she returned his caresses. Wearied by the fatigues of the journey, and by the manifold objects he had seen, he longed for quiet and rest. Ginnistan, who felt deeply attracted by the beautiful youth, took good care not to mention the draught which Sophia had given him. She led him to a retired bath, and removed his armor. Eros dipped himself in the dangerous waves, and came out again in rapture. Ginnistan chafed dry his strong limbs knit with youthful vigor. He thought with ardent longing of his beloved, and embraced the charming Ginnistan in sweet delusion. He surrendered himself carelessly to his tenderness, and fell asleep on the fair bosom of his guide.

In the mean time a sad change had taken place at home. The scribe had involved the domestics in a dangerous conspiracy. His fiendish mind had long sought occasion to obtain possession of the government of the house, and to shake off his yoke. Such an occasion he had found. His party first seized the mother and put her in irons. The father also was deprived of everything but bread and water. The little Fable heard the noise in the chamber. She hid herself behind the altar; and observing that there was a concealed door on its farther side, she opened it quickly, and discovered a staircase leading from it. She closed the door behind her, and descended the stairs in the dark. The scribe rushed furiously into the chamber, in order to revenge himself on the little Fable, and to take Sophia captive. Neither of them was to be found. The bowl was also missing, and in his wrath he broke the altar into a thousand pieces, without, however, discovering the secret staircase.

Fable continued to descend for a considerable time. At length she reached an open space adorned with splendid colonnades, and closed by a great door. All objects there were dark. The air was like one immense shadow; and a darkly beaming body stood in the sky. One could easily distinguish objects, because each figure exhibited a peculiar shade of black, and cast behind a pale glimmer; light and shade seemed to have changed their respective offices. Fable rejoiced to find herself in a new world. She regarded everything with childish curiosity. At length she reached the door, before which upon a massive pedestal reclined a beautiful Sphinx.

"What dost thou seek?" said the Sphinx.

"My possession," replied Fable.

"Whence comest thou hither?"

"From olden times."

"Thou art yet a child."

"And will be a child forever."

"Who wilt assist thee?"

"I will assist myself. Where are my sisters?" asked Fable.

"Everywhere, and yet nowhere," answered the Sphinx.

"Dost thou know me?"

"Not as yet."

"Where is Love?"

"In the imagination."

"And Sophia?"

The Sphinx murmured inaudibly to itself, and rustled its wings.

"Sophia and Love!" cried Fable triumphantly, and passed the door. She stepped into an immense cave, and joyfully reached the aged sisters, who were pursuing their wonderful occupation, by the poor light of a dimly burning lamp. They seemed not to notice their little guest, who busily hovered around them with artless caresses. At last one of them with a crabbed face roughly rebuked her.

"What wouldst thou here, idler? Who has admitted thee? Thy childish steps disturb the quiet flame. The oil is burning to waste. Canst thou not be seated, and occupy thyself usefully?"

"Beautiful aunt," said Fable, "I am no idler. But I cannot help laughing at your door-keeper. She would have taken me to her breast; but seemed to have eaten too much to rise. Let me sit before the door, and give me something to spin. I cannot see well here; and when I am spinning I must be suffered to sing and talk, which might disturb your serious cogitations."

"Thou shalt not go outside; but through a cleft of the rock a beam from the upper world pierces into a side-chamber, there thou mayest spin if thou knowest how. Here lie great heaps of old ends, spin them together. But have a care; for if thou spin lazily or break the threads, they will wind round and choke thee."

The old woman laughed maliciously and resumed her labor. Fable gathered up an armful of the threads, took distaff and spindle, and tripped singing into the chamber. She looked out through the cleft, and saw the constellation of Phoenix. Rejoicing at the happy omen, she began to spin industriously, leaving the chamber door ajar, and sang in subdued tones: –

Within your cells awaken,
Children of olden time;
Be every bed forsaken,
The morn begins to climb.

Your threadlets I am weaving
Into a single thread:
In *one* life be ye cleaving, –
The times of strife are sped.

Each one in all is living,
And all in each beside;
One heart its pulses giving.
From *one* impelling tide.

Yet spirits only are ye.
But dream and witchery.
Into the cavern fare ye,
And vex the holy Three.

The spindle turned with incredible velocity between her little feet, while she twisted the thread with both her hands. During the song, innumerable little lights became visible, which passed through the chink of the door, and spread through the cave in hideous masks. The elders continued spinning gloomily, and in expectation of the cries of distress of little Fable. But how terrified were they when a horrible nose appeared over their shoulders, and when upon looking around they beheld the whole cave filled with fearful forms, engaged in a thousand fantastic tricks. They shrunk together, howled with frightful voices, and would have turned to stone through fear, had not the scribe entered the cave bearing with him a mandrake root. The lights concealed themselves in the rocky cleft, and the cave became entirely illuminated, while the black lamp was extinguished, having been overturned in the confusion. The old hags were glad when they heard the scribe approaching; but were full of wrath against the little Fable. They called her forth, rebuked her terribly, and forbade her spinning longer. The scribe smiled grimly; because he supposed that now the little Fable was in his power, and said,

"It is good that thou art here, and art kept employed. I hope that thou receivest thy share of punishment. Thy good spirit has guided me hither. I wish thee a long life and many pleasures."

"I thank thee for thy good will," said Fable; "lo, what a good age is approaching thee. The hourglass and sickle only are wanting to make thee like in looks to the brother of my beautiful aunts. If thou needest quills, only pluck a handful of soft down from their cheeks."

The scribe threatened to attack her. She smiled and said,

"If thy beautiful locks and spiritual eyes are dear to thee, beware! think of my nails, thou hast not much more to loose."

He turned with stifled rage towards the old women, who were rubbing their eyes, and searching for their distaffs. They could not find them because the lamp was extinguished; but they vented their rage against Fable.

"Do let her go," said he spitefully, "that she may catch tarantulas to prepare your oil. I will tell you for your consolation that Eros is restlessly on the wing, and by his industry will keep your scissors busy. His mother, who has so often compelled you to spin the lengthened threads, will become a prey to the flames to-morrow."

He laughed with joy, when he saw that Fable wept at this news, and giving a piece of the root to the old people, departed chuckling. The sisters, though supplied with oil, angrily ordered Fable to go in search of tarantulas, and Fable hastened away. She pretended to open the door, slammed it noisily, and crept stealthily to the back of the cave, where a ladder was hanging down. She ascended quickly, and soon came to an aperture, which opened into the apartment of Arcturus.

The king sat surrounded by his counsellors when Fable appeared. The Northern Crown adorned his head. He held the lily in his left hand, the balance in his right. The eagle and the lion sat at his feet.

"Monarch," said Fable, bending reverently before him, "Hail to thine eternal throne! Joyful news for thy wounded heart! An early return of wisdom! Awakening to eternal peace! Rest to the restless love! Glorification of the heart! Life to antiquity and form to the future!"

The king touched her open forehead with the lily, "Whatever thou demandest shall be granted thee."

"Three times shall I petition, and when I come the fourth time. Love will be before the door. Now give me the lyre."

"Eridanus," cried the king, "bring the lyre hither."

Eridanus streamed forth murmuring from his concealment, and Fable snatched the lyre from his boiling flood.

Fable played a few prophetic strains. She sipped from the cup which the king ordered to be handed her, and hastened away with many thanks. She glided with a sweet, elastic motion over the icy sea, drawing joyful music from the strings.

The ice resounded melodiously beneath her step. She fancied the voices of the rocks of sorrow were the voices of her children seeking her, and she answered in a thousand echoes.

Fable soon reached the shore. She met her mother who appeared wasted and pale; she had grown thin and sad, and her noble features revealed the traces of a hopeless sorrow and of touching constancy.

"What has happened to thee, dear mother?" asked Fable; "thou seemest to me entirely changed; I should not know thee except by internal signs. I hoped once more to refresh myself at thy breast; I have pined after thee for a long time."

Ginnistan caressed her tenderly, and became calm and serene.

"I thought from the first," said she, "that the scribe would not take thee captive. It refreshes me to see thee. Poor and pinched are my affairs now; but I console myself with hoping that it will soon end. Perhaps I am about to have a moment of rest. Eros is near; and when he sees thee and thou speakest with him, he may tarry some time. In the mean time come to my bosom. I will give thee what I have."

She took Fable upon her lap, proffered her breast, and while smiling upon the little one who was enjoying her feast, continued, "I am myself the cause that Eros has become so wild and inconstant. But yet I repent it not, for those hours have made me immortal. I believe that his fiery caresses have strangely transformed him. Long, silver-white wings covered his glittering shoulders, and the charming fulness of his form. The strength, which swelling forth had so suddenly changed him from a youth to a man, seemed entirely to have withdrawn into his wings, and he had become again a boy. The silent glow of his face became like the dazzling fire of a will-o'-the-wisp, his holy seriousness had changed to dissembled roguishness, the significant calm to childish irresolution, the noble carriage to a droll agility. I felt irresistibly attracted to the wanton boy by an ardent passion, and suffered with pain his sneering scorn, and his indifference to my most touching prayers. I perceived that my form was changed. My careless serenity had fled, and its place filled with sorrowful anxiety and shrinking timidity. I would have hidden myself with Eros from all eyes. I had not the heart to meet his offending eye, and was overwhelmed with shame and humility. I had no thoughts but for him; and would have given my life to free him from his wantonness. Deeply as he had hurt my feelings, I was compelled to worship him.

"Since the time when he discovered himself and escaped me, I have continually been in pursuit of him, though I have conjured him touchingly and with hot tears to remain with me. He seems really intent on persecuting me. As often as I reach him, he flies away again. On every side his bow deals destruction. I have nought to do but to console the unhappy, and yet I myself need consolation. The voices of those who call me point out to me his path, and their mournful complaints, when I am compelled to leave them, deeply cut my heart. The scribe pursues us in a terrible rage, and revenges himself upon the poor wounded ones. The fruit of that mysterious night was a multitude of strange children, who look like their grandfather, and are named after him. Being winged like their father, they ever accompany him, to torment the poor ones whom his arrow wounds. But there comes the joyous procession. I must away. Farewell, sweet child. His presence excites my passion. Be happy in thy designs."

Eros passed on without Ginnistan, who hastened near him, beseeching but one look of tenderness. But he turned kindly towards Fable, and his little companions danced joyously around her. Fable was glad to see her foster-brother again, and sang a merry song to her lyre. Eros seemed as if desiring to recall some recollections of the past, and let fall his bow upon the ground. Ginnistan could now embrace him, and he suffered her tender caresses. At last Eros began to nod; he clung to Ginnistan's bosom and fell asleep, spreading over her his wings. The weary Ginnistan full of rejoicing turned not her eye from the graceful sleeper. During the song, tarantulas came forth from all sides, which drew a shining net over the blades of grass, and with sprightly movements accompanied the music upon the threads. Fable now consoled her mother, and promised to her speedy assistance. From the rocks fell back the soft echo of the music, and lulled the sleeper. From the carefully preserved vessel Ginnistan sprinkled some drops into the air, and the most delightful dreams descended upon them. Fable took the vessel and continued her journey. Her strings never were at rest, and the tarantulas followed the enchanting sounds upon their fast-woven threads.

She soon saw from afar the lofty flame of a funeral pile, which rose high above the green forest. Mournfully she gazed towards heaven; yet rejoiced when she saw Sophia's blue veil which was waving over the earth, forever covering the unsightly tomb. The sun stood in heaven, fiery-red with rage. The powerful flame imbibed its stolen light; and the more fiercely the sun strove to preserve itself, ever more pale and spotted it became. The flame grew whiter and more intense, as the sun faded. It attracted the light more and more strongly; the glory around the star of day was soon consumed, and it stood there a pale, glimmering disk, every new agitation of spite and rage aiding the escape of the flying light-waves. Finally, nought of the sun remained but a black, exhausted dross, which fell into the sea. The splendor of the flame was beyond description. It slowly ascended, and bore towards the North. Fable entered the court, which was desolate; the house had fallen. Briars were growing in the crevices of the window frames, and vermin of every kind were creeping about on the broken staircase. She heard a terrible noise in the chamber; the scribe and his associates had been devoting her mother to the flames, but had been greatly terrified by the sudden destruction of the sun.

They had in vain struggled to extinguish the flame, and had not escaped unhurt. They vented their pain and anxiety in fearful curses and wailings. But more terrified were they, when Fable entered the chamber, and rushed upon them with a furious cry, letting her anger loose upon them. She stepped behind the cradle, and her pursuers rushed madly into the web of the tarantulas, which revenged themselves by a thousand wounds. The whole crowd commenced a frantic dance, to which Fable played a merry tune. With much laughter at their ludicrous performances, she approached the fragments of the altar, and cleared them away, in order to find the hidden staircase, which she descended with her train of tarantulas.

The Sphinx asked, "what comes more suddenly than the lightning?"

"Revenge," said Fable.

"What is most transient?"

"Wrongful possession."

"Who knows the world?"

"He who knows himself."

"What is the eternal mystery?"

"Love."

"With whom does it rest?"

"With Sophia."

The Sphinx bowed herself mournfully, and Fable entered the cave.

"Here I bring you tarantulas," said she to the old sisters, who again had lighted their lamp and were busily employed. They were overwhelmed with fear, and one of them rushed upon her with the shears to murder her. Unwarily she stepped upon a tarantula, which stung her in the foot. She cried piteously; the others came to her assistance, and were likewise stung by the irritated reptiles. They could not now attack Fable, and danced wildly about.

"Spin directly for us," cried they angrily to the little one, "some light dancing dresses. We cannot move in this stiff raiment, and are nearly melted with heat. Thou must soak the thread in spider's juice that it may not break, and interweave flowers, which have grown in fire; otherwise thou shalt die."

"Right willingly," said Fable, and retired to the side-chamber.

"I will get you three fine large flies," said she to the spiders, which had fixed their airy web about the ceiling and the walls; "but you must spin for me immediately three beautiful light dresses. I will bring you directly the flowers which must be worked upon them."

The spiders were ready and began to weave busily. Fable glided up the ladder, and proceeded to Arcturus.

"Monarch," said she, "the wicked dance, the good rest. Has the flame arrived?"

"It has come," said the King. "Night is passed and the ice melts. My spouse appears in the distance. My enemy is overwhelmed. All things begin to exist. As yet I do not dare to show myself, for I am not alone King. Ask what thou wilt."

"I need," said Fable, "some flowers that have grown in fire. I know thou hast a skilful gardener, who understands rearing them."

"Zinc," cried the King, "give us flowers."

The flower gardener stepped from the ranks, bringing at vessel full of fire, and sowed shining seeds therein. Soon flowers sprang up. Fable gathered them in her apron, and returned. The spiders had been industrious, and nothing more was needed but to attach the flowers, which they immediately began to do with much taste and skill. Fable took good care not to pull off the ends which were yet hanging to the weavers.

She carried the dresses to the wearied dancers, who had sunk down dripping with perspiration, and were taking a moment's breath after their unwonted exertions. She dextrously undressed the haggard beauties, who were not backward in scolding their little servant, and put on the new dresses, which fitted excellently. While thus employed, she praised the charms and lovely character of her mistresses, who seemed really pleased with her flatteries, and the splendor of their new appearance. Having in the mean time rested themselves, they recommenced their mazy whirl, whilst they deceitfully promised little Fable a long life and great rewards. Fable returned to the chamber, and said to the spiders, "you can now eat in peace the flies which I hare brought to your web."

The spiders were soon impatient at being pulled back and forth by the distracted movements of the dancers, for the ends of the threads were still in them. They therefore ran out and attacked the dancers, who would have defended themselves with the shears, had not Fable quietly removed them. They therefore submitted to their hungry companions; who for a long time had not tasted so rich a feast, and who sucked them to the marrow. Fable looked out from the cleft in the rock, and saw Perseus with his great shield of iron. The shears flew to it, and Fable asked him to trim with them the wings of Eros, and then with his shield to immortalize the sisters, and finish the great work.

She now left the subterraneous kingdom, and flew rejoicing to Arcturus's palace.

"The flax is spun. The lifeless are again unsouled. The living will govern, the dead will shape and use. The Inmost is revealed, and the Outermost is hidden. The curtain will soon be lifted, and the play commence. Once more I petition thee; then will I spin days of eternity."

"Happy child," cried the monarch with emotion, "thou art our deliverer."

"I am only Sophia's god-daughter," said the little one. "Permit Turmaline, the flower gardener, and Gold to accompany me. I must gather up the ashes of my foster-mother; the old Bearer must again arise, that the earth may not lie in chaos, but renew her motion."

The king called all three, and commanded them to accompany the little Fable. The city was light, and in the streets was the bustle of business. The sea broke roaring upon the high cliff, and Fable went over in the king's chariot with her companions. Turmaline carefully gathered the dispersing ashes. They traversed the earth till they came to the old giant, upon whose shoulders they descended. He seemed lamed by the touch, and could not move a limb. Gold placed a coin in his mouth, and the flower-gardener pushed a dish under his loins. Fable touched his eyes and poured out her vessel upon his forehead. Soon as the water flowed from his eyes into his mouth, and over his body into the dish, a flash of life made all his muscles quiver. He opened his eyes and rose vigorously. Fable jumped up to her companion on the swelling ground, and kindly bade him good morning.

"Art thou again here, dear child?" said the old man, "thou of whom I have so continually dreamed? I always thought that thou wouldst appear before the earth and my eyes became too heavy. I have indeed been sleeping long."

"The earth is again light, as it always was for the good," said Fable. "Old times are returning. Shortly thou wilt again be among thine old acquaintances. I will spin out for thee joyous days, nor shalt thou want an help-meet. Where are our old guests, the Hesperides?"

"With Sophia. Their garden will soon bloom again, its golden fruits send forth their odor. They are now busy gathering together the fading plants."

Fable departed, and hastened to the house. It was entirely in ruins. Ivy was winding round the walls. Tall bushes shaded the ancient court, and the soft moss enwrapt the old steps. She entered the chamber. Sophia stood by the altar which had been rebuilt. Eros was lying at her feet in full armor, more grave and noble than ever. A splendid lustre hung from the ceiling. The floor was paved with variegated stones, describing a great circle around the altar, which was graced with noble and significant figures. Ginnistan bent weeping over a couch, on which the father appeared lying in deep slumber. Her blooming grace was infinitely enhanced by an expression of devotion and love. Fable handed to the holy Sophia, who tenderly embraced her, the urn in which the ashes were gathered.

"Lovely child," said she, "thy faithfulness and assiduity have earned for thee a place among the stars. Thou hast elected the immortal within thee. Phœnix is thine. Thou wilt be the soul of our life. Now arouse the bridegroom. The herald calls, and Eros shall seek and awaken Freya."

Fable rejoiced unspeakably at these words. She called her companions Gold and Zinc, and approached the couch. Ginnistan awaited full of expectation the issue of her enterprise. Gold melted coin, and filled with a glittering flood the space in which the father was lying. Zinc wound a chain around Ginnistan's bosom. The body floated upon the trembling waves. "Bow thyself, dear mother," said Fable, "and lay thy hand upon the heart of thy beloved."

Ginnistan bowed. She saw her image many times reflected. The chain touched the flood, her hand his heart; he awoke and drew the enraptured bride to his bosom. The metal became a clear and liquid mirror. The father arose; his eyes flashed lightning; and though his shape was speakingly beautiful, yet his whole frame appeared a highly susceptible fluid, which betrayed every affection in manifold and enchanting undulations.

The happy pair approached Sophia, who pronounced the words of consecration upon them, and charged them faithfully to consult the mirror, which reflected everything, in its real shape, destroyed every delusion, and ever retained the primeval type of things. She now took the urn, and shook the ashes into a bowl upon the altar. A soft bubbling announced the dissolution, and a gentle wind waved the garments and locks of the bystanders. Sophia handed the bowl to Eros, who proffered it to the others. All tasted the divine draught, and received with unspeakable joy the Mother's friendly greeting in their soul of souls. She appeared to each one of them, and her mysterious presence seemed to transfigure all.

Their expectations were fulfilled and surpassed. All perceived what they had wanted, and the chamber became an abode of the blessed.

Sophia said, "the great secret is revealed to all, and remains forever unfathomable. Out of pain is the new world born, and the ashes are dissolved into tears for a draught of eternal life. The heavenly mother dwells in all, that every child may be born immortal. Do you not feel the sweet birth in the beating of your heart?"

She poured from the bowl the remainder upon the altar. The earth trembled to its centre. Sophia said, "Eros, hasten with thy sister to thy beloved. Soon shall ye see me again."

Fable and Eros quickly departed with their train. Then was scattered over, the earth a mighty spring. Everything arose and stirred with life. The earth floated farther beneath the veil. The moon and the clouds were trailing with joyous tumult towards the North. The king's castle beamed with a lordly splendor over the sea, and upon its battlements stood the king in full majesty with all his suite. On every side they saw dust-whirls, in which familiar shapes seemed represented. Numerous bands of young men and maidens appeared hastening to the castle, whom they welcomed with exaltation. Upon many a hill sat happy couples but just awakened, in long-lost embraces; and they thought the new world was a dream, nor could they cease assuring themselves of its reality.

Flowers and trees sprang up in verdant vigor. All things seemed inspired. All spoke and sang. Fable saluted on all sides her old acquaintances. With friendly greeting animals approached awakened men. The plants welcomed them with fruits and odor, and arrayed themselves most tastefully. No weight lay longer on any human bosom, and all burdens became the solid ground on which men trod. They came to the sea. A ship of polished steel lay fastened to the shore. They stepped aboard, and cast off the rope. The prow turned to the north, and the ship cleaved the amorous waves as if on pinions, The sighing sedge ceased its murmur, as it glides gently to the shore. They hastened up the broad stairs. Love admired the royal city and its opulence. In the court the living fountain was sparkling; the grove swayed to and fro in sweetest tones, and a wondrous life seemed to gush and thrive in its swelling foliage, its twinkling fruits and blossoms. The old hero received them at the door of the palace.

"Venerable man," said Fable, "Eros needs thy sword. Gold has given him a chain, one end of which reaches down to the sea, the other encircles his breast. Take it in thy hand, and lead us to the hall where the princess rests." Eros took the sword from the hand of the old man, pressed the handle to his breast, and pointed the blade before him. The folding doors of the hall flew open, and enraptured Eros approached the slumbering Freya. Suddenly a mighty shock was felt. A bright spark sped from the princess to the sword, the sword and the chain were illumined; the hero supported the little Fable who was almost sinking. The crest of Eros waved on high. "Throw away thy sword," exclaimed Fable, "and awake thy beloved."

Eros dropped the sword, flew to the princess and kissed her sweet lips vehemently. She opened her full, dark eyes, and recognised the loved one. A long kiss sealed their eternal alliance.

The king descended from the dome, hand in hand with Sophia. The stars and the spirits of nature followed in glittering ranks. A day unspeakably serene filled the hall, the palace, the city, and the sky. An innumerable multitude poured into the spacious, royal hall, and with silent devotion saw the lovers kneel before the king and the queen, who solemnly blessed them. The king took the diadem from his head, and bound it round the golden locks of Eros, The old hero relieved him of his armor, and the king threw his mantle around him. Then he gave him the lily from his left hand, and Sophia fastened a costly bracelet around the clasped hands of the lovers, and placed her crown upon the brown locks of Freya.

"Hail to our ancient rulers!" exclaimed the people. "They have always dwelt among us, and we have not known them! All hail! They will ever rule over us. Bless us also!"

Sophia said to the new queen, "Throw the bracelet of your alliance into the air, that the people and world may remain devoted to you." The bracelet dissolved in the air, and light halos were soon seen around every head; and a shining band encircled city, sea, and earth, which were celebrating an eternal Spring-festival. Perseus entered, bearing a spindle and a little basket. He carried the latter to the new king.

"Here," said he, "are the remains of thine enemies."

A stone slab chequered with white and black squares lay in the basket, with a number of figures of alabaster and black marble.

"It is the game of chess," said Sophia; "all war is confined to this slab and to these figures. It is a memento of the olden, mournful times."

Perseus turned to Fable and gave her the spindle. "In thy hands shall this spindle make us eternally rejoice, and out of thyself shalt thou spin an indissoluble, golden thread."

Phoenix flew with melodious rustling to her feet, and spread his wings before her; she placed herself upon them, and hovered over the throne, without again descending. She sang a heavenly song and began to spin, whilst the thread seemed to wind forth from her breast. The people fell into new raptures, and all eyes were fastened on the lovely child. New shouts of exultation came from the door.

The old Moon entered with her wonderful court, and behind her the people bore in triumph Ginnistan and her bridegroom. Garlands of flowers were wound around them; The royal family received them with the most hearty tenderness, and the new royal pair proclaimed them their viceregents upon earth.

"Grant me," said the Moon, "the Kingdom of the Fates, whose wondrous mansions have arisen from the earth, even in the court of the palace. I will delight you therein with spectacles, in which the little Fable will assist me."

The king granted the prayer; the little Fable nodded pleasantly, and the people rejoiced at the novel and entertaining pastime. The Hesperides congratulated them upon the new accession, and prayed that their garden might be protected. The king gave them welcome; and so followed joyful events in rapid succession. In the mean while, the throne had imperceptibly changed to a splendid marriage-bed, over which Phœnix and the little Fable were hovering in the air. Three Caryatides of dark porphyry supported the head, while its foot rested upon a Sphinx of basalt. The king embraced his blushing bride. The people followed his example, and kissed each other. Nothing was heard but tender names and a noise of kisses.

At length Sophia said, "The Mother is among us. Her presence will render us eternally happy. Follow us into our dwelling. In the temple will we dwell forever, and treasure up the secret of the world."

> Fable spun diligently, and sang with a clear voice:
> Established is Eternity's domain,
> In Love and Gladness melts the strifeful pain;
> The tedious dream of grief returneth never;
> Priestess of hearts Sophia is forever.

Novalis

Novalis

Sophie von Kühn

HENRY OF OFTERDINGEN

✳

PART SECOND

THE FULFILMENT

THE FULFILLMENT

THE CLOISTER, OR FORE-COURT

ASTRALIS

Upon a summer morning was I young;
Then felt I for the first my own life-pulse,
And while in deeper raptures Love dissolved,
My sense of life unfolded; and my longing
For more entire and inward dissolution,
Was every moment more importunate.
My being's plastic power is delight;
I am the central point, the holy source,
Whence every longing stormfully outflows,
And where again, though broken and dispersed,
Each longing calmly mingles into one.
Ye know me not, ye saw me not becoming. –
Who witnessed me upon that happy eve,
When, a night-wanderer yet, I found at length
For the first time myself? Then flowed there not
A shudder of sweet rapture over you?
Entirely hid in honey-cups I lay;
I breathed a fragrance, calmly waved the flowers
In golden morning air. An inner gushing
Was I, a gentle striving, all things flowed
Through me and over me, and light I rose.
Then sank the first dust-seed within the shell, –
That glowing kiss when risen from the feast!

Backward I ebbed upon my inmost life –
It was a flash, – my powers already swell,
And move the tender petals and the bell,
And swiftly, from beneath my being's spring,
To earthly senses thoughts were blossoming.
Yet was I blind, but stars began to sweep
In light across my being's wondrous deep;
Myself I found as of a distant clime,
Echo of olden as of future time.
From sadness, love and hopefulness created,
The growth of memory was but a flight,
And mid the dashing billows of delight,
Then too the deepest sorrow penetrated. –
The world in bloom around the hillock clings, –
The Prophet's words were changed to double wings;
Matilde and Henry were alone united
Into one form, into one rapture plighted;
New-born I rose, to Heaven gladly leaping,
For then the earthly destinies were blent
In one bright moment of transfiguration;
And Time, no more his ancient title keeping,
Again demanded what it once had lent.
Forth breaks the new creation here,
Eclipsing the glow of the brightest sphere.
Behold through ruins ivy-streaming
A new and wondrous future gleaming,
And what was common hitherto,
Appeareth marvellous and new.
Love's realm beginneth to reveal,
And busy Fable plies her wheel.
To its olden play each nature returns,
And a mighty spell in each one burns;
And so the Soul of the world doth hover
And move through all, and bloom forever.
For each other all must strive,
One through the other must ripen and thrive;
Each is shadowed forth in all,
While itself with them is blending,
And eagerly into their deeps doth fall,
Its own peculiar essence mending,
And myriad thoughts to life doth call.
The dream is World, the world is Dream,
And what already past may seem,
Itself is yet in distance moulding;

But Fancy first her court is holding,
Freely the threads at her pleasure weaving,
Much veiling here, much there unfolding,
And then in magical vapor leaving.
Life and death, rapture and sadness,
Are here in inmost sympathy, –
Who yieldeth himself to love's deep madness,
From its wounds is never free.
In pain must every bond be riven
That winds around the inner eye,
The orphaned heart with woe have striven,
Ere it the sullen world can fly.
The body melteth in its weeping,
Its bitter sighs the bosom burn;
The world a grave becometh, keeping
The heart, like ashes in an urn.

In deep thought a pilgrim was walking along a narrow foot-path which ran up the mountain side. Noon had passed. A strong wind whistled through the blue air. Its dull and ever-changing sounds lost themselves as they came. Had it perhaps flown through the regions of childhood, or through other whispering lands? They were voices whose echo sounded in his heart; yet the pilgrim did not appear to recognise them. He had now reached the mountain where he hoped to find a limit to his journey. Hoped? No longer did he cherish hope. Terrible anxiety, the sterile coldness of indifferent despair, urged him to seek the wild horrors of the mountains; the most toilsome path soothed the tumult of his soul. He was weary and silent. He noticed not the gradual accumulation of nature around him, as he sat upon a stone and cast his eye backward. It seemed as if he were or had been dreaming. A splendor whose limit he could not define opened before him. His cheeks were soon wet with tears, as his feelings suddenly broke loose; he would have wept himself away in the distance, that no trace of his existence might remain. Amid his deep-drawn sighs he seemed to recover; the soft, serene air penetrated him. The world was again present to his senses, and thoughts of other times began to speak to him consolation.

In the distance lay Augsburg with its towers; far on the horizon glimmered the mirror of the fearful, mysterious stream. The mighty forest bowed with grave sympathy towards the wanderer; the notched mountain rested meaningly upon the plain, and both seemed to say, "Hasten on, O stream, thou dost not escape us. I will follow thee with winged ships. I will break thee, restrain thee, and swallow thee up in my bosom! O pilgrim, confide in us! Even he is our enemy whom we ourselves begat; let him make haste with his booty, he escapes us not."

The poor pilgrim thought of olden times and their unspeakable delights; but how heavily did those dear recollections pass through his mind. The broad hat concealed a youthful face; it was pale as a night-flower. The balmy sap of youthful life had changed to tears, his swelling breath to deep sighs; an ashy paleness had usurped all color.

On one side upon the declivity of the hill, he thought he saw a monk kneeling under an old oak tree. "Might not that possibly be the old chaplain?" he conjectured, without much surprise at the idea. The monk appeared larger and more unshapely the nearer he approached. He now discovered his mistake. It was an isolated rock, over which a tree was bending. With silent emotion he clasped the stone in his arms, and with loud sobbing pressed it to his breast. "O that yet your speech was preserved, and that the Holy Mother would give me some token! Am I then entirely miserable and abandoned? Dwells there then in this desert no holy one who would lend me his prayer? Dear father, at this time pray thou for me!"

As he so thought to himself, the tree began to wave; the rock emitted a hollow sounds and as from a great depth beneath the earth, clear, sweet voices were heard singing: –

Her heart was full of gladness,
For gladness knew she best;
She nothing knew of sadness,
With darling at her breast.
She showered him with kisses,

She kissed his cheek so warm, –
Encircled was with blisses
Through darling's fairy form.

The soft voices seemed to sing with infinite pleasure. They repeated the verse several times. All was quiet again, when the astonished pilgrim heard some one speaking to him from the tree:–

"If thou wilt play a song in honor of me upon thy lute, a little maiden will come for it; take her with thee and leave her not. Think of me when thou comest to the emperor. I have chosen this abode, that I may remain with my little child; let a strong, warm dwelling be built for me here. My little one has conquered death; trouble not thyself, I am with thee. Yet a while thou wilt remain upon earth, but the little girl will console thee, until thou also diest and enterest into our joy."

"It is Matilda's voice!" exclaimed the pilgrim, and fell upon his knees in prayer. Then pierced through the branches a lengthened ray unto his eyes, and through it in the distance he beheld a small but wonderful splendor, not to be described, only to be depicted with a skilful pencil. It was composed of extremely delicate figures; and the most intense pleasure and joy, even a heavenly happiness, everywhere rayed forth from it, so that even the inanimate vessels, the chiselled capitals, the drapery, the ornaments, everything visible, seemed not so much like works of art, as to have grown and sprung up together like the full-juiced herb. Most beautiful human forms were passing to and fro, and appeared kind and gracious to each other beyond measure. Before all was standing the pilgrim's beloved one, and it seemed as if she would have spoken to him; yet nothing could be heard, and the pilgrim only regarded with ardent longing her pleasant features, as she beckoned to him so kindly and smilingly, and laid her hand upon her heart. The sight was infinitely consoling and refreshing, and the pilgrim remained along while steeped in holy rapture, until the vision disappeared. The sacred beam had drawn up all pain and trouble from his heart, so that his mind was again clear and cheerful, his spirit free and buoyant as before. Nought remained but a silent, inward longing, and a sound of sadness in the spirit's depths; but the wild torments of solitude, the sharp anguish of unspeakable loss, the terrible sense of a mournful void, had passed away with all earthly faintness, and the pilgrim again looked forth upon a world teeming with expression. Voice and language renewed their life within him, all things seemed more known and prophetic than before, so that death appeared to him a high revelation of life, and he viewed his own fleeting existence with child-like and serene emotion. The future and the past had met within him, and formed an eternal union. He stood far from the present, and the world was now for the first time dear to him, when he had lost it, and was there only as a stranger, who would yet wander but a while through its diversified and spacious halls. It was now evening, and the earth lay before him like an old beloved dwelling, which he had found again after long absence. A thousand recollections recurred to him; every stone, every tree, every hillock, made itself recognised. Each was the memorial of a former history.

> The pilgrim snatched his lute, and sang: –
> Love's tears, love's glowing,
> Together flowing,
> Hallow every place for me,
> Where Elysium quenched my longing,
> And in countless prayers are thronging,
> Like the bees around this tree.
>
> Gladly is it o'er them bending,
> Thither wending,
> Them protecting from the storm;
> Gratefully its leaves bedewing,
> And its tender life renewing,
> Wonders will the prayers perform.
>
> E'en the rugged rock is sunken,
> Joy-drunken,
> At the Holy Mother's feet.
> Are the stones devotion keeping,

Should not man for her be weeping
Tears and blood in homage meet?

The afflicted hither stealing
Should be kneeling;
Here will all obtain relief.
Sorrow will no more be preying,
Joyfully will all be saying:
Long ago we were in grief.

On the mountain, walls commanding
Will be standing;
In the vales will voices cry,
When the bitter times are waking:
Let the heart of none be aching,
Thither to those places fly!

Oh, thou Holy Virgin Mother!
With another
Heart the sorrowing wanders hence.
Thou, Matilda, art revealing
Love eternal to my feeling,
Thou, the goal of every sense.

Thou, without my questions daring,
Art declaring
When I shall attain to thee.
Gaily in a thousand measures
Will I praise creation's treasures,
Till thou dost encircle me.

Things unwonted, wonders olden!
To you beholden,
Ever in my heart remain.
Memory her spell is flinging,
Where light's holy fountain springing
Washed away the dream of pain.

During this song he had noticed nothing, but as he looked up, there appeared a young girl standing upon the rock, who kindly greeted him like an old acquaintance, and invited him to go to her dwelling, where she had already prepared an evening meal for him. Her whole behavior and carriage towards him were friendly. She asked him to tarry a few moments, while she stepped under the tree, and looking up with an indescribable smile, shook many roses from her apron upon the grass. She knelt silently by his side, but soon arose and led the pilgrim on.

"Who has told thee about me?" asked the pilgrim.

"Our mother."

"Who is thy mother?"

"The Mother of God."

"How long hast thou been here?"

"Since I came from the tomb."

"Hast thou already been dead?"

"How could I else be living?"

"Livest thou entirely alone here?"

"An old man is at home, yet I know many more who have lived."

"Wouldst thou like to remain with me?"

"Indeed I love thee."

"How long hast thou known me?"

"O! from olden times; my former mother, too, told me about thee."

"Hast thou yet a mother?"

"Yes; but really the same."

"What is her name?"

"Maria."

"Who was thy father?"

"The Count of Hohenzollern."

"Him I also know."

"Thou shouldst know him well, for he is also thy father."

"My father is in Eisenach."

"Thou hast more parents."

"Whither are we going?"

"Ever homewards."

They had now reached a roomy spot in the wood, where some decayed towers were standing beyond deep ravines. Early shrubbery wound about the old walls, like a youthful garland around the silvery head of an old man. While contemplating the gray stones, the tortuous clefts, and the tall, ghastly, shapes of rock, one looked into immensity of time, and saw the most distant events, collected in short but brilliant minutes. So appears to us the infinite space of heaven, clad in dark blue; and like a milky glimmer, stainless as an infant's cheeks, appears the most distant array of its ponderous and mighty worlds. They walked through an old doorway, and the pilgrim was not a little astonished when he found himself entirely surrounded by strange plants, and saw all the charms of the most beautiful garden hidden beneath the ruins. A small stone house built in recent style, with large windows, lay in the rear. There stood an old man behind the broad-leafed shrubbery, employed in tying the drooping branches to some little props. His female guide led the pilgrim to him, and said, "Here is Henry, after whom you have inquired so often."

As the old man turned around, Henry fancied that he saw the miner before him.

"This is the physician Sylvester," said the little girl.

Sylvester was glad to see him, and said, "it is a long time since I saw your father. We were both young then. I was quite solicitous to teach him the treasures of the Fore-time, the rich legacies bequeathed to us by a world too early separated from us. I noticed in him the tokens of a great artist; his eye flashed with the desire to become a correct eye, a creative instrument; his face indicated inward constancy and persevering industry. But the present world had already taken hold of him too deeply; he would not listen to the call of his own nature. The stern hardihood of his native sky had blighted in him the tender buds of the noblest plants; he became an able mechanic, and inspiration seemed to him but foolishness."

"Indeed," said Henry, "I often observed a silent sadness within him. He always labored from mere habit, and not for any pleasure. He seems to feel a want, which the peaceful quiet and comfort of his life, the pleasure of being honored and beloved by his townsmen, and consulted in all important affairs of the city, cannot satisfy. His friends consider him very happy; but they know not how weary he is of life, how empty the world appears to him, how he longs to depart from it; and that he works so industriously not so much for the sake of gain, as to dissipate such moods."

"What I am most surprised at," replied Sylvester, "is that he has committed your education entirely into the hands of your mother, and has carefully abstained from taking any part in your development, nor has ever held you to any fixed occupation. You can happily say that you have been permitted to grow up free from all parental restraints; for most men are but the relics of a feast which men of different appetites and tastes have plundered."

"I myself know not," replied Henry, "what education is, except that derived from the life and disposition of my parents, or the instruction of my teacher, the chaplain. My father with all his cool and sturdy habits of thought, which leads him to regard all relations like a piece of metal or a work of art, yet involuntarily and unconsciously exhibits a silent reverence and godly fear before all incomprehensible and lofty phenomena, and therefore looks upon the blooming growth of the child with humble self-denial. A spirit is busy here, playing fresh from the infinite fountain; and this feeling of the superiority of a child in the loftiest matters, the irresistible thought of an intimate guidance of the innocent being who is just entering on a course so critical, the impress of a wondrous world, which no earthly currents have yet obliterated, and then too the sympathizing memory of that golden age when the world seemed to us clearer, kindlier, and more unwonted, and the almost visible spirit of prophecy attended us, – all this has certainly won my father to a system the most devout and discreet."

"Let us seat ourselves upon the grass among the flowers," said the old man interrupting him. "Cyane will call us when our evening meal is ready. I pray you continue your account of your early life. We old people love much to hear of childhood's years, and it seems as if I were drinking the odor of a flower, which I had not inhaled since my infancy. Tell me first, however, how my solitude and garden please you, for these flowers are my friends; my heart is in this garden. You see nothing that loves me not, that is not tenderly beloved. I am here in the midst of my children, like an old tree from whose roots, has sprouted this merry youth."

"Happy father," said Henry, "your garden is the world. The ruins are the mothers of these blooming children; this manifold animate creation draws its support from the fragments of past time. But must the mother die, that the children may thrive? Does the father remain sitting alone at their tomb, in tears forever?"

Sylvester gave his hand to the sighing youth, and then arose to pluck a fresh forget-me-not, which he tied to a cypress branch and brought to him. The evening wind waved strangely in the tops of the pines which stood beyond the ruins, and sent over their hollow murmur. Henry hid his face bedewed with tears upon the neck of the good Sylvester, and when he looked again, the evening star arose in full glory above the forest.

After some silence, Sylvester began; "You would probably like to be at Eisenach among your friends. Your parents, the excellent countess, your father's upright neighbors, and the old chaplain make a fair social circle. Their conversation must have produced an early influence upon you, particularly as you were the only child. I also imagine the country to be very striking and agreeable."

"I learn for the first time," said Henry, "to esteem my native country properly, since my absence, and the sight of many other lands. Every plant, every tree, every hill and mountain has its own horizon, its peculiar landscape, which belongs to it, and explains its whole structure and nature. Only men and animals can visit all countries; all countries are theirs. Thus together they form one great region, one infinite horizon, whose influence upon men and animals is just as visible, as that of a more narrow circuit upon the plant. Hence men who have travelled, birds of passage, and beasts of prey, are distinguished among other faculties, for a remarkable intelligence. Yet they certainly possess more or less susceptibility to the influence of these circles, and of their varied contents and arrangement. The attention and composure necessary to contemplate properly the alternation and connexion of things, and then to reflect upon and compare them, are in fact wanting to most men. I myself often feel how my native land has breathed upon my earliest thoughts imperishable colors, and how its image has become a peculiar feature of my mind, which I am ever better explaining to myself, the deeper I perceive that fate and mind are but names of one idea."

"Upon me," said Sylvester, "living nature, the emotive outergarment of a landscape, has always produced a most powerful effect. Especially I am never tired of examining most carefully the different natures of plants. All productions of the earth are its primitive language; every new leaf, every particular flower, is everywhere a mystery, which presses outward; and since it cannot move itself at love and joy, nor come to words, becomes a mute, quiet plant. When we find such a flower in solitude, is it not as if everything about it were glorified, and as if the little feathered songsters loved most to linger near it? One could weep for joy, and separated from the world, plant hand and foot in the earth, to give it root, and never abandon the happy neighborhood. Over all the sterile world is spread this green, mysterious carpet of love. Every Spring it is renewed, and its peculiar writing is legible only to the loved one, like the nosegay of the East; he will read forever, yet never enough, and will perceive daily new meanings, new delightful revelations of loving nature. This infinite enjoyment is the secret charm, which the survey of the earth's surface has for me, while each region solves other riddles, and has always led me to divine whence I came and whither I go."

"Yes," said Henry, "we began to speak of childhood's years, and of education, because we are in your garden; and the revelation of childhood, the innocent world of flowers, imperceptibly brought to our thoughts and lips the recollection of old acquaintanceship. My father is also very fond of gardening, and spends the happiest hours of his life among the flowers. This has certainly kept his heart open towards children, since flowers are their counterpart. The teeming opulence of infinite life, the mighty powers of later times, the splendor of the end of the world, and the golden future which awaits all things, we here see closely entwined, but still to be most plainly and clearly in tender youthfulness. All-powerful love is already working, but does not yet enflame; it is no devouring fire, but a melting vapor; and however intimate the union of the tenderest souls may be, yet it is accompanied by no intense excitement, no consuming madness, as in brutes. Thus is childhood below here nearest to the earth; as on the other hand clouds are perhaps the types of the second, higher childhood, of the paradise regained; and hence they so beneficently shed their dew upon the first."

"There is indeed something very mysterious in the clouds," said Sylvester, "and certain overcloudings often have a wonderful influence upon us. Trailing over our heads, they would take us up and away in their cold shades; and when their form is lovely and varied, like an outbreathed wish of our soul, then the clearness and the splendid light, which reigns upon earth, is like a presage of unknown, ineffable glory. But there are also dark, solemn, and fearful overcloudings, in which all the terrors of old night appear to threaten. The sky seems as if it never would be clear again; the serene blue is hidden; and a wan copper hue upon the dark gray ground awakens fear and anxiety in every bosom. Then when the blasting beams shoot downwards, and with fiendish laughter the crashing thunder-peals fall after them, we are struck to our souls; and unless there arises the lofty consciousness of our moral superiority, we fancy that we are delivered over to the terrors of hell and all the powers of darkness. They are echoes of the old, unhuman nature, but awakening voices too of the higher nature of divine conscience within us. The mortal totters to its base; the immortal grows more serene and recognises itself."

"Then," said Henry, "when will there be no more terror or pain, want or evil in the universe?"

"When there is but one power, the power of conscience; when nature becomes chaste and pure. There is but one cause of evil, – common frailty, – and this frailty is nothing but a weak moral susceptibility, and a deficiency in the attraction of freedom."

"Explain to me the nature of Conscience."

"I were God, could I do so; for when we comprehend it. Conscience exists. Can you explain to me the essence of poetry?"

"A personality cannot be distinctly defined."

"How much less then the secret of the highest indivisibility. Can music be explained to the deaf?"

"If so, would the sense itself be part of the new world opened by it? Does one understand facts only when one has them?"

"The universe is separated into an infinite system of worlds, ever encompassed by greater worlds. All senses are in the end but one. One sense conducts, like one world, gradually to all worlds. But everything has its time and its mode. Only the Person of the universe can detect the relations sustained by our world. It is difficult to say, whether we, within the sensuous limits of corporeity, could really augment our world with new worlds, our sense with new senses, or whether every increase of our knowledge, every newly acquired ability, is only to be considered as the development of our present organization."

"Perhaps both are one," said Henry. "For my own part, I only know that Fable is the collective instrument of my present world. Even Conscience, that sense and world-creating power, that germ of all Personality, appears to me like the spirit of the world-poem, like the event of the eternal, romantic confluence of the infinitely mutable common life.

"Dear pilgrim," Sylvester replied, "the Conscience appears in every serious perfection, in every fashioned truth. Every inclination and ability transformed by reflection into a universal type becomes a phenomenon, a phase of Conscience. All formation tends to that which can only be called Freedom; though by that is not meant an idea, but the creative ground of all being. This freedom is that of a guild. The master exercises free power according to design, and in defined and well digested method. The objects of his art are his, and he can do with them as he pleases, nor is he fettered or circumscribed by them. To speak accurately, this all-embracing freedom, this mastership of dominion, is the essence, the impulse of Conscience. In it is revealed the sacred peculiarity, the immediate creation of Personality, and every action of the master, is at once the announcement of the lofty, simple, evident world – God's word."

"Then is that, which I remember was once called morality, only religion as Science, the so called theology in its proper sense? Is it but a code of laws related to worship as nature is to God, a construction of words, a train of thoughts, which indicates, represents the upper world, and extends it to a certain point of progress – the religion for the faculty of insight and judgment – the sentence, the law of the solution and determination of all the possible relations which a personal being sustains?"

"Certainly," said Sylvester, "Conscience is the innate mediator of every man. It takes the place of God upon earth, and is therefore to many the highest and the final. But how far was the former science, called virtue or morality, from the pure shape of this lofty, comprehensive, personal thought! Conscience is the peculiar essence of man fully glorified, the divine archetypal man (Urmensch.) It is not this thing and that thing; it does not command in a common tongue, it does not consist of distinct virtues. There is but one virtue, – the pure, solemn Will, which, at the moment of decision chooses, resolves instantaneously. In living and peculiar oneness it dwells and inspires that tender emblem, the human body, and can excite all the spiritual members to the truest activity."

"O excellent father!" exclaimed Henry, "with what joy fills me the light which flows from your words! Thus the true spirit of Fable is the spirit of virtue in friendly disguise; and the proper spirit of the subordinate art of poetry is the emotion of the loftiest, most personal existence. There is a surprising selfness (Selbstheit) between a genuine song and a noble action. The disfranchised conscience in a smooth, unresisting world, becomes an enchaining conversation, an all-narrating fable. In the fields and halls of this old world lives the poet, and virtue is the spirit of his earthly acts and influences; and as this is the indwelling divinity among men, the marvellous reflex of the higher world, so also is Fable. How safely can the poet now follow the guidance of his inspiration, or if he possesses a lofty, transcendent sense, follow higher essences, and submit to his calling with child-like humility. The higher voice of the universe also speaks within him, and cries with enchanting words to kindlier and more familiar worlds. As religion is related to virtue, so is inspiration to mythology; and as the history of revelation is treasured in sacred writings, so the life of a higher world expresses itself in mythology in manifold ways, in poems of wonderful origin. Fable and history sustain to each other the most intimate relations, through paths the most intricate, and disguises the most extraordinary; and the Bible and mythology are constellations of one orbit."

"What you say is perfectly true," said Sylvester; "and now you can probably comprehend that all nature subsists by the spirit of virtue alone, and must ever become more permanent. It is the all-inflaming, the all-quickening light in the embrace of earth. From the firmament, that lofty dome of the starry realm, down to the ruffling carpet of the varied meadow, all things will be sustained by it, united to us and made comprehensible; and by it the unknown course of infinite nature's history will be conducted to its consummation."

"Yes; and you have often as beautifully shown, before now, the connexion between virtue and religion. Everything, which experience and earthly activity embrace, forms the province of Conscience, which unites this world with higher worlds. With a loftier sense religion appears, and what formerly seemed an incomprehensible necessity of our inmost nature, a universal law without any definite intent, now becomes a wonderful, domestic, infinitely varied, and satisfying world, an inconceivably interior communion of all the spiritual with God, and a perceptible, hallowing presence of the only One, or of his Will, of his Love in our deepest self."

"The innocence of your heart," Sylvester replied, "makes you a prophet. All things will be revealed to you, and for you the world and its history will be transformed into holy writ, just as the sacred writings evince how the universe can be revealed in simple words, or narratives, if not directly, yet mediately by hinting at and exciting higher senses. My connexion with nature has led me to the point where the joy and inspiration of language have brought you. Art and history have made me acquainted with nature. My parents dwelt in Sicily, not far from the famous Mount Ætna. Their dwelling was a comfortable house in the ancient style, hidden by old chestnut trees near the rocky shore of the sea, and affording the attraction of a garden stocked with various plants. Near were many huts, in which dwelt fishermen, herdsmen, and vine-dressers. Our chambers and cellar were amply provided with everything that supports and gives enjoyment to life, and by well bestowed labor, our arrangements were agreeable to the most refined senses. Moreover there was no lack of those manifold objects, whose contemplation and use elevate the mind above ordinary life and its necessities, preparing it for a more suitable condition, and seem to promise and procure for it the pure enjoyment of its full and proper nature. You might have seen there marble statues, storied vases, small stones with most distinct figures, and other articles of furniture, the relics perhaps of other and happier times. Also many scrolls of parchment lay in folds upon each other, in which were treasured, in their long succession of letters, the knowledge, sentiments, histories, and poems of that past time, in most agreeable and polished expressions. The calling of my father, who had by degrees become an able astrologer, attracted to him many inquiring visiters, even from distant lands; and as the knowledge of the future seemed to men a rare and precious gift, they were led to remunerate him richly for his communication; so that he was enabled, by the gifts he received, to defray the expenses of a comfortable and even luxurious style of life."

• • •

The author advanced no farther in the composition of this second part, which he called "The Fulfilment," as he had called the first "The Expectation," because all that was left to anticipation in the latter was explained and fulfilled in the former. It was the design of the author to write, after the completion of Ofterdingen, six romances for the statement of his views of physical science, civil life, commerce, history, political science, and of love; as his views of poetry had been given in Ofterdingen. I need not remind the intelligent reader, that the author in this poem has not adhered very closely to the time or the person of that well known Minnesinger, though every part brings him and his time to remembrance. It is an irreparable loss, not only to the friends of the author, but to the art itself, that he could not have finished this romance, the originality and great design of which would have been better developed in the second than in the first part. For it was by no means his object to represent this or that occurrence, to embrace one side of poetry, and explain it by figures and narrative; but it was his intention, as is plain from the last chapter of the first part, to express the real essence of poetry and explain its inmost aim.

To this end nature, history, war, and civil life, with their usual events, are all transformed to poetry, as that is the spirit which animates all things.

I shall endeavor as far as possible, from my memory of conversations with my friend, and from what I can discover in the papers he has left, to give the reader some idea of the plan and subject-matter of the second part of this work.

To the poet, who has apprehended the essence of his art at its central point, nothing appears contradictory or strange; to him all riddles are solved. By the magic of fancy he can unite all ages and all worlds; wonders vanish, and all things change to wonders. So is this book written; and the reader will find the boldest combinations, particularly in the tale which closes the first part. Here are renewed all those differences by which ages seem separated, and hostile worlds meet each other. The poet wished particularly to make this tale the transition-point to the second part, in which the narrative soars from the common to the marvellous, and both are mutually explained and restored; the spirit of the prologue in verse should return at each chapter, and this state of mind, this wonderful view of things should be permanent. By this means the invisible world remains in eternal connexion with the visible. This speaking spirit is poetry itself; but at the same time the sidereal man who is born from the love of Henry and Matilda. In the following lines, which should have their place in Ofterdingen, the author has expressed in the simplest manner the interior spirit of his works:

> When marks and figures cease to be
> For every creature's thoughts the key,
> When they will even kiss or sing
> Beyond the sage's reckoning,
> When life, to Freedom will attain,
> And Freedom in creation reign,
> When Light and Shade, no longer single,
> In genuine splendor intermingle,
> And one in tales and poems sees
> The world's eternal histories, –
> Then will our whole inverted being
> Before a secret word be fleeing.

The gardener, who converses with Henry, is the same old man who had formerly entertained Ofterdingen's father. The young girl, whose name is Cyane, is not his child, but the daughter of the Count of Hohenzollern. She came from the East; and though it was at an early age, yet she can recollect her home.

She has long lived a strange life in the mountains, among which she was brought up by her deceased mother. She has lost in early life a brother, and has narrowly escaped death in a vaulted tomb; but an old physician rescued her in some peculiar way. She is gentle, and kind, and very familiar with the supernatural. She tells the poet her history as she had heard it once from her mother. She sends him to a distant cloister, whose monks seem to be a kind of spirit-colony; everything is like a mystic, magic lodge. They are the priests of the holy fire in youthful minds. He hears the distant chant of the brothers; in the church itself, he has a vision. With an old monk Henry converses about death and magic, has presentiment of death – and of the philosopher's stone; visits the cloister-garden and the churchyard, concerning which latter I find the following poem: –

Praise ye now our still carousals,
Gardens, chambers decked so gaily,
Household goods as for espousals,
Our possessions praise.
Mew guests are coming daily,
Some late, the others early;
On the spacious hearth forever
Glimmereth a new life-blaze.

Thousand vessels wrought with cunning,
Once bedewed with thousand tears,
Golden rings and spurs and sabres,
Are our treasury;
Many gems of costly mounting
Wist we of in dark recesses,
None can all our wealth be counting,
Counts he even ceaselessly.

Children of a time evanished,
Heroes from the hoary ages,
Starry spirits high excelling,
Wondrously combine,
Graceful women, solemn sages,
Life in all its motley stages,
In one circle here are dwelling,

In the olden world recline.

None is evermore molested;
None who joyously hath feasted,
At our sumptuous table seated,
Wisheth to be gone.
Hushed is sorrow's loud complaining,
Wonders are no longer greeted,
Bitter tears no longer raining,
Hour-glass ever floweth on.

Holy kindness deeply swelling,
In blest contemplation buried,
Heaven in the soul is dwelling
With a cloudless breast;
In our raiment long and flowing
Through spring-meadows are we carried,
Where rude winds are never blowing,
In this land of perfect rest.

Pleasing lure of midnight hours
Quiet sphere of hidden powers,
Rapture of mysterious pleasure,
These alone our prize;
Ours alone that highest measure,
Where ourselves in streamlets pouring,
Then in dew-drops upward soaring,
Drink we as we flow or rise.

First with us grew life from love;
Closely like the elements
Do we mangle Being's waves,
Foaming heart with heart.
Hotly separate the waves,
For the strife of elements
Is the highest life of love,
And the very heart of hearts.

Whispered talk of gentle wishes
Hear we only, we are gazing
Ever into eyes transfigured,
Tasting nought but mouth and kiss;
All that we are only touching,
Change to balmy fruits and glowing,

Change to bosoms soft and tender,
Offerings to daring bliss.

The desire is ever springing,
On the loved one to be clinging,
Round him all our spirit flinging,
One with him to be, –
Ardent impulse ever heeding
To consume in turn each other,
Only nourished, only feeding
On each other's ecstasy.

So in love and lofty rapture
Are we evermore abiding,
Since that lurid life subsiding,
In the day grew pale;
Since the pyre its sparkles scattered,
And the sod above us sinking,
From around the spirit shrinking
Melted then the earthly veil.

Spells around remembrance woven,
Holy sorrow's trembling gladness,
Tone-like have our spirits cloven,
Cooled their glowing blood.
Wounds there are, forever paining;
A profound, celestial sadness,
Within all our hearts remaining,
Us dissolveth in one flood.

And in flood we forth are gushing,
In a secret manner flowing
To the ocean of all living,
In the One profound;
And from out His heart while rushing,
To our circle backward going,
Spirit of the loftiest striving
Dips within our eddying round.

All your golden chains be shaking
Bright with emeralds and rubies,
Flash and clang together making,
Shake with joyous note.
From the damp recesses waking,

From the sepulchres and ruins,
On your cheeks the flush of heaven,
To the realm of Fable float.

O could men, who soon will follow
To the spirit-land, be dreaming
That we dwell in all their joyance,
All the bliss they taste,
They would burn with glad upbuoyance
To desert the life so hollow, –
O, the hours away are streaming,
Come, beloved, hither haste.

Aid to fetter the Earth-spirit,
Learn to know the sense of dying,
And the word of life discover;
Hither turn at last.
Soon will all thy power be over,
Borrowed light away be flying,
Soon art fettered, O Earth-spirit,
And thy time of empire past.

This poem was perhaps a prologue to a second chapter. Now an entirely new period of the work would have opened; the highest life proceeding from the stillest death; he has lived among the dead and conversed with them. Now the book would have become nearly dramatic, the epic tone, as it were, uniting together and simply explaining the single scenes. Henry suddenly finds himself in Italy, distracted, rent with wars; he sees himself the leader of an army. All the elements of war play in poetic colors. With an irregular band, he attacks a hostile city; here appears in episode the love of a noble of Pisa for a Florentine maiden. War-songs – "a great war, like a duel, noble, philo-sophical, human throughout. Spirit of the old chivalry; the tournament. Spirit of bacchanalian sadness.[4] Men must fall by each other, – nobler than to fall by fate. They seek death. – Honor, fame, is the warrior's joy and life. The warrior lives in death and like a shade. Desire for death is the warrior-spirit. Upon the earth is war at home; it must be upon earth." – In Pisa Henry finds the Son of Frederick the Second, who becomes his confidential friend. He also travels to Loretto. Several songs were to follow here.

The poet is cast away on the shores of Greece by a tempest. The old world with its heroes and treasures of art fills his mind. He converses with a Grecian about morality. Everything from ancient times is present to him; he learns to understand the old pictures and histories. Conversation upon Grecian polity and mythology.

After becoming acquainted with the heroic age and with antiquity, he visits the Holy Land, for which he had felt so great a longing from his youth. He seeks Jerusalem, and acquaints himself with Oriental poetry. Strange events among the infidels detain him in desert regions; he discovers the family of the eastern girl (see Part I.): the manners and life of nomadic tribes. – Persian tales, recollections of the remotest antiquity. The book during all these various events was to retain its characteristic hue, and recall to mind the blue flower: throughout, the most distant and distinct traditions were to be knit together, Grecian, Oriental, Biblical, Christian, with reminiscences of and references to both the Indian and Northern mythology. – The Crusades. – Life at sea. – Henry visits Rome. Roman history.

Sated with his experiences, Henry at length returns to Germany. He finds his grandfather, a profound character; Klingsohr is in his society. An evening's conversation with them.

Henry joins the court of Frederick, and becomes personally acquainted with the emperor. The court would have made a worthy appearance, portraying the best, greatest, and most remarkable men, collected from the whole world, whose centre is the emperor himself. Here appears the greatest splendor, and the truly great world. German character and German history are explained. Henry converses with the emperor concerning government and the empire; obscure hints of America and the Indies. The sentiments of a prince, – the mystic emperor, – the book, "De tribus impostoribus."

Henry having now, in a new and higher method than in the

Expectation, lived through and observed nature, life, and death, war, the East, history, and poetry, turns back into his mind as to an old home. Front his knowledge of the world and of himself arises the impulse for expression; the wondrous world of fable now draws the nearest, because the heart is fully open to its comprehension.

In the Manesian collection of Minnesingers, we find a rather obscure rival song of Henry of Ofterdingen and Klingsohr with other poets; instead of this, jousting, the author would have represented another peculiar poetic contest, the war of the good and evil principles in songs of religion and irreligion, the invisible world contrasted with the visible. "Out of Enthusiasm the poets in bacchanalian intoxication contend for death." The sciences are poetized; mathematics also enters the lists. The plants of India are commemorated in song; new glorification of Indian mythology.

This is Henry's last act upon the earth; the transition to his own glorification. This is the solution of the whole work, the *Fulfilment* of the allegory which concludes the First Part. Everything is explained and completed, supernaturally and yet most naturally. The partition between Fiction and Truth, between the Past and the Present has fallen down. Faith, Fancy, and Poetry lay open the internal world.

Henry reaches Sophia's land, in Nature, such as might be allegorically painted; after having conversed with Klingsohr concerning certain singular signs and omens. These are mostly awakened by an old song which he hears by chance, and in which is described a deep water in a secluded spot. The song excites within him long forgotten recollections; he visits the water, and finds a small golden key, which a raven had stolen from him some time before, and which he had never, expected to find. An old man had given it to him soon after Matilda's death, with the injunction that he should carry it to the emperor, who would tell him what to do with it. Henry seeks the emperor, who is highly rejoiced and gives him an ancient manuscript, in which it is

▶ 188

written that the emperor should give it to that man who ever brought him a golden key; that this man would discover in a secret place an old talisman, a carbuncle for his crown, in which a space was yet left for it. The place itself is also described in the parchment. After reading the description, Henry takes the road to a mountain, and meets on the way the stranger who first told him and his parents concerning the blue flower; he converses with him about Revelation. He enters the mountain and Cyane trustingly follows him.

He soon reaches that wonderful land in which air and water, flowers and animals, differ entirely from those of earthly nature. The poem at the same time changes in many places to a play. "Men, beasts, plants, stones and stars, the elements, sounds, colors, meet like one family, act and converse like one race. Flowers and brutes converge concerning men. The world of fable is again visible; the real world is itself regarded as a fable." He finds the blue flower; it is Matilda, who sleeps and has the carbuncle. A little girl, their child, sits by a coffin, and renews his youth. "This child is the primeval world, the close of the golden time." "Here the Christian religion is reconciled with the Heathen. The history of Orpheus, of Psyche, and others are sung."

Henry plucks the blue flower, and delivers Matilda from her enchantment, but she is lost to him again; he becomes senseless through pain, and changes to a stone. "Edda (the blue flower, the Eastern Maiden, Matilda) sacrifices herself upon the stone; he is transformed to a melodious tree. Cyane hews down the tree and burns herself with him. He becomes a golden ram. Edda, Matilda, is obliged to sacrifice it. He becomes a man again. During these metamorphoses he has the very strangest conversations."

He is happy with Matilda, who is both the Eastern Maiden and Cyane. A joyous spirit-festival is celebrated. All that has past was Death, the last dream and awakening. "Klingsohr comes again as king of Atlantis. Henry's mother is Fancy, his father, Sense. Swaning is the Moon; the miner is the antiquary and at the same time Iron. The emperor Frederick is Arcturus. The Count of Hohenzollern and the merchants also return." Everything flows into an allegory. Cyane brings the stone to the emperor; but Henry is now himself the poet of the fabulous tale which the merchants had formerly related to him.

The blissful land suffers yet again by enchantment, while subjected to the changes of the Seasons. Henry destroys the realm of the Sun. The whole work was to close with a long poem, only the beginning of which was composed.

THE NUPTIALS OF THE SEASONS

Deep buried in thought stood the new monarch. He was recalling
    Dreams of the midnight, and every wonderful tale,
Which gathered he first from the heavenly flower, when stricken
    Gently by prophecy, love all-subduing he felt.
He thought still he heard the accents deeply impressive,
    Just as the guest was deserting the circle of joy;
Fleeting gleams of the moon illumined the clattering window,
    And in the breast of the youth there raged a passionate glow.
Edda, whispered the monarch, what is the innermost longing
    In the bosom that loves? What his ineffable grief?
Say it, for him would we comfort, the power is ours, and noble
    Be the time when thou art the joy of heaven again. –
"Were the times not so cold and morose, if were united
    Future with Present, and both with the holy Past time;
Were the Spring linked to Autumn, and the Summer to Winter,
    Were into serious grace childhood with silver age fused;
Then, O spouse of my heart, would dry up the fountain of sorrow,
    Every deep cherished wish would be secured to the soul."
Thus spake the queen, and gladsomely clasped her the radiant
                       beloved:
    Thou hast uttered in sooth to me a heavenly word,
Which long ago over the lips of the deep-feeling hovered,
    But on thine alone first pure and in season did light.
Quickly drive here the chariot, ourselves we will summon
    First the times of the year, then all the seasons of man. –

They ride to the sun, and first bring the Day, then the Night;
then to the North, for Winter, then to the South, to find Summer;
from the East they bring the Spring, from the West the Autumn.

Then they hasten after Youth, next to Age, to the Past and to the Future.

This is all I have been able to give the reader from my own recollection, and from scattered words and hints in the papers of my friend. The accomplishment of this great task would have been a lasting memorial of a new poesy. In this notice I have preferred to be short and dry, rather than expose myself to the danger of adding anything from my own fancy. Perhaps many a reader will be grieved at the fragmentary character of these verses and words, as well as myself, who would not regard with any more devout sadness a piece of some ruined picture of Raphael or Corregio.

L. Tieck.

NOTES

I

This *rifacimento* of Arion's story is not mere mythological twaddle. As allegories abound, and as in fact there is a suspicion that the whole Romance may be only an allegory, an "Apotheosis of Poetry," – the reader must keep open his internal eye.

Arion is the Spirit of Poetry as embodied in any age, whether in a single voice, or many. This the age always attempts to drown, – seldom with applause. The sailors are the exponents of an age, or its critics. In the case of Arion, they belonged to a certain tribe of Philistines, – not yet extinct.[5] There is a deep significance in the fact, that they resolutely stopped their ears against the Poet's song. The treasures of the Poet are his ideas of the good and the beautiful, which he fetches from his far home; for he comes, "not in entire forgetfulness." The fact, that Arion preferred jumping overboard to being converted into a heave-offering, is typical of the self-extinguishment and natural dissolution of the true soul, born into a humanity which is not its counterpart, which cannot answer to it. Those providential dolphins are a grateful posterity, which preserve not only the Poet's treasures, but his memory. The conflict among the sailors, too, has a deep meaning, hidden also in that old, wonderful myth of the Kilkenny cats.

But an allegory has many sides, like a genuine symphony. Each reader will interpret all of them best from his own point of view. Should Henry himself turn out to be Arion, the feat would only be one of inverted transmigration, and not more extraordinary than the regular method.

II

An opportunity is taken to introduce some further remarks of the author concerning History. They are found among a multitude of fragments, arranged under the three heads of Philosophical, Critical, and Moral; an amorphous heap of sayings, generally of great beauty and power. The present have little connexion with the text, but will be their own excuse. The total of his remarks will be seen to hint at a theory of History, with which most school-histories and respectable annals are in no wise infected.

'Luck or fate is talent for history. The sense for apprehending occurrences is the prophetic, and luck the divining instinct. (Hence the ancients justly considered a man's luck one of his talents.) We take delight in divination. Romance has arisen from the want of history.

'History creates itself. It first arises through the connexion of the past with the future. Men treat their recollections much too negligently.

'The historian organizes the historical Essence. The data of history are the mass, to which the historian gives form, while giving animation. Consequently history always presupposes the principles of animation and organization; and where they are not antecedent there can be no genuine historical *chef d'œuvre*, but only here and there the traces of an accidental animation, where a capricious genius has ruled.

'The demand, to consider this present world the best, is exactly analogous to that which would consider my own wedded wife the best and only woman, and life to be entirely for her and in her. Many similar demands and pretensions are there, which he who dutifully acknowledges, who has a discriminating respect for everything that has transpired, is historically religious, the absolute Believer and Mystic of history, the genuine lover of Destiny. Fate is the mysticised history. Every voluntary love, in the common signification, is a religion, which has and can have but one apostle, one evangelist and disciple, and can be, though not necessarily, an extra-religion (Wechsel-religion.)

'There is a series of ideal occurrences running parallel with reality. They seldom coincide. Men and chances usually modify the ideal occurrence, so that it appears imperfect, and its results likewise. Thus it was in the Reformation. Instead of Protestantism appeared Lutheranism.

'What fashions the man, but his *Life-History*? In like manner nothing fashions great men, but the *World's-History*.

'Many men live better in the past and future time, than in the present.

'The Present indeed is not at all comprehensible without the Past, and without a high degree of culture, an impregnation with the highest products, with the pure spirits of the present and of previous ages; all which assimilating guides and strengthens the human prophetic glance, which is more indispensable to the human historian, to the active, ideal elaborator of historic facts, than to the grammatical and rhetorical annalist.'

III

Novalis seems here to rehearse his whole poetic creed; or rather, he seems to be reviewing his own poems. What he deprecates, are the faults he most avoids. He is distinguished for extreme simplicity, both in style and language; and the thoughts, though lofty and sometimes vast, are yet fresh, chaste, and comprehensible. They have a domestic sublimity. They indicate simply an infinite expansion of the poet's heart, whose mild and primeval denizens are undisturbed by the forced, the foreign, or the shadowy. They have a oneness of design, and are finished and luminous to the most minute criticism. If we say that Novalis wrote as he was inspired, never attempting to superinduce what was only galvanic upon the true life, and never daring to write when he was not inspired, we both describe his genius and discover the secret of his beauty.

With one or two exceptions, the present romance is an unfavorable specimen of his poetic powers. The subjects of most of the songs require only that luminous simplicity alluded to, and are only fine examples of a lyrical style, with a few glimpses of his true genius. "Astralis," the poem that introduces the second part, is unlike the rest of the volume, being an irregular, mystic embodyment of the hero's destinies, – a recapitulation of the past and a presentiment of the future. The romance is unfavorable, excepting one or two prose passages of great sublimity, much resembling the "Hymns to the Night," one or two of which are given below. The dream at the close of the sixth chapter may be particularly designated. "The image of Death, and of the River being the Sky in that other and eternal Country, seems to us a fine and touching one: there is in it a trace of that simplicity, that soft, still pathos, which are characteristics of Novalis, and doubtless the highest of his specially poetic gifts." But it is in his Spiritual Songs that we gain a glimpse of his true genius. They are eminently devotional, and indiscriminately addressed to the Father, the Son, and the Holy Virgin. A translation of the mass of them would form a most desirable hymn book for the Christian, though, to be sure, it would be very graceless to supplant worthy old Dr. Watts. But they are very sweet and touching, and full of pious fervor. We have been struck with the similarity of their tone to those of George Herbert, who stands with the Father and the Son at the very door of his heart, with tearful and familiar supplication for them to enter.

"Geusz, Vater, Ihn gewaltig aus,
Gib Ihn aus deinem Arm heraus:
Nur Unschuld, Lieb' und süsze Scham
Hielt Ihn, dasz er nicht längst schon kam.

"Treib' Ihn von dir in unsern Arm,
Dasz er von deinem Hauch noch warm;
In schweren Wolken sammle ihn,
Und lasz Ihn so hernieder ziehn."

Among his promiscuous poems is a beautiful lyric, representing the triumph of Faith over Sorrow, under the symbol of a beautiful child bringing to him a wand, beneath whose touch the Queen of Serpents yields to him the "precious jewel."

The following is the first Hymn to the Night:

"What living, sense-endowed being loves not, before all the prodigies of the far extending space around him, the all-rejoicing light with its colors, its beams and billows, its mild omnipresence, as waking day? The restless giant-world of the stars, swimming with dancing motion in its azure flood. Inhales it as its life's inmost soul; the sparkling, ever-resting stone, the sensitive, imbibing plant, and the wild, burning, many-shaped animal, inhale it; but before all, the glorious stranger, with the speaking eyes, the uncertain gait, and the gently closed, melodious lips. Like a king of earthly nature, it summons each power to countless transformations, ratifies and dissolves treaties in infinite number, and suspends its heavenly image on every earthly being. Its presence alone reveals the wondrous splendor of creation's realms.

"I turn aside to the holy, ineffable, mysterious Night. Far away lies the world, sunk in a depth profound waste and lonely is its place. O'er the chords of the bosom waveth deep sadness. I will dissolve into dew drops, and mingle myself with the ashes. Distance of memory, wishes of youth, dreams of childhood, the short joys and vain hopes of a whole long life, flit by me in robes of gray, like evening clouds after sunset. In other spaces Light has pitched its merry tents. Will it never return to its children, who are waiting for it with the trusting faith of innocence?

"What swells now so forebodingly beneath the heart, and swallows up the soft air of sadness? Hast thou also a pleasure in us, sombre Night? What bringest thou beneath thy mantle, that with viewless power winds its way to my soul? A costly balsam is dripping from thy hand, from thy bunch of poppy. The drooping pinions of the mind thou bearest upward. Dimly and ineffably we feel ourselves moved; a solemn countenance do I see, in pleasing terror, that gently and full of devotion bendeth towards me, and showeth dear youth hid in the infinite locks of the mother. How poor and childish Light now appears to me! How welcome and blessed the farewell of day! Only for this, because Night alienates from thee thy servants, didst thou sow in the regions of space the luminous balls, to proclaim thy omnipotence, thy return, in the times of thy absence. More heavenly than yonder twinkling stars appear the infinite eyes that Night opens in us. Their sight extends farther than the palest of that numberless host; unbeholden to Light, they gaze through the depths of a loving spirit, which fills a loftier space with unspeakable rapture. Praised be the Queen of the world, the high announcer of holy spheres, the nurse of blessed love! She sends me thee, O dearly beloved, lovely sun of the Night. Now I awake, for I am Thine and Mine; thou hast announced to me Night as my life, thou hast made me a man. Consume my body with a spirit-glow, that in ether I may mingle more closely with thee, and be thou my bridal night forever."

The Beloved was Sophia; concerning whom he writes as follows: –

"It is for me a mournful duty to inform you that Sophia is no more. After unspeakable sufferings, borne with exemplary resignation, she died on the 10th of March, at half past nine in the morning. She was born on the 17th of March, 1783, and on the 15th of March, 1795, I gained from her the assurance, that she would be mine. She has suffered since the 7th of November, 1795. Eight days before her death I left her with the strongest conviction, that I should never see her again. I could not have endured to look impotently upon the terrible struggle of blooming youth down-stricken, the fearful anguish of the heavenly creature. Fate have I never feared. For three previous weeks I saw its menaces. It has become evening about me, whilst I was yet gazing into the morning-red. My sorrow is boundless, like my love. For three years had she been my hourly thought. She alone has bound me to life, to my country, and to my occupations. With her loss I am separated from everything, for I scarcely have myself any longer. But it has become evening, and it seems to me, as if I soon were about to depart, and so would I gladly be tranquil, and see around me only kind, friendly faces, and live entirely in her spirit, gentle and kindhearted, as she was.

"Cherished by me, as my own immortal Sophia, will be the friendship, the assiduity with which you strove to render her last days serene. Sophia still treasures your kindnesses with the warmest gratitude, and I have felt a silent impulse to express to you this gratitude, united with my own. You will pardon it to my love, when I tell you, that your attention to Sophia's wishes, and that half year's residence with her, now first has made you really dear to me.... I must cling to the past, as I have nothing more to expect from the future. Farewell, and be happier than

Your friend,
HARDENBERG."

But how soon does his grief become holy, and therefore a joy! The letter is chiefly valuable as an introduction to the third Hymn to the Night: –

"Once as I shed bitter tears, when my hope dissolved into pain flowed away, and I stood alone by the barren hillock, which hid in a dark, narrow space the form of my life; alone, as none had been before, driven by unspeakable anguish, powerless, nothing left but a thought of misery; – as I then looked about after aid, could neither move forward nor backward, but clung to a fleeting, extinguished life, with infinite longing, – then came from the blue distance, from the heights of my old blessedness, a breath as of twilight, and at once the tie of birth, the chain of Light, was rent asunder. Away flew the glory of earth, and with it my sorrow; the sadness rushed together into a new, unfathomable world; thou, Night's-inspiration, slumber of heaven, camest over me. Gently the scene rose aloft; above it floated my unfettered, new-born Spirit The hillock became a dust-cloud, and through it I saw the transfigured features of my Beloved. Eternity lay in her eyes; I grasped her hands, and the tears became a glittering, indissoluble tie. Thousands of years flew away in the distance, like tempest-clouds. Upon her neck I wept enrapturing tears at the thought of this new life. – It was the first and only dream, and since then do I feel an eternal, unchangeable faith in the heaven of Night, and its Sun my Beloved."

Such is the melting tenderness, which is a chief element of his poetry, such the cunning drug that embalms his genius!

FOOTNOTES

1. *Mährchen.*

2. *Mutter* or *Metallmutter* is the gang or matrix that contains the ore.

3. *Mährchen.*

4. *Bacchischen Wehmuth*; the sadness that drives to dissipation, not the Elysium of the morning after.

5. The word *Critic* is derived from the Hebrew word *executioner*; collectively, *executioners and runners*, from the root *kridik, to cut.* Thus it gradually came to mean, to cut and run. It is somewhat remarkable that the secondary meaning of the noun is *Philistine.* See Gesenius in voc.; who also adds, "the conjecture is not improbable that the Philistines sprang from Crete, and that *Caphtor* signifies *Kridik* Comp. Michælis Spicil. J. 1. p. 292-308. Supplemm. p. 1328." The proverbial character of the Cretans is well known.

The Rabbi Ben Hillel, who was of the tribe of Onagrites, defended the oral traditions of the Jews against certain persons, who were disposed to sniff somewhat. In his writings, the venerable Rabbi was accustomed to designate them as Philistines – *mais nous avons change tout cela* – and, in a felicitous allusion to the ancient narrative, insinuated that the extraordinary discomfiture of so many Philistines by a certain jaw-bone was explained upon the well known principle in Homœopathy, whereby any nuisance is abated by the application of homo--geneous substances. This was in the infancy of that science. But the learned Rabbi in his strictures did not anticipate the retort of his opponent Judas Haggadosh, who called Ben Hillel *the would-be jaw-bone.*

TRANSCENDENT POETRY:
A NOTE ON NOVALIS

The world must be romanticized.

Novalis, *Pollen and Fragments* (56)

Poetry is what is truly and absolutely real, this is the kernel of my philosophy. The more poetic, the more true.

Novalis[1]

Novalis is the most mystical of the German Romantic poets. He is at once the most typical and the most unusual of the German Romantic poets – indeed, of all Romantic poets.[2] He is supremely idealistic, far more so than Johann Wolfgang von Goethe or Heinrich Heine. He died young, which makes him, like Percy Bysshe Shelley and John Keats, something of a hero (or martyr). He did not write as much as Shelley, but his work, like that of Keats or Arthur Rimbaud, promised much. For Michael Hamburger, Novalis' work is almost totally idealistic: 'Novalis's

1 Novalis: *Works* (Minor), III, 11
2 See Richard Faber, 1970; Heinz Ritter: "Die geistlichen Lieder des Novalis. Ihre Datierung und Entstehung", *Jahrbuch der deutschen Schiller–Gesellschaft*, IV, 1960, 308–42; Friedrich Hiebel: *Novalis*, Francke, Bern 1972; Curt Grutzmacher, 1964; Géza von Molnár, 1970; John Neubauer, 1972; Bruce Haywood, 1959.

philosophy, then, is not mystical, but utopian. That is why his imaginative works are almost wholly lacking in conflict. They are a perpetual idyll'.[3] It's true, Novalis' work is supremely idealistic, and utopian. But it is also mystical, because it points towards the invisible, unseen, unknown, and aims to reach that ecstatic realm. He wrote:

> The sense of poetry has much in common with that for mysticism. It is the sense of the peculiar, personal, unknown, mysterious, for what is to be *revealed*, the necessary-accidental. It represents the unrepresentable. It sees the invisible, feels the unfeelable, etc... The sense for poetry has a close relationship with the sense for augury and the religious sense, with the sense for prophecy in general.[4]

Novalis was born Georg Philipp Friedrich von Hardenberg on May 2, 1772 in Oberwiederstedt. He studied law between 1790 and 1794 at Jena, Wittenberg and Leipzig. There he met many of the leading literary lights, such as Johann Wolfgang von Goethe, Johann Gottfried Herder, Jean Paul (Johann Paul Friedrich Richter), the Schlegels, Ludwig von Tieck and Friedrich Wilhelm Joseph Schelling. Later, in 1797, Novalis studied at the Mining Academy in Freiburg. He began publishing in 1798. His chief works include: *Faith and Love or the King and the Queen, Pollen, The Novices at Sais, Heinrich von Ofterdingen, Christendom or Europa* and *Hymns To the Night.*[5] He was engaged to Sophie von Kühn from 1794-97, and to Julie von Charpentier from 1798 to his death in 1801. He died on March 25, 1801 in Weißenfels, from tuberculosis.

Novalis was passionately in love with his beloved, Sophie,

---

3 M. Hamburger: *Reason and Energy*, 97
4 Novalis: *Novalis Schriften*, 3, 686
5 The translator of this edition of *Hymns To the Night*, George MacDonald (1824-95), was influenced by Novalis. MacDonald's works included *Phantastes* (1858), *Lilith* (1895), *Bannerman's Boyhood* and the *Curdie* children's stories: *The Princess and the Goblin* (1872) and *The Princess and Curdie* (1882). Lewis Carroll and John Ruskin were among MacDonald's literary friends. The Scottish fantasist was a significant influence on J.R.R. Tolkien and C.S. Lewis, among others.

whom he had met in October, 1794, when she was twelve. They were engaged in March, 1795 (Sophie was 13; Novalis was 22). Novalis was devastated when she died on March 19, 1797, two days after her fifteenth birthday. 'My main task should be', he wrote, 'to bring everything into a relationship to [Sophia's] idea.'[6]

After the death of Sophia von Kühn, Novalis wrote to Karl Wilhelm Friedrich Schlegel from Tennstedt, near Grüningen, where she was buried:

> You can imagine how I feel in this neighbourhood, the old witness of my and her glory. I still feel a secret enjoyment to be so close to her grave. It attracts me ever more closely, and this now occasionally constitutes my indescribable happiness. My autumn has come, and I feel so free, usually so vigorous – something can come of me after all. This much I solemnly assure you as become absolutely clear to me what a heavenly accident her death has been – the key to everything – a marvellously appropriate event. Only through it could various things be absolutely resolved and much immaturity overcome. A simple mighty force has come to reflection within me. My love has become a flame gradually consuming everything earthly.[7]

Sophie von Kühn was for Novalis something like Dante Alighieri's Beatrice Portinari or Francesco Petrarch's Laura de Noyes, or Maurice Scève's Délie; that is, a soul–image or *anima* figure, someone pure and holy. Further, Sophie the person fused for Novalis with 'Sophia' of Gnostic philosophy, the Goddess about whom C.G. Jung has written so eloquently.

> My favourite study [wrote Novalis in 1796] has the same name as my fiancée. Sophie is her name – philosophy is the soul of my life and the key to my inner-most self. Since that acquaintance, I also have become completely amalgamated with that study.[8]

Sophia is the Goddess of Wisdom; she is an incarnation for poets and mystics of the Black Goddess, a deity who presides over the

6 Novalis: ib, 4, 37
7 Novalis, in, 4, 220
8 Novalis, letter to Friedrich Schlegel, 8 July 1796, in *Novalis Schriften*, op.cit., 4, 188

unknown, the dark things, occultism and witchcraft. Novalis was very interested in the occult, in magic and hermeticism, in Neoplatonism, alchemy, theosophy, the *Qabbalah*, and other belief systems. Novalis was fascinated by the invisible realm, the things that are unseen but he knows are there, which is the realm of occultism. As he writes: 'We are bound nearer to the unseen than to the visible.'[9]

Apart from his small collection of lyrics, and his *Hymnen an die Nacht*, one of Novalis' major works was his (unfinished) *Blütenstaub* (*Pollen*) and *Glauben und Liebe* (*Faith and Love*), collections of philosophical fragments. These together form an æsthetics of religion, and a mysticism of poetry.

✳

Some notes on German Romanticism are worth making here: the world of German Romantic poetry holds many of the same tenets as that of British and French Romanticism. The term 'Romanticism' means for me here a lyrical, emotional, religious and self-conscious form of art which can be applied to many modern artists, as well as the Romantics themselves.[10]

One of the key elements of Romantic poetry, of German Romantic poetry especially, and of all poetry generally, is the concept of unity. For the poet, all things are connected together.

> In our mind [wrote Novalis], everything is connected in the most peculiar, pleasant, and lively manner. The strangest things come together by virtue of one space, one time, an odd similarity, an error, some accident. In this manner, curious unities and peculiar connections

---

9 Novalis: *Pollen*, 125.
10 On Romanticism, see Jürgen Habermas: *The Philosophical Discourse of Modernity*, tr. Frederick Lawrence, MIT Press, Cambridge Mass., 1987. On German Romanticism, see David Simpson *et al*, eds: *German Aesthetic and Literary Criticism*, Cambridge University Press, 3 vols, 1984–5; H.G. Schenk: *The Mind of the European Romantics*, Constable, 1966; M.H. Abrams: *Natural Supernaturalism: Tradition and Revolution in Romantic Literature*, Norton, New York, 1971; Marshall Brown, 1979; Philippe Lacoue–Labarthe & Jean-Luc Nancy, eds, 1988; Azade Seyhan: *Representation and its Discontents: The Critical Legacy of German Romanticism*, University of California Press, Berkeley, 1992.

originate – one thing reminds us of everything, becomes the sign of many things. Reason and imagination are united through time and space in the most extraordinary manner, and we can say that each thought, each phenomenon of our mind is the most individual part of an altogether individual totality.[11]

What connects everything is the poet's sensibility, awareness, imagination, talents, feelings, call them what you will. Poetry is very much like Western magic in this respect. Magicians speak of the cardinal rule of hermeticism and magicke as being the hermetic tenet of the Emerald Table of Hermes Trismegistus: *as above, so below*. This dictum applies to poetry as much to magic. Basically, the view is that all things are one even as they are separate/ different/ scattered everywhere. Sufi mystics speak of 'unity in multiplicity' and 'multiplicity in unity', the 'unity' for them being Allah. For poets and magicians, founded in the Western Neoplatonic, Renaissance, humanist, magical tradition, 'the One' is only occasionally identified with God.

For (the Romantic) poets, the *as above, so below* worldview means that inner and outer are identical, that what happens inside, psychologically, is mirrored and influences the outer, physical world. The two worlds interconnect and influence each other. As Novalis writes: 'What is outside me, is really within me, is mind – and vice versa'.[12] Further, the world is a continuum for the poet, so that colours are associated with particular planets, say, or angels, or flowers, or metals. This view of the oneness of all things occurs not only in Romantic poetry, but in most of poetry, from Sappho in the ancient world onwards. It is, partly, the basis for the 'pathetic fallacy', the ubiquitous poetic metaphor, where Sappho can say that erotic desire is like a wind shaking oak trees on a mountainside.

The Romantic philosophy of unity develops into Charles Baudelaire's 'theory of correspondences', which was later taken up by Arthur Rimbaud, Stéphane Mallarmé and Paul Valéry.

11 Novalis, *Novalis Schriften*, 3, 650-1.
12 Novalis, *Novalis Schriften*, 3, 429

Friedrich Schlegel, one of the major theorists of Romantic poetry, speaks of Romantic art as unifying poetry and philosophy, which is one of the hallmarks of Romantic poetry, German or otherwise. 'Romantic poetry is a progressive universal poetry', wrote Schlegel.[13] He argued for a new mythology of poetry, a universal mythopœia, which would connect all things together, a 'hieroglyphic expression of nature around us'.[14]

Folklore and fairy tales are another element: much of German Romanticism uses all kinds of folklore – the Grimms, for instance, with their very influential collection, *Children's and Household Tales,* and their collecting (and rewriting) of fairy tales. Ludwig von Tieck's works contain much fantastic material, and he uses fairy tales in his fictions, including Charles Perrault's *Puss in Boots* fairy tale in his *Der gestiefelte Kater.*[15] A.W. Schlegel wrote: 'Myth, like language, generally, a necessary product of the human poetic power, an arche-poetry of humanity'.[16]

Novalis wrote of fairy tales: 'All fairy tales are dreams of that homelike world that is everywhere and nowhere.'[17] Figures such as Isolde and Tristan, Tannhäuser, of Arthurian legend, appear in German Romantic poetry. Romanticism also employs all manner of hermetic or occult thought, from Gnosticism (in Novalis's philosophy), Qabbalism, Rosicrucianism, alchemy, magic, astronomy, etc (in Franz Brentano's *Die Romanzen vom Rosenkrantz,* alchemy in Johann Wolfgang von Goethe's *Faust,* etc).

The Hellenism of German Romanticism ties in with (and is

---

13 F. Schlegel: *Kritische Friedrich Schlegel Ausgabe* , Schöningh, Paderborn, 1958, II, 182
14 F. Schlegel, in ib., II, 318
15 See Rolf Stamm: *Ludwig Tieck's späte Novellen* , Kohlhamer, Stuttgart, 1973; Raimund Belgardt: "Poetic Imagination and External Reality in Tieck", *Essays in German Literature Festschrift,* ed. Michael S. Batts, University of British Columbia Press, 1968, 41-61; Rosemarie Helge: *Motive und Motivstrukturen bei Ludwig Tieck*, Kummerle, Göppingen, 1974
16 A.W. Schlegel: *Kritische Ausgabe der Verlesungen* , ed. Ernst Behler & Frank Jolles, Schöningen, Paderborn, 1989-, I, 49
17 Novalis, *Novalis Schriften*, 2. 564

inextricable from) the paganism of Romanticism. The German Romantics, like their British counterparts, exalted pagan beliefs, though theirs was a stylized, self-conscious form of paganism, which took up certain beliefs or rites and ignored others. Heinrich Heine wrote that the first Romantics

> acted out of a pantheistic impulse of which they themselves were not aware. The feeling which they believed to be a nostalgia for the Catholic Mother Church was of deeper origin than they guessed, and their reverence and preference for the heritage of the Middle Ages, for the popular beliefs, diabolism, magical practices, and witchcraft of that era... all this was a suddenly reawakened but unrecognized leaning toward the pantheism of the ancient Germans.[18]

The paganism of Romanticism is a part of pantheism, as in the Classicism of painters such as Nicolas Poussin and Claude Lorrain, or nature worship. Heinrich Heine called pantheism 'the secret religion of Germany'.[19]

The Romantics, including Novalis, exalted nature (German Romanticism had its 'Naturphilosophie', a non-scientific notion stemming partly from the work of Friedrich Wilhelm Joseph Schelling and Georg Wilhelm Friedrich Hegel). But, again, nature is mediated through the highly self-conscious and heavily stylized mechanisms of poetry. Images of nature abound in most forms of Romantic poetry. Nature is the backdrop to their poetic out-pourings, but it is always nature seen from the vantage point of culture.[20]

German Romantic poetry, like all Romantic poetry (like all poetry, one might say), has idealistic and utopian elements. German Romantic poetry, in particular, is marked by a vivacious, sometimes over-developed idealism (and utopianism), which comes as much from the philosopher Plato as from Immanuel

18 H. Heine: *Salon II*, 1852, 250-1

19 H. Heine: *Works*, 3, 571

20 Novalis has a fascinating view of nature as the mother, a refuge: 'the reason why people are so attached to Nature is probably that, being spoilt children, they are afraid of the father and take refuge with the mother'.

Kant. 'Transcendental idealism' is a term often applied to German Romantic poetics. 'I call transcendental all knowledge which is not so much occupied with objects as with the mode of our cognition of objects', remarked Kant in the *Critique of Pure Reason*,[21] underlining the subjectivity (as with René Descartes) that is at the centre of post-Renaissance philosophy. There is a philosophy, Johann Gottlieb Fichte argued, that is beyond being and beyond consciousness, a philosophy that aims for 'the absolute unity between their separateness.'[22]

✳

Novalis, like the other (German) Romantics, believed in the magical/ religious unity of the world. For him, all things were united, in one way or another. Novalis was one of the first artists to bring together many seemingly diverse practices and philosophies. Leonardo da Vinci had drawn together botany, biology, anatomy, natural science, engineering, mathematics and other strands of thought in his Renaissance art, and Novalis did the same. The metaphysical synthesis was called *Totalwissenschaft*, a total knowledge.

Novalis learnt much from Friedrich Schlegel, during his time at Jena, one of the centres of German Romanticism. Schlegel wrote at length of the unifying spirit of art, where poetry and philosophy merge: the aim of Romantic poetry, Schlegel asserted, was not only 'to unite all the separate species of poetry and put poetry in touch with philosophy and rhetoric', but also to

> use poetry and prose, inspiration and criticism, the poetry of art and the poetry of nature; and make poetry lively and sociable, and life and society poetic; poeticize wit and fill and saturate the forms of art with every kind of good, solid matters for instruction, and animate them with the pulsation of humour.[23]

Novalis' philosophy may be called 'transcendent philosophy',

21 Immanuel Kant: *Werke*, de Gruyter, Berlin, 1968, III, 43
22 J. Fichte, letter, 23 June 1804, quoted in E. Behler, 19
23 F. Schlegel, *Gespräch über die Poesie, Kritische Friedrich Schlegel Ausgabe*, Schöningh, Paderborn, 1958, 182

as his poetry might be called 'transcendent poetry'. He called it 'magisch', 'Magie', his 'magic idealism'.[24] It is a mixture of poetry and philosophy, a poetry of philosophy and a philosophy of poetry.[25] 'Transcendental poetry is an admixture of poetry and philosophy,'[26] he writes. And again: 'Poetry is the champion of philosophy... Philosophy is the theory of poetry.' (ib., 56) Poetry becomes philosophy, and philosophy becomes poetry. Or as he put it: 'Die Welt wird Traum, der Traum wird Welt' ('World becomes dream, dream becomes world'). Friedrich Schlegel wrote in the *Athenæum* (fragment 451): 'Universality can attain harmony only through the conjunction of poetry and philosophy'.[27]

Kept by Novalis as a collection of fragments, *Pollen* has affinities with the maxims of Friedrich Nietzsche, the thoughts in Blaise Pascal's *Pensées*, with Jacob Boehme's writings and other mystical collections. It is worth quoting from some of these fragments, which show Novalis at his most idealistic and pithy. His statements summarize the (German) Romantic position on poetry, and the basics of all poetics. First of all, he muses on interiority:

> Toward the Interior goes the arcane way. In us, or nowhere, is the Eternal with its worlds, the past and future... The seat of the world is there, where the inner world and the outer world touch... The inner world is almost more mine than the outer. It is so heartfelt, so private – man is given fullness in that life – it is so native.[28]

Here Novalis heads straight for one of the prime realms of mysticism: the inner world, the life of the spirit, the imagination, the soul. His distinction, and then fusion, of inner and outer is the beginnings of modern psychology. It is also one of the key aspects

24 Novalis: *Works* (Minor), Paris, 1837, III
25 See Manfred Frank: "Die Philosophie des sogenannten "magischen Idealismus"", *Euph*, LXIII, 1969, 88–116; Karl Heinz Volkmann–Schluck, 1967, 45–53; Theodor Haering, 1954; G. Hughes, 66; Manfred Dick, 1967, 223–77; Hugo Kuhn: *Text und Theorie*, Metzler, Stuttgart 1967
26 Novalis: *Pollen and Fragments*, 57
27 F. Schlegel, *Lucinde and the Fragments*, tr. Peter Firchow, University of Minnesota Press, Minneapolis 1971, 240
28 Novalis: *Pollen and Fragments*, 50–53

of poetry. For the poet, the inner, psychic or spiritual world is as real and as important, and nourishing, as the outer, public world. The two in fact are part of a continuum, both flowing into each other, like the *yin–yang* dualism of Chinese mysticism. The one informs the other in art. They are not separated, that is the key point. They form a unity. As Novalis wrote in his poem 'Know Yourself' (the title comes from the basic tenet of Greek hermeticism): 'There is only one'.[29]

In magic and hermeticism, the fundamental tenet is 'as above, so below', which, in the modern era, becomes the psychological 'as outside, so inside'. Poets have long known about this inside–outside pairing. In William Shakespeare's plays, the external setting of a scene – the opening of *Macbeth*, for instance – indicates the characters' inner feelings. Further, in Shakespeare's Elizabethan theatre, there were few props, and little scenery on stage, so the words became full of images, painting pictures in the audience's mind. Hence, in a different way, inner and outer became fused.

For Novalis, rightly, the seat of the soul is precisely that poetic space where 'the inner world and the outer world touch' (150). It was Rainer Maria Rilke who fully developed this inner–outer unity in his lyrics. Rilke is, as we have said, the poet most like Novalis in German poetry. Rilke had his notion of the Angel (in the *Duino Elegies*). The Rilkean Angel is essentially a shaman, and Novalis also speaks at length in his collections of fragments of the poet as shaman. He does not use the term 'shaman', but his 'sorcerer' or 'genius' or 'prophet' is basically the archaic shaman, the angelic traveller to other worlds, the vatic mouthpiece of his/her cult, the dancing, drumming, musical figure, like Dionysius or Orpheus, who knows how to fly, who can climb the World Tree, who can penetrate the invisible.[30] Novalis writes:

---

29 Novalis: *Pollen*, 137
30 See Mircea Eliade, *Myths, Dreams and Mysteries*, Harper & Row, New York, 1975; *Shamanism: Archaic Techniques of Ecstasy*, Princeton University Press, New Jersey, 1972; Weston La Barre: *The Ghost Dance*, Allen & Unwin 1972

> The sorcerer is a poet. The prophet is to the sorcerer as the man of taste is to the poet... The genuine poet is all-knowing... (50–1)

As Weston La Barre notes in *The Ghost Dance*, there is not much difference between the artist, the genius, the criminal, the psychotic and the mad person. Novalis notes:

> Madness and magic have many similarities. A magician is an artist of madnesses. (79)

Similarly, William Shakespeare wrote in *A Midsummer Night's Dream*: 'The lunatic, the lover and the poet,/ Are of imagination all compact.' (V.i.7) In Shakespeare's art, there are deep connections between lovers, lunatics, poets – and fools. They are all caught up with some kind of 'madness', some kind of 'abnormal', 'extraordinary' subjectivity. Their goals may be different, but they are all connected psychologically. Similarly, for Novalis, as for so many poets, love can be seen as a madness, and there is a narrow dividing line between the religious maniac and the fool. There is the 'holy fool' figure in Russian history, the 'trickster god' in ancient mythology, and King Lear's clown, the court jester who is allowed to transgress the boundaries that others are not allowed to cross.

Novalis as a poet sees the unity of all things, so he writes: 'All barriers are only there for the traversing' (87). This is the Romantic poet talking here: this is a very Romantic notion, it seems, this perception that barriers are there to be transgressed. This is the poet as social rebel speaking, knowing that art must go to extremes. Thus, madness, poetry, idiocy, genius and love form a continuum which is life itself.

In Novalis's *œuvre*, love and mysticism, the secular and the sacred, art and religion, fuse. Thus, in Novalis' 'magic idealism', we hear of the mysticism of love, or the religious nature of art. In this he is no different from other Romantics, such as William Wordsworth or Victor Hugo. For Novalis, life itself is sacred. 'Our whole life is a divine service', he writes (124). In this Novalis is in accord with writers such as D.H. Lawrence, who regarded life itself as holy, or the artist and sculptor Eric Gill, or the cult of the Australian aborigines.

The religion of the aborigines is the 'eternal dreamtime', the mythic, timeless state. For them, life was sacred, and life was sacralized by rituals that include singing. The Australian Bushmen speak of 'singing the world into life'. Rainer Maria Rilke wrote in his *Sonnets For Orpheus*: 'song is existence.' The figure of Orpheus, the mythological poet–as–shaman, features prominently, though he is sometimes hidden, in the works of poets such as Novalis (in his story *Heinrich von Ofterdingen*), Rilke and Arthur Rimbaud. Orpheus' song is his art, and his *raison d'être*. Novalis also wrote of music, and its relation to poetry and religion. The notion of the 'music of the spheres', the celestial harmonies that drive the cosmos, is central to Western religion. For Dante Alighieri, God was at the centre of the concentric circles or wheels of the universe. He was at the heart of the *Rosa Mystica*. For Novalis, the 'One' of Neoplatonism now has many names. In Hinduism it is Brahma; in Taoism it is the Tao; in Zen Buddhism it is Pure Reality; in Tibetan mysticism it is the Clear Light of the Void; and in Islam it is Allah.

Simply being alive, as Mircea Eliade notes, was a sacred act:

In the most archaic phases of culture, *to live as a human being* was in itself *a religious act*, since eating, sexual activity, and labour all had a sacramental value. Experience of the sacred is inherent in man's mode of being in the world.[31]

D.H. Lawrence wrote extensively of 'being alive', about real 'livingness'. In *Etruscan Places* he defined it in a way of which Novalis would surely approve:

To the Etruscan all was alive...They [the Etruscans] felt the symbols and danced the sacred dances. For they were always in touch, physically,

---

31 Mircea Eliade, *Ordeal by Labyrinth*, University of Chicago Press 1984, 154

with the mysteries.[32]

Novalis speaks often of 'mysteries' too. For the occult, hermetic, Neoplatonic, religious artist, there must always be some 'mystery' behind everything. No matter how far you go, there must always be something mysterious behind it. It was true for the participants in the ancient Eleusian Mysteries, and it is the same for Romantic poets. The world is not a machine, nor is it limited. It must be infinite, for, behind everything, there is yet more mystery. There are no limits, yet it is the poet's task to find the limits, and to explore the boundaries.

Novalis looked back to early Christianity, to Neoplatonism and to Greek religion. Like most Romantics, Novalis was very nostalgic. But he might have looked back also to many Hindu sects, to Tantric cults, to Sufi mystics and poets, to Australian aborigines, to the shamans of Siberia and North America, to the Chinese Taoists (Chuang-tzu, Lao-tzu), or to the Confucians (Confucius, Mencius), or to the Zen Buddhist masters (Hui-Neng, Dogen, Jakuin), or to the Ancient Greeks of Epicurus, Heraclitus or Empodecles' day.

What is the purpose of Novalis' cult of 'transcendent poetry'? More life, basically. This was Rainer Maria Rilke's great goal, his Holy Grail: life and more life, more and more of life. That is our goal, Rilke claimed. Poetry is a way of enabling us to be more alive, say Novalis and Rilke:

Poetry is the great art of constructing transcendental health... Poetry is generation. All compositions must be living individuals. (*Pollen*, 50)

Rainer Maria Rilke says similar things about poetry. In a letter to his Polish translator, Witold von Hulewicz, of November 13, 1925, Rilke explained his notion of the angel: a being that shows us how to be painfully but blissfully alive, living in the transcendent realm of 'the Open', as Rilke called that special

[32] D.H. Lawrence: *Mornings in Mexico and Etruscan Places*, Penguin 1960, 147–9

poetic place. We must be

> Transformed? Yes, for our task is to stamp this provisional, perishing earth into ourselves so deeply, so painfully and passionately, that its being may rise again, "invisibly", in us.[33]

All you have to do in life is to be. Be what, exactly? Just *be*, says Rainer Maria Rilke: 'all we basically have to do is to *be*, but simply, earnestly, the way the earth simply is', he wrote in *Letters on Cézanne*.[34] To simply *be* is really difficult, as Novalis and Rilke admit. Yet it is the goal. To realize, as the Hindu mystics put it, that Thou Art That (*tat tvam asi*). As Novalis commented:

> Art of becoming all–powerful. Art of realizing our intentions totally. (118)

Total fulfilment – it's a tall order, perhaps, but only this ontological totality will do for Novalis. He is supremely idealistic while at the same being totally honest, and totally simple, and totally ordinary. He is optimistic, it seems, when he writes:

> All is seed. (73)

Yet he is also being quite realistic, knowing, as an artist does, that *anything* can be used in art. A transcendent, total art can include *everything*. Nothing is exempt from art, not even nothingness itself. Indeed, nothingness is a large element of some art (Samuel Beckett's compressed texts, for instance, or Ad Reinhardt's black–on–black paintings), as it is a key component in Buddhism and Taoism.

Novalis' idealistic philosophy is all–inclusive. 'All is seed', he writes. *All*. Or, again, in a different fashion:

> All must become nourishment. (65)

33 Rilke: *Duino Elegies*, tr. J.B. Leishman & Stephen Spender, Hogarth Press, 1957, 157
34 Rilke: *Letters on Cézanne*, ed. Clara Rilke, Cape, 1988

Or, again, in a different way, he says:

All can become experiment – all can become an organ. (88)

Meister Eckhart, the German mediæval mystic whose mystical philosophy is in tune with Rainer Maria Rilke's and Novalis' philosophies, wrote:

The seed of God is in us... The seed of a pear tree grows into a pear tree, a hazel seed into a hazel tree, a seed of God into God.[35]

Much of alchemy, hermeticism, witchcraft, Qabbalism and Neo-platonism is concerned with healing, nourishment and rebirth. It was one of Novalis' chief concerns. The philosophical fragments state the basic view of nourishment in a variety of ways. The fragments are deeply poetic. Although they are written in prose, they are clearly poetry. One of Novalis' most powerful sentences is:

Everything can become magical work. (73)

This statement is itself magical. For Novalis, art is for the enrichment of life. Whatever art may do, Novalis says, it must enrich us. 'To enliven all is the aim of life', he asserts (64).

∗

Love features prominently in Novalis' philosophy of poetry and poetry of philosophy. Love – and sex. For, under Novalis' sophisticated sophisms, there is sex. An eroticism which is that fundamental *jouissance* of the text in Romanticism is found in Novalis's work. For Novalis, love and philosophy are aspects of the same mystery. 'It is with love as with philosophy', he writes (*Pollen*, 57). He evokes the *eroticism* of philosophy, something which Plato may have understood subconsciously, but which

---

35 Quoted in James M. Clark & John V. Skinner: *Meister Eckhart*, London 1953, 151

Novalis brings into the foreground:

> In the essential sense, philosophizing is – a caress – a testimony to the inner love of reflection, the absolute delight of wisdom. (53)

For Novalis, the highest form of love is spiritual, of course. In this he is in harmony with those other great poets of love, such as Dante Alighieri, Francesco Petrarch, Guido Guinicelli, Guido Cavalcanti and Bernard de Ventadour. For the mediæval troubadours and *stilnovisti*, human love was transcended in stature and significance by spiritual love. In personal terms, this meant that the human, flesh–and–blood beloved, Petrarch's Laura, Dante's Beatrice, Novalis' Sophie, was surpassed, spiritually, and even transcended physically in some cases, by the figure of the Virgin Mary. Novalis too, like Dante and Petrarch, raised the Mother of God above his Sophie as a beloved.

> By absolute will power, love can be gradually transmuted into religion.[36]

This is a familiar pose with (usually male) poets, this worldly renunciation in favour of religious love. 'What I feel for Sophie', Novalis wrote, 'is religion, not love' (ib., 295).

Friedrich Nietzsche had a theory that the more tragic tragedy becomes, the more sensual it becomes. In other words, tragedy has a sensual dimension which increases as the sense of tragedy increases. William Shakespeare's tragedies are his most erotic works. Think of the erotic entanglements of love and death in *Macbeth,* or *King Lear*. Novalis too spoke of the erotic quality of intensity and absolutism. Power is an aphrodisiac, it is said: the powerful people are those who can go to extremes. Tragic characters go to extremes – Macbeth, Beatrice, Othello – they push against their ontological boundaries. They practice a kind of absolutism or extremism that seems particularly Romantic. Novalis notes the sensuality of power and extremism in his

---

36 Novalis, *Works* (Minor) II, 299

fragments, as when he claims:

All absolute sensation is religious. (197)

Tragic power and political power is sexual and seductive, and so is magical power. Novalis writes:

Magic is like art – to wilfully use the sensual realm. (119)

Magicians throughout history have been erotic figures: Aleister Crowley, Georg Gurdjieff, Merlin, Paracelsus. The eroticism of magic is obvious: witchcraft, for instance, was and is regarded very much in sexual terms. Witchcraft was a heresy, certainly, that disturbed the Church for religious reasons, but many of the accusations brought against witchcraft were of a sexual nature.

More 'ordinary' – that is, bourgeois, heterosexual, traditional – are the views of Novalis on love such as this:

Every beloved object is the focus of a paradise... One touches heaven, when one touches a human body. (30, 59)

This neatly summarizes the links between love and religion that have been described throughout history, from the Biblical *Song of Songs* onwards. Novalis says that you touch heaven when you touch a body. This is what the troubadours said, that making love was heavenly, that to enter a woman was to enter heaven. William Shakespeare said it, John Donne said it, John Keats said it, and Robert Graves said it in the British poetic tradition; Sappho and C.P. Cavafy said it in the Greek tradition; Ovid, Dante Alighieri and Giuseppe Ungaretti said it in the Italian tradition; Novalis, Joseph Freiherr von Eichendorff, Ludwig von Tieck and Rainer Maria Rilke said it in the German tradition; Alexander Pushkin, Fyodor Tyutchev, Arseny Tarkovsky and Anna Akhmatova said it in the Russian tradition.

Not all of Novalis' eroticism was cerebral, philosophic and 'idealistic'. He produced obvious eroticism at times, the sensual love of a beloved which centres on the body:

> Wonderful powers of the bodily appearance – the beautiful lineaments
> – the form – the voice – the complexion – the musculature and elasticity
> – the eyes, the senses of touch, of feeling – the outer nature – the angles –
> the closed–off spaces – the darkness – the veil. Through the selection of
> clothing the body becomes yet more mystical. (116)

In Novalis' *Hymns To the Night*, the night itself is a vast, erotic, maternal, deep, dazzling space, the place of Henry Vaughan's 'deep, but dazzling darkness', the darkness of occultism and præternaturalism, the night that is the Goddess, the Mother Night of mythology, the Gnostic Night which is embodied in the Goddess Sophia, Wisdom, the night of shamanic flights. Rainer Maria Rilke in his *Duino Elegies*, wrote lyrically of this erotic night that whirls about humans and is full of angels:

> But, oh, the nights – those nights when the infinite wind
> eats at our faces! Who is immune to the night, to Night,
> ever–subtle, deceiving? Hardest of all, to the lonely,
> Night, is she gentler to lovers?[37]

Rainer Maria Rilke's poetic night is a bliss space which is clearly the external metaphor or image of the poet's inner space. It is a space of the invisible, where the Rilkean 'Open' can flourish. Novalis' night is similarly mythical:

> Downward I turn
> Toward the holy unspeakable
> Mysterious Night
> …The great wings of the spirit lift you aloft
> And fill us with joy
> Dark and unspeakable,
> Secret, as you yourself are,
> Joy that foreshadows
> A heaven to us.
> …Heavenly as flashing stars
> In each vastness
> Appear the infinite eyes

37 R. Rilke: *Duino Elegies*, tr. Stephen Cohn, Carcanet Press 1989, 21

Novalis, in his opening section of the *Hymns To the Night*, begins with that universal journey of heroes: into the underworld. It is a primary myth, this descent. In mythology it is often to Hell: Dante, Orpheus, Jesus, and Isis: they descend into the under- world. Of course, by Novalis' epoch, this nocturnal realm was identified with the inner spaces. Novalis knew that the descent into an external, mythic space was the expression of an inner, psychic descent.

When he has made the shamanic journey into the unknown, invisible, dark realm, he finds... what? His beloved, his Muse, the Queen of the Night: veritably, the Black Goddess:

Praise the Queen of the World
The highest messenger
Of the holy world,
The one who nurtures
Holy love.
You come, Beloved –,
The Night is here –
My soul is enchanted –
The earthly day is past
And you are mine again.
I gaze into your deep dark eyes
And see nothing but love and ecstasy.
We sink upon the altar of Night
Upon the soft bed –
The veil drops
And kindled by your heated touch
The flame of the sweet offering
Glows. (140-1)

Novalis here describes the basic story or myth of Western culture: the descent and return, the journey to fundamental ontologies, the resacralization of life, symbolized by a spiritual union expressed in erotic terms. At the heart of the *Hymnen an die Nacht* is this erotic–spiritual union, an ecstatic fusion of dualities. It

---

38 Novalis: *Pollen*, 138–140

is also a poetic expression of lust, of masculinist desire. For, simply, the poet goes into the Night and he makes loves to it.

In Novalis' 1800 poem, despite the Christian and theological aspects of the work, the feminine, magical dimension is continually exalted. For Novalis, the Night is a womb out of which the Son of Light, Jesus, is born; but also, our era, the Christian epoch, is born from Mother Night. Novalis uses the typical mechanisms of shamanism – the night flight or spiritual journey – as a mythic descent and return. In section three of *Hymns to the Night,* his soul soars over the world, in the typical fashion of archaic shamanism, which is the basis of all religion:

> You night raptures,
> Heavenly slumbers came over me
> The scene itself gently rose higher – my unbound, newborn
> Soul soared over the scene. The hill became a dust cloud
> and through the cloud I saw the clear features of my Beloved –
> In her eyes rested Eternity... (143)

Although he sees the mythic Night as Christian, a gathering darkness after the Light or Day of Greece, Novalis continually emphasizes the feminine, maternal aspects of this mythical Night. Novalis' Night, like Rainer Maria Rilke's, is a supremely female space: 'She bears *you* – motherly', he writes (143);

> The dark ocean's
> Blue depths
> Were a Goddess' womb.

There is much idealism in this view of a feminized soul-space, a mythic 'dreamtime' over which the Goddess presides. The upsurge of hope in the *Hymns To the Night* is very powerful:

> And into heaven's
> Infinite distance
> Filled with the lustrous world
> Into the heart of the highest spaces,
> The soul of the world withdrew

With her powers
To wait for the dawn
Of new days
And the higher destiny of the world. (150-1)

By the end of the poem, the transition is made, from the dark, maternal, feminine realm of Night to the bright, rational, masculine realm of Day or Light. 'We sink into the Father's heart', writes the poet, in the last line (159). But it is an ambiguous ending, for the new form of the feminine, the Virgin Mary, is not the erotic Black Goddess of ancient times.

Novalis describes the basic emotional displacement of the psychoanalysis of childhood: the movement of the child away from the mother towards the father; from intuition to ratiocination; from emotion to reason; from dependency to independence, from femininity to masculinity; from immaturity to maturity; from the semiotic realm to the symbolic realm (the Law of the Father).

Novalis simply trades in the usual poetic fare: the associations of darkness with the feminine, light with the masculine, and so on. He employs the age-old dichotomies of Western culture, where, after a night of ecstasy, the Night is renounced in favour of the Day. It is familiar rhetoric. Novalis, though, raises it to new heights because of his energy and idealism. *Hymns To the Night* is an exuberant poetic sequence, shot through and powered by flashes of inspiration and enthusiasm. It is a poem that exists all on its own. There is nothing else quite like it – not in German Romanticism, nor in poetry throughout history. It combines elements of the theological exegesis, the courtly *canso*, the philosophical tract, utopian and idealistic mysticism, and a fervent lyrical poetry.

Hymnen an die Nacht is a poem that embellishes the norms of Western culture – heterosexuality, theology, Christianity, and philosophy without much developing them or questioning them. It is an uncritical poem, which re-states what is already known – and felt – about Western culture. Ambiguity and doubt are not high in the poetic mix: *Hymnen an die Nacht* is a mystical poem, and about the certainty of the mystical experience. After their ecstasy, mystics feel utterly sure of their faith, their God, their duty, their life. They trust their mystical ecstasy, as one must trust one's own experiences in life. Romanticism, as we have seen, is founded on subjectivity. The Romantic poets, whether of France, Germany, Britain, America or Italy, unfailingly trust their own experiences. Indeed, artists must. Novalis' *Hymns To the Night* is constructed out of the basic, unshakeable faith in the poetic self.

✳

Novalis continues to be read, as do Heinrich Heine, Johann Wolfgang von Goethe, both Schlegels, Friedrich Schiller and Friedrich Hölderlin. There is a richness in poets such as Goethe and Novalis that endures. Glyn Hughes writes of Novalis:

> The sustaining interest in the reading of Novalis's works is the sense of contact with a mind of visionary intensity and total commitment. The poetic achievement is in the momentary glimpses of ideal reality: what, in other contexts, we should call epiphanies. (61)

Novalis' *Hymns To the Night* articulates the rebirth at the heart of Romanticism, that self–invention which always goes to the heart of life by way of speaking of fundamental experiences – of love, death, birth and rebirth. From the womb of the Virgin Mother the shining self is reborn. Novalis' poetics, like those of Johann Wolfgang von Goethe, Friedrich Hölderlin, Heinrich Heine or Friedrich Schlegel, are those of a spiritual rebirth, a resacralization of life, a renaissance of life, in short. This is the goal of not just the Romantic poets, but of most poets throughout history.

BIBLIOGRAPHY

BY NOVALIS

Recommended books are marked with an asterisk.

Novalis Schriften. Die Werke Friedrichs von Hardenberg , ed. Richard
Samuel, Hans-Joachim Mähl & Gerhard Schulz, Kohlhammer,
Stuttgart, 1960-88 *
Pollen and Fragments: Selected Poetry and Prose, tr. Arthur Versluis,
Phanes Press, Grand Rapids, 1989 *
Hymns to the Night and Other Selected Writings , tr. Charles E. Passage,
Bobbs-Merrill Company, Indianapolis, 1960
Hymns to the Night, Treacle Press, New York, NY, 1978 *
Novalis: Fichte Studies, ed. J. Kneller, Cambridge University Press,
Cambridge, 2003
Notes For a Romantic Encyclopedia, tr. D. Wood, State University of New
York Press, New York, 2007

ON NOVALIS

Henri Clemens Birven. *Novalis, Magus der Romantik*, Schwab, Büdingen,
1959
B. Donehower, ed. *The Birth of Novalis*, State University of New York
Press, New York, 2007
Sara Frierichsmeyer. *The Androgyne In Early German Romanticism:
Friedrich Schlegel, Novalis and the Metaphysics of Love* , Bern, New
York, 1983
Curt Grutzmacher. *Novalis und Philippe Otto Runge*, Eidos, Munich 1964
Bruce Haywood. *The Veil of Imagery: A Study of the Poetic Works of
Friedrich von Hardenburg*, Harvard University Press, Cambridge,

Mass., 1959

Frederick Heibel. *Novalis: German Poet, European Thinker, Christian Mystic*, AMS, New York, 1969

L. Johns. *The Art of Recollection In Jena Romanticism* , Niemeyer, Tübingen, 2002

Alice Kuzniar. *Delayed Endings: Nonclosure In Novalis and Hölderlin* , University of Georgia Press, Athens, 1987

Géza von Molnar. *Novalis's Fichte Studies*, Mouton, The Hague 1970

— . *Romantic Vision, Ethical Context: Novalis and Artistic Autonomy* , University of Minnesota Press, Minneapolis 1987

Bruno Müller. *Novalis – der dichter als Mittler*, Lang, Bern, 1984

John Neubauer. *Bifocal Vision: Novalis's Philosophy of Nature and Disease* , Chapel Hill 1972

— . *Novalis*, 1980

I. Nikolova. *Complementary Modes of Representation In Keats, Novalis and Shelley*, Peter Lang, New York, 2001

Nicholas Saul. *History and Poetry In Novalis and In the Tradition of the German Enlightenment*, Institute of Germanic Studies, 1984

OTHERS

Gwendolyn Bays. *The Orphic Vision: Seer Poets from Novalis to Rimbaud*, University of Nebraska Press, Lincoln, 1964 *

Ernst Behler. *German Romantic Literary Theory*, Cambridge University Press, 1993 *

Ernst Benz. *The Mystical Sources of German Romantic Philosophy* , tr. B. Reynolds & E. Paul, Pickwick, Allison Park, 1983

G. Birrell. *The Boundless Presence: Space and Time In the Literary Fairy Tales of Novalis and Tieck*, 1979

Richard Brinkmann, ed. *Romantik in Deutschland*, Metzler, Stuttgart, 1978

Manfred Brown. *The Shape of German Romanticism*, Cornell University Press, Ithaca, 1979

K. Calhoun. *Fatherland: Novalis, Freud and the Discipline of Romance*, 1992

Manfred Dick. *Die Entwicklung des Gedankens der Poesie in den Fragmenten des Novalis*, Bouvier, Bonn, 1967, 223-77

Hans Eichner. *Friedrich Schlegel*, Twayne, New York, 1970

R.W. Ewton. *The Literary Theory of A.W. Schlegel* , Mouthon, The Hague, 1971

Richard Faber. *Novalis: die Phantasie an die Macht*, Metzler, Stuttgart 1970

Walter Feilchenfeld. *Der Einfluss Jacob Böhmes auf Novalis*, Eberia, Berlin, 1922

Theodor Haering. *Novalis als Philosoph*, Kohlhammer, Stuttgart, 1954

Michael Hamburger. *Reason and Energy: Studies In German Literature*, Weidenfeld & Nicolson, 1970 *

Heinrich Heine. *The Complete Poems of Heinrich Heine*, tr. Hal Draper, Suhrkamp/ Insel, Boston, 1982

—. *The North Sea*, tr. Vernon Watkins, Faber, 1955

Friedrich Hölderlin. *Poems and Fragments*, tr. Michael Hamburger, Routledge & Kegan Paul, 1966

Glyn Tegai Hughes. *Romantic German Literature*, Edward Arnold, 1979 *

Philippe Lacoue-Labarthe & Jean-Luc Nancy, eds. *The Literary Absolute: The Theory of Literature In German Romanticism*, State University of New York Press, Albany, 1988

D. Mahoney. *The Critical Fortunes of a Romantic Novel*, 1994

J. Neubauer. *Novalis*, 1980

W. O'Brien. *Novalis*, 1995

Ritchie Robertson. *Heine*, Peter Halban, 1988

Helmut Schanze. *Romantik und Aufklärung, Unterschungen zu Friedrich Schlegel und Novalis*, Carl, Nürnberg, 1966

—. ed. *Friedrich Schlegel und die Kunstheorie Seiner Zeit*, Wissenschaftliche Buchgesellschaft, Darmstadt, 1985

Elizabeth Sewell. *The Orphic Voice: Poetry and Natural History*, Routledge, 1961*

Karl Heinz Volkmann-Schluck. "Novalis' magischer Idealismus", *Die deutsche Romantik*, ed. Hans Steffen, 1967, 45-53

WEBSITES

Aquarium	novalis.autorenverzeichnis.de
Novalis Gesellschaft	novalis-gesellschaft.de
International Novalis Society	ula.org/s/or/en

Beauties, Beasts, and Enchantment

CLASSIC FRENCH FAIRY TALES

Translated and with an Introduction
by Jack Zipes

A collection of 36 classic French fairy tales translated by renowned writer Jack Zipes.
Cinderella, Beauty and the Beast, Sleeping Beauty and *Little Red Riding Hood* are among the
classic fairy tales in this amazing book.
Includes illustrations from fairy tale collections.
Jack Zipes has written and published widely on fairy tales.

'Terrific... a succulent array of 17th and 18th century 'salon' fairy tales'
- *The New York Times Book Review*

'These tales are adventurous, thrilling in a way fairy tales are meant to be... The translation
from the French is modern, happily free of archaic and hyperbolic language... a fine and
sophisticated collection' - *New York Tribune*

'Enjoyable to read... a unique collection of French regional folklore' - *Library Journal*

'Charming stories accompanied by attractive pen-and-ink drawings' - *Chattanooga Times*

Introduction and illustrations   612pp.   ISBN 9781861712510 Pbk   ISBN 9781861713193 Hbk

Arseny Tarkovsky

Selected Poems

Arseny Tarkovsky is the neglected Russian poet, father of the acclaimed film
director Andrei Tarkovsky. This new book gathers together many of Tarkovsky's
most lyrical and heartfelt poems, in Virginia Rounding's new, clear translations. Many
of Tarkovsky's poems appeared in his son's films, such as *Mirror, Stalker, Nostalghia*
and *The Sacrifice*. There is an introduction by Rounding, and a bibliography of both
Arseny and Andrei Tarkovsky.

Illustrated. Bibliography and notes.
ISBN 9781861711144 Pbk   ISBN 9781861712660 Hbk

CRESCENT MOON PUBLISHING

web: www.crmoon.com e-mail: cresmopub@yahoo.co.uk

ARTS, PAINTING, SCULPTURE

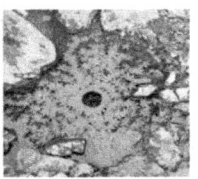

The Art of Andy Goldsworthy
Andy Goldsworthy: Touching Nature
Andy Goldsworthy in Close-Up
Andy Goldsworthy: Pocket Guide
Andy Goldsworthy In America
Land Art: A Complete Guide
The Art of Richard Long
Richard Long: Pocket Guide
Land Art In the UK
Land Art in Close-Up
Land Art In the U.S.A.
Land Art: Pocket Guide
Installation Art in Close-Up
Minimal Art and Artists In the 1960s and After
Colourfield Painting
Land Art DVD, TV documentary
Andy Goldsworthy DVD, TV documentary
The Erotic Object: Sexuality in Sculpture From Prehistory to the Present Day
Sex in Art: Pornography and Pleasure in Painting and Sculpture
Postwar Art
Sacred Gardens: The Garden in Myth, Religion and Art
Glorification: Religious Abstraction in Renaissance and 20th Century Art
Early Netherlandish Painting
Leonardo da Vinci
Piero della Francesca
Giovanni Bellini

Fra Angelico: Art and Religion in the Renaissance
Mark Rothko: The Art of Transcendence
Frank Stella: American Abstract Artist
Jasper Johns
Brice Marden
Alison Wilding: The Embrace of Sculpture
Vincent van Gogh: Visionary Landscapes
Eric Gill: Nuptials of God
Constantin Brancusi: Sculpting the Essence of Things
Max Beckmann
Caravaggio
Gustave Moreau

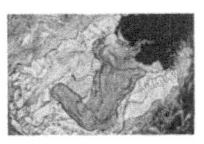

Egon Schiele: Sex and Death In Purple Stockings
Delizioso Fotografico Fervore: Works In Process 1
Sacro Cuore: Works In Process 2
The Light Eternal: J.M.W. Turner
The Madonna Glorified: Karen Arthurs

LITERATURE

J.R.R. Tolkien: The Books, The Films, The Whole Cultural Phenomenon
J.R.R. Tolkien: Pocket Guide
Tolkien's Heroic Quest
The *Earthsea* Books of Ursula Le Guin
Beauties, Beasts and Enchantment: Classic French Fairy Tales
German Popular Stories by the Brothers Grimm
Philip Pullman and *His Dark Materials*
Sexing Hardy: Thomas Hardy and Feminism
Thomas Hardy's *Tess of the d'Urbervilles*
Thomas Hardy's *Jude the Obscure*
Thomas Hardy: The Tragic Novels
Love and Tragedy: Thomas Hardy
The Poetry of Landscape in Hardy
Wessex Revisited: Thomas Hardy and John Cowper Powys
Wolfgang Iser: Essays and Interviews
Petrarch, Dante and the Troubadours
Maurice Sendak and the Art of Children's Book Illustration
Andrea Dworkin
Cixous, Irigaray, Kristeva: The *Jouissance* of French Feminism
Julia Kristeva: Art, Love, Melancholy, Philosophy, Semiotics and Psychoanalysis
Hélene Cixous I Love You: The *Jouissance* of Writing
Luce Irigaray: Lips, Kissing, and the Politics of Sexual Difference
Peter Redgrove: Here Comes the Flood
Peter Redgrove: Sex-Magic-Poetry-Cornwall
Lawrence Durrell: Between Love and Death, East and West
Love, Culture & Poetry: Lawrence Durrell
Cavafy: Anatomy of a Soul
German Romantic Poetry: Goethe, Novalis, Heine, Hölderlin
Feminism and Shakespeare
Shakespeare: Love, Poetry & Magic
The Passion of D.H. Lawrence
D.H. Lawrence: Symbolic Landscapes
D.H. Lawrence: Infinite Sensual Violence
Rimbaud: Arthur Rimbaud and the Magic of Poetry
The Ecstasies of John Cowper Powys
Sensualism and Mythology: The Wessex Novels of John Cowper Powys
Amorous Life: John Cowper Powys and the Manifestation of Affectivity (H.W. Fawkner)
Postmodern Powys: New Essays on John Cowper Powys (Joe Boulter)
Rethinking Powys: Critical Essays on John Cowper Powys
Paul Bowles & Bernardo Bertolucci
Rainer Maria Rilke
Joseph Conrad: *Heart of Darkness*
In the Dim Void: Samuel Beckett
Samuel Beckett Goes into the Silence
André Gide: Fiction and Fervour
Jackie Collins and the Blockbuster Novel
Blinded By Her Light: The Love-Poetry of Robert Graves
The Passion of Colours: Travels In Mediterranean Lands
Poetic Forms

POETRY

Ursula Le Guin: Walking In Cornwall
Peter Redgrove: Here Comes The Flood
Peter Redgrove: Sex-Magic-Poetry-Cornwall
Dante: Selections From the Vita Nuova
Petrarch, Dante and the Troubadours
William Shakespeare: Sonnets
William Shakespeare: Complete Poems
Blinded By Her Light: The Love-Poetry of Robert Graves
Emily Dickinson: Selected Poems
Emily Brontë: Poems
Thomas Hardy: Selected Poems
Percy Bysshe Shelley: Poems
John Keats: Selected Poems
Joh n Keats: Poems of 1820
D.H. Lawrence: Selected Poems
Edmund Spenser: Poems
Edmund Spenser: Amoretti
John Donne: Poems
Henry Vaughan: Poems
Sir Thomas Wyatt: Poems
Robert Herrick: Selected Poems
Rilke: Space, Essence and Angels in the Poetry of Rainer Maria Rilke
Rainer Maria Rilke: Selected Poems
Friedrich Hölderlin: Selected Poems
Arseny Tarkovsky: Selected Poems
Arthur Rimbaud: Selected Poems
Arthur Rimbaud: A Season in Hell
Arthur Rimbaud and the Magic of Poetry
Novalis: Hymns To the Night
German Romantic Poetry
Paul Verlaine: Selected Poems
Elizaethan Sonnet Cycles
D.J. Enright: By-Blows
Jeremy Reed: Brigitte's Blue Heart
Jeremy Reed: Claudia Schiffer's Red Shoes
Gorgeous Little Orpheus
Radiance: New Poems
Crescent Moon Book of Nature Poetry
Crescent Moon Book of Love Poetry
Crescent Moon Book of Mystical Poetry
Crescent Moon Book of Elizabethan Love Poetry
Crescent Moon Book of Metaphysical Poetry
Crescent Moon Book of Romantic Poetry
Pagan America: New American Poetry

MEDIA, CINEMA, FEMINISM and CULTURAL STUDIES

J.R.R. Tolkien: The Books, The Films, The Whole Cultural Phenomenon
J.R.R. Tolkien: Pocket Guide
The *Lord of the Rings* Movies: Pocket Guide
The Cinema of Hayao Miyazaki
Hayao Miyazaki: *Princess Mononoke*: Pocket Movie Guide
Hayao Miyazaki: *Spirited Away*: Pocket Movie Guide
Tim Burton : Hallowe'en For Hollywood
Ken Russell
Ken Russell: *Tommy*: Pocket Movie Guide
The Ghost Dance: The Origins of Religion
The Peyote Cult
Cixous, Irigaray, Kristeva: The *Jouissance* of French Feminism
Julia Kristeva: Art, Love, Melancholy, Philosophy, Semiotics and Psychoanalysis
Luce Irigaray: Lips, Kissing, and the Politics of Sexual Difference
Hélene Cixous I Love You: The *Jouissance* of Writing
Andrea Dworkin
'Cosmo Woman': The World of Women's Magazines
Women in Pop Music
HomeGround: The Kate Bush Anthology
Discovering the Goddess (Geoffrey Ashe)
The Poetry of Cinema
The Sacred Cinema of Andrei Tarkovsky
Andrei Tarkovsky: Pocket Guide
Andrei Tarkovsky: *Mirror*: Pocket Movie Guide
Andrei Tarkovsky: *The Sacrifice*: Pocket Movie Guide
Walerian Borowczyk: Cinema of Erotic Dreams
Jean-Luc Godard: The Passion of Cinema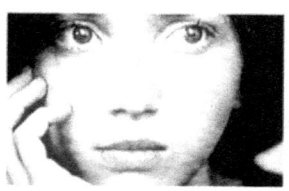
Jean-Luc Godard: *Hail Mary*: Pocket Movie Guide
Jean-Luc Godard: *Contempt*: Pocket Movie Guide
Jean-Luc Godard: *Pierrot le Fou*: Pocket Movie Guide
John Hughes and Eighties Cinema
Ferris Bueller's Day Off: Pocket Movie Guide
Jean-Luc Godard: Pocket Guide
The Cinema of Richard Linklater
Liv Tyler: Star In Ascendance
Blade Runner and the Films of Philip K. Dick
Paul Bowles and Bernardo Bertolucci
Media Hell: Radio, TV and the Press
An Open Letter to the BBC
Detonation Britain: Nuclear War in the UK
Feminism and Shakespeare
Wild Zones: Pornography, Art and Feminism
Sex in Art: Pornography and Pleasure in Painting and Sculpture
Sexing Hardy: Thomas Hardy and Feminism

The Light Eternal is a model monograph, an exemplary job. The subject matter of the book is beautifully organised and dead on beam. (Lawrence Durrell)
It is amazing for me to see my work treated with such passion and respect. (Andrea Dworkin)

CRESCENT MOON PUBLISHING
P.O. Box 1312, Maidstone, Kent, ME14 5XU, Great Britain. www.crmoon.com

cresmopub@yahoo.co.uk   www.crescentmoon.org.uk